Granny's Chips

by

Randolph Moreau

PublishBritannica
London   Baltimore

© 2003 by Randolph Moreau.
All rights reserved. No part of this book may be reproduced, stored in a retrieval system, or transmitted in any form or by any means without the prior written permission of the publishers, except by a reviewer who may quote brief passages in a review to be printed in a newspaper, magazine, or journal.

First printing

ISBN: 1-4137-0794-7
PUBLISHED BY PUBLISHBRITANNICA
www.publishbritannica.com
London   Baltimore

Table of Contents

Chapter One–A Letter..5

Chapter Two–A House..14

Chapter Three–The Road to Monte Carlo............................29

Chapter Four–Maure...44

Chapter Five–Midnight Mayhem.....................................61

Chapter Six–A Gothik Revival.......................................71

Chapter Seven–A Daughter's Grief..................................69

Chapter Eight–Revelations and a Plan..............................106

Chapter Nine–A Princely Icon......................................117

Chapter Ten–The Arrival..138

Chapter Eleven–Settling Accounts..................................155

Chapter Twelve–A Father's Tale....................................172

Chapter Thirteen–The Best Laid Plans..............................184

Chapter Fourteen–Final Accounting................................191

Chapter One ~
A Letter

The Eurostar wasn't very crowded; it was too early. Few people felt like waking up before sunrise to make the 6:04 from Waterloo to the Gare du Nord, even on a Friday. Marc Balanger found his assigned first class car and boarded. He placed his laptop and the LV Monogram tote, containing the few things he'd brought with him from Montréal, in the overhead. He took his place, a seat on the right of the aisle facing the engine. He stretched out his legs, arranging his tall slender frame more comfortably. He caught his reflection in the window and smiled, allowing himself a brief moment of self-satisfaction.

The seat opposite the small table that separated him from any potential companion was empty and he hoped that it would remain that way. Marc had just survived his 6th divorce, and was headed to his new home in the south of France, to lick his wounds, finish his latest novel, and start again. He was hoping for a quiet London-Paris leg of his journey.

Major life changes usually bring with them a period of analysis, self or otherwise. Marc was facing several major changes at the same time; the end of a five-year relationship, returning to Europe to live after an absence of more than five years in Canada, and the realization that his youth was definitely over. He had passed his forty-fifth birthday six months ago.

Yet, he was still fit, guarding his taut swimmer's build. His classic features were framed by a thick mass of fine chestnut hair, naturally streaked with blond and red highlights. He wore it long, just below the collarbone, its natural waves usually pulled into a ponytail at the base of the neck. He thought he still had quite a few good years left;

this feeling of loss and failure would pass. He was rich, successful in his profession, and famous; things would get better.

The night before had been pleasant enough. He'd dined with his dearest friend and confidant, Stephen Hampstead, who had collected him when his Canadian flight arrived at Heathrow. They had passed a quiet evening, playing the could have, should have, would have game, Marc suffering only minor jetlag from the day's Atlantic crossing. It had been easy to convince his friend to come and join him in France. Stephen would finish shooting the last episode of the Majors of Tilford today, and had no projects starting till June. A nice long vacation in the south of France, with its sun and beaches, was just what Stephen loved the most.

Marc settled back into his seat, slipped on his reading glasses, and opened the book he'd brought with him to read on the journey; a mystery by Peter Mayle. He was content, his surroundings beginning to melt away, dissolving into the world of murder and intrigue in the art world. His reverie was short lived. An attractive man in his early thirties, fashionably but conservatively dressed, broke his concentration.

"Good morning," his softly accented English betrayed his Parisian origins. "I don't mean to disturb you, but I see by my seat number that we will be traveling together."

Marc looked up and smiled politely, without answering.

"My name is Laurent Teyssier," he said, having placed his small LV Damier carry-on in the overhead.

"Pleasure," Marc replied, looking over his glasses. An English mother and his university years in England had provided him a perfect BBC-accented speech.

"Au contraire, Monsieur Balanger," the young man said, placing a book on the table between them. "The pleasure is mine."

Marc was forced to look up from his novel; he noticed that his companion's book was one of his. "Murder in Paradise" was the first novel he had written after leaving university. It was the story of murder and scandal set against a backdrop of the international set on the Côte d'Azur of the 1930's.

GRANNY'S CHIPS

"Mystery fan, I see," Marc commented wryly, as the young man took his seat.

"Actually," he replied. "I'm a Balanger fan." His smile was charming, and his way was definitely winning. "But I promise, I won't bother you…that is, if you would prefer to read. I've got a very good book with which to pass the time."

It was Marc's turn to smile. He couldn't very well be rude to a fan, so he closed his book and slid it over to the side, under the window. "I'm sorry, I didn't mean to be rude." Marc, regarded by all and sundry as a particular charmer himself, slid into the celebrated author mode. He removed his glasses and put them in the LV case next to the book. "I'm just a little tired still, jet lag…flew in from Canada yesterday."

"Please, if you need a little sleep, I won't be offended," his companion replied.

"This is the opinion of someone who has never slept with me before," Marc replied, laughing. "Seriously though, I never sleep in public if I can avoid it. You see, Monsieur Teyssier…"

"Laurent, please Monsieur Balanger."

"Very well…Laurent…you see, I snore rather badly, which is embarrassing for me and annoying for my fellow passengers."

"I snore myself," he admitted sheepishly.

"Well then," Marc added smiling. "For the sake of our fellow passengers, we must do our best to keep each other awake."

The train began its rocking motion as it pulled out of the station.

The waiter appeared to take their beverage order. "Something to drink, messieurs?"

"Monsieur Balanger?" Laurent deferred verbally.

"Marc, please," Marc replied to his traveling companion. Turning to the waiter he requested a mimosa.

"I'll have the same," Laurent gave his order in turn.

As the Eurostar rolled towards Ashford, Marc warmed up to the pleasant young man seated across from him. The truth be known, he enjoyed the company of a pleasant companion when traveling, provided he was not overly tired. He discovered that Laurent Teyssier was a native Parisian, an architect by profession. Younger than he by more than a decade, Laurent was not only charming, but quite attractive in that sporty actor-model kind of way.

His high cheekbones and full lips, the aquiline nose, separating wide crystal blue eyes, combined to give him an otherworld sort of attraction. His full tawny-coloured mane, clipped into one of those careless longish *sauvage* cuts, further accentuated the look of a magazine cover male. Something extremely useful in his profession Marc thought.

By the time they entered the Channel Tunnel on the other side of Ashford, they had shared a meal, a good English breakfast and multiple mimosas. Marc was certain that the diversion of a pleasant traveling companion for the trip to Paris, was exactly what he needed to help him transition from his lovely Victorian home on the Carrée St Louis in Montréal to his, as yet unseen, new home in southern France.

It was his turn to reveal some things about himself, and to his surprise, he found that he was enjoying doing so.

"So, Marc," Laurent asked. "How long were you in Montréal?"

"Five years and six months," Marc replied wistfully. "Most of them happy, although the last six months were rather difficult."

"I see a relationship that did not work out in your past," Laurent responded, adopting a fortune-teller tone.

"And you would be correct. I am recently and sadly divorced," Marc said with a sigh. "That's why I decided to return to my roots. My parents live near Aix en Provence, I have a sister in Paris and a brother near Bordeaux."

"So, where will you be living then?"

"Paris in the winter…I have a small apartment on the rue Montpensier…near St Tropez, the rest of the year." Marc laughed in spite of himself. "Actually my new home is about 4 kilometres from the village of Lorgues."

"I know the area, it is quite beautiful there, very picturesque."

"Yes, so I hear," Marc replied. "It's a hard, life I know, but someone has to live it," he added with a grin.

By the time the Eurostar pulled into the Gare du Nord, Marc felt they had established a genuine and very pleasant rapport. So when Laurent suggested they exchange cards, Marc did so willingly. They said farewell, as fellow travelers on a pleasant voyage always do, with a warm handshake and a promise to stay in touch.

"Galerie Montpensier, rue Montpensier," Marc gave the address of his Paris flat to the driver. He wondered, as the taxi pulled into the bustling traffic of Paris, whether they would see each other again.

His Paris apartment was in the back quadrangle of the Palais Royal, which formed one of Paris' most enchanting hidden gardens. Three sides of the quadrangle were apartments above chic little boutiques and restaurants, the fourth end closed off the garden with the Ministry of Culture. The apartment itself was smallish, two bedrooms, sitting room, dinning room, small kitchen and only one bath. These were spread over three levels, but they were filled with light as one side of the apartment opened onto the garden and the other onto the rue Montpensier itself.

His bedroom faced the garden, and it was here that he wrote when in Paris, watching groups of men playing "pétanque" on their lunch hour, elegant Parisiennes shopping in one of the numerous antique dealers, or bureaucrats and artists eating on one of the terrace restaurants, which were interspersed here and there, among the interior galleries that ringed three sides of the quadrangle's ground floor.

Marc had a special fondness for this apartment because it was small. When he was in Paris he could shop for himself and cook his own meals. He could not, however, receive the myriad guests, friends and family, who were always around in other places he lived. That was perhaps the reason he kept the apartment. It was the sanctuary away from the public life that his work and family position frequently shoved him into.

He was in the shower when the phone rang; he let the answering machine do its job. It rang three times more before he dried off, dressed, and pulled his long chestnut hair, just beginning to grey at the temples, into its trademark ponytail. Grabbing a pack of Players Light off the bureau, he descended the stairs to the living room on the ground floor. He poured himself a Pernod, adding some water from the pitcher on the small elegant console that served as his bar. Lighting a cigarette, he walked over to the small Louis XVI writing table on which rested the phone, his Paris address book and an assortment of silver framed photos of family and friends.

He loved the little table, with its fine fruitwood veneer and ormolu mounts. He had inherited it from his grandmother. Whenever he touched it, he would remember her sitting, writing notes and invitations to her friends. The image of the beautifully coiffed and dressed Parisienne, looking up from her correspondence to smile at her favourite grandson, still made him feel warm and at home. Sitting at that desk, she had shared with him much of her wit and wisdom, and the experiences of her own fascinating life. It was a memory he still cherished; his grandmother at her writing desk, and he in a comfortable wing chair, the same chair that was now placed beside the table.

He pushed the playback button on the telephone's built-in answering machine, and grabbing a pad and pen from the drawer of the writing desk prepared to jot down the caller's numbers.

"Très cher," the first message began. He immediately recognized the soft melodious Parisian accent of his sister Chantal. "Welcome back. I'm in the office today, but will be home tomorrow afternoon. Stop by then, and I'll give you the keys, map, and all the needed details for your new place. I took the liberty of sending Marie over to tidy up your apartment and put some things in the fridge to get you through the next couple of days. I would invite you for dinner this evening, but I know you'd just plead jet lag and stay at home. Call me when you get settled, and we will arrange a time for tomorrow. Bisous mon cher, j'attends de tes nouvelles."

The thought of his sister made him smile, they had been close as children. Although he had lived a gypsy's life between England, France, and North America since going to university, they remained close. As he once spoiled her, his dear and only little sister, she now spoiled him, and it was particularly needed at the moment.

The second message was from Sean, his rare-book dealer friend in Boston. "Please give Mr. Karpov a call to let him know when you will be arriving in Monte Carlo. He will send a driver to collect you." The soft Anglo-Irish accent of Sean's voice was modulated with a bit of urgency. "He seems quite anxious to get that letter…and thanks again for carrying it over for me, I owe you one. My best to friend Stephen…sorry about the divorce."

The third call was from the limousine service, letting him know that the car and driver were confirmed. It would pick him up at his apartment to go the Gare du Nord to collect Stephen, then on from there, to the Gare de Lyons, where they would catch their train to Nice. The vehicle would be a 4-passenger sedan, and would arrive at his apartment promptly at 11 on Sunday.

"Marc, this is Laurent," the fourth message began. Marc's ears perked up, he was surprised to say the least. "Sorry to bother you, I suppose you must be sleeping off the jet lag by now. I was wondering if you would like to have dinner tomorrow night. I hope you won't think I'm being presumptuous, but I really enjoyed our conversation on the train, and thought perhaps you might consider our getting together before you leave for the Côte d'Azur on Sunday. Please give me a call when you get up, I'll be around all day, since I'm working from home."

Marc cleared the messages and picked up the receiver. Settling comfortably in his favourite wing chair, he dialled his sister's office. He arranged to meet her at her apartment on Saturday afternoon around 2:00, for a late lunch. That would leave him plenty of time to have a long chat, pick up what he needed, and still have dinner with Laurent that evening. Calling Laurent, he agreed to dinner at 8:00 at Le 3, a restaurant not too far from his apartment. The choice of restaurant was telling, and it was Laurent's choice, not his.

The third call meant going back upstairs to his bedroom. The number for Mr. Karpov, Sean's client, and the letter that they seemed to think was so important, was in the tote he'd brought with him from Montréal. Taking the phone (how he loved the cordless life of the 21st century), he went back up the stairs to his bedroom. He put the tote on the large, canopied and draped iron bed, opened it and retrieved the plain brown envelope containing Mr. Karpov's treasured letter.

Opening the letter, Marc pulled out the slip of paper with Karpov's information on it. Scribbled in Sean's hasty handwriting was a number. Sitting on the bed he dialled the number, and waited as the phone rang at the other end. A man's voice answered. "Karpov," the heavily accented voice replied.

"Monsieur Karpov," Marc began. "This is Marc Balanger, a friend of Sean Sweeney."

"Ah, Monsieur Balanger," Karpov replied. "I have been anxiously awaiting your call."

"I have the letter which Sean purchased for you at the Sotheby's auction in New York last week. I've just arrived in Paris this afternoon, and I had a message from Sean to phone and let you know when I will be arriving in Monte Carlo. I'll be taking the TGV from Paris on Sunday afternoon, we'll be arriving in Monte Carlo around 7:50 or thereabouts. I'm traveling with a friend of mine Stephen Hampstead."

"Wonderful, wonderful," Karpov replied. "Of course you and Mr. Hampstead will dine with us aboard my little boat. You know I saw Mr. Hampstead in your wonderful play in the West End several years ago. It will be a pleasure to have to such famous artists as yourselves as guests aboard the Rosenkranz."

"I'm certain the pleasure will be ours, Mr. Karpov." Marc responded as politely as one can to a perfect stranger.

"My driver, Malinkov, will collect you at the station." Karpov's tone changed from that of a charming host to one of serious gravity. "I know you will take care of my little letter Monsieur Balanger. Mr. Sweeney assures me that you are most trustworthy. You see, the letter was written by a Georgian Prince with close connections to the Tsar Nicholas II. As a collector of Russian imperial artefacts, I have long sought this letter. It is a most important part of our imperial legacy."

"You need not worry Monsieur Karpov," Marc replied. "I assure you it will be well cared for. As a collector myself, I understand your concerns."

"You are a collector, Monsieur Balanger?" Karpov's voice sounded almost ominous.

"Yes. I have accumulated quite a collection of small Greco-Roman bronzes. I must plead ignorance, however, about your countries great treasures. I acquired my own interest from my summers with my family in Provence, which as you know was heavily settled by the Greeks and Romans."

"Indeed, Monsieur Balanger, Greco-Roman…" Karpov's voice mellowed. "I shall enjoy talking with you, collector to collector."

"Well, then, Mr. Hampstead and I will see you on Sunday evening, Monsieur Karpov."

"Yes, Sunday evening. Au revoir, Monsieur Balanger."

What could be in that letter that was so important, Marc asked himself. He pulled the letter out of the envelope. It was only one sheet, enclosed in a transparent plastic sleeve. The paper itself was engraved with a coat of arms on one side. The page had yellowed with age. It was written by hand, on both sides, some paragraphs in French, the language of the Russian imperial aristocracy, some paragraphs in Russian.

Marc examined the letter rather quickly, he was surprised at the excellent quality of the French paragraphs, but not knowing Russian, ignored those. It was from a Prince Felix Andronikov to a Prince Andrei Barataev, either a relative or close friend, judging from the contents of the French paragraphs. The letter was dated March 1, 1917, and had been sent from St Petersburg. News of his wife, Elena and the birth of their daughter, Aleksandra, various bits and pieces about their new home in St Petersburg, just finished. Talk of the war with Germany, and the political events of the previous month, were also commented on. Yet there was nothing in the French paragraphs to indicate that the letter held great importance for a collector. Pity he didn't read Russian, he thought.

Marc replaced the letter in its envelope, went downstairs and prepared a light supper. It was just another curiosity, and frankly, one that didn't interest him overmuch.

Chapter Two ~
A House

Chantal's apartment was on the left bank, on the second floor of a Haussmann building facing the Louvre. It was walking distance, albeit a lengthy one, from his apartment. The day was sunny and bright, and the weather, although still a bit brisk, was perfect for a walk. Marc left his apartment around one and strolled through the Place de Carrousel, across the Pont de Carrousel, and down the Quai Voltaire to the charming building where his sister, her husband Edward, and their little boy, Marc-Édouard had lived for the past few years. He took his time, savouring the early spring air and soaking in the feeling of his favourite city.

Chantal had prepared a late lunch, and over pâté aux truffles, Coquilles St Jacques, and a tasty pêche Melba, washed down with a bottle of Tattinger, they talked about summers in Provence, the parents, the brother, Jean-Charles, their careers, in short all the pleasant things in life. Chantal and Edward tactfully avoided the divorce, for which Marc was grateful, and after dinner he and Chantal retired to her studio to talk about the house.

He liked this room and could see why his sister had so wanted the apartment, actually two apartments which they had made into one. The view from her workroom was the façade of the Louvre, stately and elegant by day, a picture out of a fairy tale in the beautiful illumination of the night. The ceilings were high, the mouldings were graceful, and the fireplace, in which a low fire was burning, was warm and cozy in spite of its ornately carved marble mantel.

It was furnished with pieces that their grandmother had left Chantal, uniquely feminine, quintessentially French. As she watched his sister gathering the papers pertaining to the house, he could not help but

GRANNY'S CHIPS

admire her svelte blonde beauty, wrapped in a peach coloured silk, decorated lightly with a long strand of granny's pearls. He looked away from his talented and much admired sister and sifted through a group of ink and watercolour designs scattered across the surface of her worktable; necklaces she was preparing for one of her clients, a jeweller on the Place Vendôme.

"Nice these," Marc commented. "Bocheron or Chaumet?"

"Enough about work," she smiled the disarming smile that, since childhood, signalled a change of subject. "Let's talk about your new house." She gestured to a pair of large, comfortable Louis XV armchairs. Casually she walked over to the tall double windows overlooking the Seine; she opened them wide.

"I know you're dying for a cigarette, so please feel free." She crossed over to the chairs and sat facing Marc, placing the papers on the small Louis quinze table that served to hold cups, glasses, the apartment's only ashtray, and whatever nécessaires two people would need, sitting before a cozy fire.

"As I told you when we spoke, it's near Lorgues, about 40 km north of St Tropez, only 4 km from the village. You have room for family and friends, as you requested; there are eleven bedrooms, four more than your place in Montréal, so you won't have to squeeze anyone in. Have you decided to keep the house on the Carrée St Louis?"

"I don't know yet, I guess it depends on..." Marc felt a small shadow of the recent past cloud the sun filled room.

"No matter," Chantal interrupted quickly, seeking to avoid what was still a very delicate subject. Artfully, she changed the topic, returning to a description of his new home. "There are 5 reception rooms, the library has beautiful fruitwood paneling, with lots of bibliothèques for your books, and some glass fronted cupboards for your *trophies*," as she called his assortments of literary awards. "All built- in, of course."

"The dinning room and main salon are charming; both have twin sets of arched French doors, which open onto a terrace that runs along the entrance front of the house. The informal sitting room is large, but it's decorated in a very cozy manner. The music room is wonderful, filled with light, and there's a wonderful baby grand in rosewood."

"The views are wonderful. From the master suite you look out on the village of Lorgues, which is built on a hill about 4 kilometres from the house. There is a comfortably-sized sitting room adjoining your bedroom with the same view. A lovely park surrounds the house and there is a formal garden in the back. The pool, just beyond the formal garden, is fantastic: a long rectangle with a little cottage style pool house at one end."

"There is a wonderful Provencal fitted kitchen. The only drawback to the place is the number of bathrooms; there are only seven, so some people will have to share when the house is full."

"The housekeeper and caretaker have agreed to stay on, pending your approval, of course. The housekeeper, Brigitte Trochet is married to a local carpenter, and lives with him in Lorgues. The caretaker, Luc Doumé, lives in one of the two staff flats on the ground floor. You have the other one free for your man, Renaud."

Marc was looking over the plans as she spoke, it was a truly wonderful house, spacious enough for family and friends, and yet there was enough privacy for him to work uninterrupted. "You've done a splendid job, très chère. How much land goes with the house?"

"About 30 acres…the usual outbuildings, garage for 4 cars, a farm house and barn. The farm is currently leased," she added. "The lease runs out in 2005. The park, which makes up about five acres of the property, is beautifully wooded. Aside from the formal garden and the pool area, there is a nice size lake with a gothik bagatelle and a surrounding meadow, great for picnics."

"Chantal, it sounds idyllic!" Marc lit another cigarette, the grey cloud of the recent past was rapidly fading. "Like Papa's place near Aix."

Marc smiled at the memories of those childhood summers. Each year, returning from school, he used to adventure around the chateau that had so long been a part of his family, discovering new nooks and crannies previously unknown.

The new house with its pink-stuccoed walls, broad front terrace, nicely paneled library and quiet country surroundings, was really perfect for him. "Chantal, the house looks beautiful. What can I say?…It's perfect."

"It does have a *bit of a history*," she added, smiling mischievously.

"What kind of history?" Marc responded warily.

"Well," she began with a slight grin. "On the surface it's uncomplicated enough. The house was built as a simple chateau around 1750 for a gentleman silk merchant from Draguignon. It remained in their family till the early part of the last century." Chantal grinned impishly, teasing. "Then a Russian émigré family, the Andronikov, bought it. They lived there until two years ago when Princess Aleksandra Andronikov passed away. Amazing woman by all accounts, she lived to be 84. You bought it from her estate."

"So where's the 'bit of history?'" Marc asked. His interest suddenly piqued; it was a Felix Andronikov who was the author of the letter he was carrying to Sean Sweeney's client, Karpov, on Sunday.

"Apparently, or so rumour has it, Prince Felix, Princess Aleksandra's father, was in possession of a fabulous collection of jewels: enormous diamonds, emeralds, and rubies, some as big as hen's eggs, *and* a treasure trove of jewelled bibelots. He supposedly brought it with him when he fled Russia with his little family. It is said that he secreted the treasure on the property," Chantal paused a moment, waiting for Marc to react, but he remained poker faced. "Now here comes the interesting part, Prince Felix was murdered in Nice, a few years after he bought the house. He left a large sum of money, in a Swiss bank, of course…"

"Of course," Marc interjected, still wearing his poker face.

"His wife, the Princess Elena, did have a rather impressive collection of jewels…which I might add, neither she nor her daughter Aleksandra are reputed to have ever sold…none of the Andronikov family jewels that were part of the estate qualify as extraordinary…impressive, perhaps, but not extraordinary."

"And just how would you know that très chère?" Mark interrupted, sounding a note of disbelief.

"I saw them with my own eyes," she beamed.

"What?"

"They were sold at auction just a few months ago, here in Paris." Chantal couldn't resist dropping a real mystery in her brother's lap. "The housekeeper, Madame Trochet, told me that the heirs to the estate gave the house and the property a very thorough search for the treasure before the house was put on the market, much to the exasperation of the estate's trustees."

"So Prince Felix died before revealing the treasure's hiding place," Marc leaned forward. "Sounds like a good plot for a new mystery."

"Exactly what I was thinking," Chantal smiled. "Now, if I may return from our *bit of history* to the present, Madame Trochet and Doumé the caretaker, will both be there when you arrive on Monday. We drove your XLS down to sign the papers on the house last week, so you have a car waiting, and I asked Brigitte to pick up a few things so that you won't go hungry on your first day or two. Since Tuesday is market day in Lorgues, I thought you might enjoy doing your own shopping for the long term. Lorgues is a charming village, complete with a medieval walled old town. The market is extraordinary, and being low on provisions will give you and Stephen a reason to get out and discover your new surroundings."

"No next day lazing about the pool?"

"You have plenty of time for that. You need to get out, meet your neighbours, even if the closest ones are 4 kilometres away."

"As you say, Madame," Marc grinned back at her. She really did know him well. When faced with a bit of trauma in his life, he usually sequestered himself away for a time; not always the best way to bounce back.

"Now, I've arranged for a rental car for you when you and Stephen arrive in Monte Carlo. The confirmation and the driving instructions are in here," she said, handing him a white envelope. "So all that's left to do is to move into your new home and enjoy it."

Marc remained quiet about the Andronikov connection, the letter and his new house. The French paragraphs made no mention of anything remotely resembling a treasure, but the Russian paragraphs, what could they reveal! And what was Karpov's interest in all this? Why was this letter so important to him? He kept his poker face.

Questions without answers…"Does Katya speak Russian?" Katya was his brother's wife; her family had immigrated to France from Russia just after the revolution.

"You know, I believe she does, why?" Chantal laughed. "Got a Russian treasure map?"

"Of course not." Marc brushed the question away with a wry little smile. "But you did say when we first talked about the house, that the contents were included in the sale; less a few personal mementos. I assume that means the books in the library are still in the house."

"Actually, yes, the books were included in the sale," she replied with reflection.

"Maybe there are some things in the collection she would like to have."

"You're up to something." Chantal replied, a bit of concern creeping into her voice. "And, you're not telling."

"Dearest sister," Marc replied sardonically. "I promise, if I find a treasure buried in the back garden, you will be the first to know."

Just at that moment, the door to Chantal's work-room burst open and his nephew and namesake, the precocious fair-haired six year old Marc-Édouard burst in. "Maman, je veux dire au revoir à mon oncle Marc avant dodo."

"Sorry, but he was rather insistent." Chantal's husband, Edward, a tall attractive Englishman brought up the rear.

"We were just finishing up anyway." Marc smiled warmly, hoisting his nephew up on to his knees. "I have a dinner engagement this evening, so I really do need to be going."

"I'll give you a lift," Edward interjected. "With all these papers and keys, it will be easier for you."

"Great idea, I don't want to drop anything along the way." He kissed his nephew, once on each cheek, the requisite bisous exchanged in France between family and close friends, and lowered him back to the floor. Standing up, collecting the maps, deed, pictures, keys, and various other miscellanies that were now his as the new proprietor of the Chateau de Maure, he bid his farewells to his sister and nephew. "You must both promise to come south very soon. I've got plenty of room," he added, with a slight chuckle and a quick glance in Chantal's direction.

Back in his own apartment, Marc glanced at his watch. It was five o'clock. If he hurried, he could still get to the FNAC before it closed. If memory served, the FNAC at Forum les Halles was open till seven.

He got the number from the operator and dialled, asking for the computer software department. He asked if they had a program for doing rudimentary translations from Russian to French, or from Russian to English. He was in luck. They had Russian to French and they were open till seven.

Quickly, he reserved a copy, headed out the door to the Métro, and made his way over to Paris' electronics, music, book, and computer superstore to retrieve it. While there, he grabbed a Russian-French dictionary on CD. What one did not have, surely the other would.

He was starting to feel the beginnings of a challenge, of excitement. Yet, freshly showered, dressing for dinner, he cautioned himself.

"Probably nothing," he muttered aloud.

He selected a camel-coloured cashmere sweater, pulling it over the navy blue silk shirt he had decided to wear for the evening. Casual, Laurent had said; relief, was what Marc had thought.

The camel and navy combination went well with the pleated charcoal trousers he had put on. Pulling on a pair of black Bally deerskin moccasins, he surveyed himself in the mirror. Not bad for a man in his mid forties, he mused; too bad this was just a friendly dinner engagement, the hint of a mystery always made him a little randy.

He took the métro for the one stop from the Palais Royal/Musée du Louvre to the Hotel de Ville. The restaurant on the rue Ste-Croix-de-la-Bretonnerie was not far from the Hotel de Ville stop, and his shoes were comfortable. The evening was quite pleasant as he had added a lightweight charcoal leather jacket on his way out the door.

Down the rue de Rivoli, up the rue Vielle du Temple, Marc found himself musing over the Karpov-Andronikov connection. He kept telling himself that it had to be sheer coincidence, yet the "rumour" Chantal told him today at lunch continued to plague him with its odd puzzle, not the least of which, was the way in which the princess had treated her heirs.

Laurent was waiting in the corridor of the restaurant that led from the street to the courtyard dinning area; the tawny good looks of his dinner companion were accentuated by his black turtleneck and black jeans. Laurent extended his hand in welcome. His long graceful fingers encircled Marc's hand in a firm, strong grip. "Would you care to sit in the courtyard, or would you prefer to sit indoors?" Teyssier smiled, as he shook Marc's hand.

"Let's try the courtyard." Marc retrieved his hand. "It really is quite pleasant this evening, especially when one considers the climate from which I have just come."

"Deux personnes, dans la cour, s'il vous plait," Laurent said to the waiter. "I take it Montréal is still quite cold this time of year."

"Montréal!" Marc spoke wistfully, as they sat down at their table. "It's a wonderful city; uniquely French, uniquely North American, the people are incredibly warm, wonderfully friendly…I fell in love with one…but the winter's are long and cold."

As if in concert, both men reached into their pockets and extracted their respective cell phones, putting them on the table. Marc looked at Laurent; they both began to laugh.

"Guilty as charged," Laurent smiled, slightly embarrassed. "I guess it's the curse of the modern man, the need for instant communication."

"Instant access, instant interruption," Marc smile faded. "You know, I can't think of anyone who might phone that can't wait until later." Reaching over to his phone, he pushed the power button, turning it off.

"Ditto," Laurent, still smiling, turned off his phone, too. " But we should still leave them on the table," he added, with a little grin.

"Otherwise people will think we're not *cellulaire solvable*."

Marc laughed in turn. Status in the first decade of the twenty-first century mandated that *everyone* have a cell phone, the French had a particularly pithy way of phrasing it.

"Quelque chose à boire, messieurs?" their waiter asked, as he placed the menus in front of them.

"I'll have a Pernod without ice," Marc replied.

"Make that two," Laurent added.

"Now that's a surprise!" Pernod, Ouzo, Pastis, Ricard, or Raki, whatever one called it; the anise based liquor was his favourite drink, but seldom anyone else's. Marc was one of the few he knew that had such a fondness for the beverage.

"Ah, but I'm full of surprises," Laurent replied, a bit too mischievous for Marc's comfort.

"Well, yes...right," Marc shifted in his chair, glancing down at the menu. "What shall we have for dinner?"

They perused the menu, Laurent making suggestions. In the end, Marc decided on escargots for starters, with a filet of beef and sauce béarnaise to follow. Laurent selected a timbale of aubergine, tomato, and goat cheese followed by a grilled salmon steak with an herb and lemon sauce. They placed their order when the waiter returned with the drinks.

Marc added water to his drink, and taking a large sip, asked one of the more dreaded question of the 21st century, "Do you mind if I smoke?"

"No, no, not at all," Laurent replied smiling. "I've been known to smoke now and again myself." He noticed that Marc was still somewhat hesitant. "No, really, it doesn't bother me. My father smoked. Actually, I rather like the smell; it reminds me of him. He always had a cigarette before dinner, a cigar after."

"Had?"

"Yes," Laurent said quietly. "He passed away when I was rather young. He liked to fly, you see...he had a small plane...one day, there was an unexpected storm."

"I'm very sorry." Marc pulled out a pack of Player's Light, and

GRANNY'S CHIPS

took a cigarette from the package.

"Both of your parents are still living?" Laurent reached across the table, lighting Marc's cigarette with a match from a packet in the ashtray.

"Yes, they live in the country, near Aix en Provence...married 50 years in September, and still very happy." Marc smiled at the thought of them. They are quite a couple...quite a handful, too. "So," Marc turned his full attention to his dinner companion. "You rang." He tried to sound nonchalant.

"Yes," Laurent replied, returning to the present. "Do you mind?" He added, tapping the cigarette pack, an implied question in his gesture. He was feeling just a bit nervous.

"Not at all," Marc replied, pulled a gold Dupont from his jacket pocket, lighting Laurent's cigarette. "I'm always exchanging cards with people on the train. Usually neither of us phones. I must say...it was a pleasant surprise...I'm glad you did."

"Well, I'm going to be in the south, myself," Laurent began, offering the obvious excuse. "The office phoned yesterday after I spoke with you. They told me that a proposal we made to a client for a job in St Tropez has been accepted. I'm going down to do the final drawings and contract the workmen."

Laurent paused a moment, taking a sip of his drink, looking for a little "Dutch courage". "I thought the two of us...you and I...we might get together in St Tropez, as we'll both be there. Perhaps...perhaps I could see your new house."

"Ah, is this a business dinner then? Architect, potential client?"

"No...honestly," Laurent floundered, but only momentarily. "You did say if I ever came that way..." he took a deep drag of the cigarette.

"Actually," he continued, sidestepping the subject. "My client has just purchased a little house in St Tropez, in the village, close to the harbour, and she wants it redone before she moves in. The place needs an overhaul, so to speak, knocking out walls, enlarging rooms, you know, changing an old Provencal town house into a 21st century hideaway. Anyway, I'm flying down on Monday. I'll be there for six to eight weeks...she wants it ready for early June."

"Well then, we'll have plenty of time to get better acquainted, if indeed that's where you're headed," Marc said, jumping off the edge of the inevitable and all too precipitous cliff.

Laurent looked Marc directly in the eye. After all, they *were* both adults. "That's exactly where I'm headed."

"Ah," Marc said, taking in a very deep breath. "Saved by the starters," he said, as the waiter placed their appetizers in front of them.

"Perhaps…perhaps not," Laurent replied, with a slightly wicked grin. The chase was on, and Laurent was determined not to loose.

"You know, this conversations is beginning to sound remarkably like one of those period drawing room comedies I wrote for the London stage."

"*Don't do that*, I know, I saw the French version when it played at the Odéon."

"So you're just having me on," Marc smiled wryly.

"Perhaps…perhaps not." Laurent's tone had grown even more mischievous.

They both laughed, it was unavoidable. Had Marc written it, it would have been written that way, laughter included.

Dinner progressed, the food was excellent, the wine, equally good. Although Marc did talk a little about his new house: pink stuccoed stone, wonderfully paneled library, and so on, Laurent did most of the talking. Marc, determined not to rewrite one of his own plays, was happy to be an observer of Laurent's efforts at a scenario for two characters in a Paris restaurant.

What he learned about Laurent, among other things, was that he had his own firm, which was officed on the rue de Rivoli in the same building as the Antiquités du Louvre, a stone's throw from Marc's apartment. Impressive for a young man of thirty-four; a fact of which Marc also became aware.

His father had been in the government, a Senator, his mother was an interior designer. It was his mother's interests, which he came to share as a young child that led him to architecture. After his father's death, Laurent had only been 10 at the time, he and his mother had moved to Paris permanently. This is where he grew up.

"My mother remarried when I was twelve. She married a Russian painter who defected during the mid 70's, perhaps you've heard of him, Sergei Reisky." His manner of speaking was boyish, a young man strolling down memory lane.

"I remember when they first met; she had been doing an apartment for a Madame Karpov, whose husband was a diplomat at the Russian embassy. Because of the connection, she and my father were invited to a party at the embassy. It was to celebrate the opening of an exhibition of contemporary Russian art at the Petit Palais."

At the mention of Karpov's name, Marc's ears perked up. They had progressed from one of his period drawing room comedies to one of his mystery novels, and this one was beginning to really grab his attention. "Would you like to have a cognac? I think one is in order," Marc signalled the waiter.

"Yes, thank you. I think I'll have another cigarette, too, that is if you don't mind."

"Please." Marc offered Laurent the open pack. "Deux cognac, s'il vous plait," he said to the waiter, as the young man cleared away their plates."

"Oui, monsieur," the waiter replied.

"Et l'addition aussi, s'il vous plait," Laurent handed the waiter a credit card. He looked at Marc. "You are my guest this evening," he added in a tone that would brook no discussion.

"Thanks." Marc was surprised, but not so much so that he dropped the thread he was trying to unravel. He steered the conversation back to its original subject. "You were talking about your stepfather and the Karpovs."

"Yes, I remember I was around six at the time. He was introduced to my parents, and maman was very impressed with him and with his work. One day, he, Sergei that is, slipped past his "escorts" as he calls them, and presented himself at the Canadian embassy asking for asylum,"

He paused, while the waiter served the Cognac. He verified the bill, added the tip, signed the receipt and retrieved his credit card.

"He came back to Paris for an exhibition of his work at a gallery on the rue Callot, I guess I was around 11. He and mother met again, and...well, a year later they married. That's how I came to learn Russian."

Marc almost dropped his cigarette. "You speak Russian?" he asked, trying to sound casual.

"Yes, actually I read it better than I speak it. Sergei has a passion for his country's literature, and thought the only way to appreciate it was to read it in the original. Oddly enough, I have a knack for languages, so I picked it up over the years with his help."

"My God!" Laurent glanced at his watch. "Look at the time. I've been talking too much, haven't I?"

"No, you haven't...honestly," Marc replied, with a reassuring touch on Laurent's arm. "But you have a plane to catch in the morning, and I've got to catch a train in the afternoon...which is just to say that it is getting late. We're both off to the south tomorrow, and there's packing to be done, apartments to close up...and..."

"And," Laurent pronounced the word as if it were a period, a punctuation mark. He knew if were going to make a move it had to be now. Taking a deep breath, he took the plunge, "Look, we're both over twenty-one..."

"Considerably, in my case," Marc added with a sense of impending doom.

"I am extremely attracted to you and I think you're attracted to me."

"Yes?" Marc replied, a question in his response. He was beginning to feel a sense of relief, but relief mingled with apprehension. He had felt the attraction the moment he had looked up from his book on the Eurostar, but he'd managed to keep it under wraps until now.

"I realize that you have, as they say, 'just fallen off a horse', and that you need some time. But I have plenty of time." Building his business had left Laurent little time for a personal life. But this was one attraction he was determined not to let go. "Your new house is only an hour or so from St Tropez, and my work only keeps me busy for four or five hours a day."

"Laurent," Marc reached across the table, touching Laurent's hands with his. "Permit me to write the end of this scene, after all, that is what I do for a living."

"OK," he gripped Marc's hands tightly. *I'm not letting you go* washis only thought, and he was determined to let his actions show it.

"As you say, I do need time…I loved Francois more than I've ever loved anyone else in my life. I don't understand why it didn't work out; I don't think I'll ever understand. It hurts when I think about it, when I try to understand…but I know I'll eventually get better, that's why I came home…to speed up the process."

Marc paused a moment to let his words sink in. However, he did not try to release Laurent's grip. "I must make one thing absolutely clear…I'm no man's diversion, nor will any man be mine; I still believe in love, even at my age, even with all the disappointments. If love's what you have on offer, well…we shall see what we shall see."

"Then this is our first date?" Laurent smiled determinedly.

Marc had to laugh. There was no denying it, Laurent had charmed and seduced. There was a real possibility here; he'd be a fool not to admit it. "Yes," he smiled, releasing his hand from Laurent's grip. "This is our first date."

They stood up and walked through the courtyard, down the corridor to the street.

"Can I walk you to a taxi?" Laurent asked tentatively.

Marc took Laurent's hand and entwined their fingers. "Like this?"

"Yes," Laurent gripped his hand firmly. "Just like this."

"You just made points, Monsieur Teyssier," Marc smiled wryly. "A rather large number of points."

"Let's walk slowly…please."

"Oh yes," Marc replied. "Very slowly."

Marc went straight to the letter as soon as he returned to his apartment. The entire walk home he had been trying to tie today's loose threads together. No mean feat, considering the company in which he was.

The threads were really quite tangled now: Andronikov and Karpov, the Chateau de Maure, a letter, a murder, a buried treasure. And exactly what was Laurent's connection to all this? In truth, there was a connection, however tentative and far reaching, to Karpov. He wondered if there was a Karpov connection to the Andronikov buried somewhere as well. One thing was certain, at least with regard to Laurent, if there were more than meets the eye, he would find out soon enough.

He took the letter out of Karpov's envelope and walked over to his "all in one" as he often called it, the printer cum scanner cum fax. The letter was hermetically sealed in a plastic sleeve to protect it from damp or tearing. It would, however, scan fairly well, or so Marc hoped. The plastic was quite transparent.

Scanning completed, Marc opened the document file and checked the results. The scanned document was quite legible. Both sides of the page came through without any bleeding of the text from the opposite side.

Putting the letter back in its envelope, and the envelope back into his briefcase, he turned back the duvet and the sheet, tossed his clothes on a nearby chair, and crawled into bed. He was really tired, and sleep was not long in coming.

Chapter Three~
The Road to Monte Carlo

Marc rose early the next morning. Copious quantities of coffee and orange juice, and more than the usual amount of cigarettes accompanied his organization of the papers, keys and sundries for the new house.

He slipped the front door keys to the house and the spare keys to the car Chantal had already driven down, into the inside pocket of his briefcase. The maps, house plans, and photos he put in a large envelope, and carefully labelled it with Chateau de Maure on the outside. He didn't want to confuse it with the envelope he was carrying to Mr. Karpov.

He put his copy of the deeds to the house and the farm, the inventory lists of its contents, those of the farm and other outbuildings, together with the lease for the farm and contracts for the staff into another brown envelope. This one he labelled legal documents. Then he slipped all three envelops into his briefcase.

He took the tickets for the train journey, both Canadian and French passports and the confirmation for the rental car in Monte Carlo, and slipped them into the front pocket of the briefcase, and closed it up.

That done, he opened the doors to the small chest that served to hold the host of miscellaneous office supplies, which he kept in his sitting room, and pulled out the case for his laptop. The *precious letter* was now scanned onto its hard drive, and he wasn't about to leave that behind. He had just zipped it up when the phone rang.

Marc picked up the receiver, it was the car hire agency; they were ringing to confirm that the driver would be there promptly at eleven. He glanced at his watch, it was ten o'clock; he felt rather pleased with himself. Everything was organized; the suitcases packed with spring clothes from his Paris closets were in the entryway. He was showered, dressed and ready to walk out the door.

He was about to go down the stairs to the kitchen, which was in the basement, to wash up the breakfast things when the phone rang again.

"Monsieur Balanger?"

"Renaud!" Marc was quite surprised. "Either you're up very early or very late."

"Very early, monsieur," he replied.

"My God, it must be four a.m. in Montréal!"

"Just after four, monsieur," Renaud replied. "I wanted to reach you before you left for Monte Carlo."

"Is everything alright, Renaud?"

"Oh yes, monsieur," he replied. "I just thought you should know that everything you wanted sent to France has been packed or crated, and the movers will be coming on Tuesday morning. I will be flying from Dorval on Tuesday evening, there is a brief stop over in Paris, but I'll be in Nice by nine a.m. on Wednesday. That should put me in St Raphael by Wednesday noon if the trains are running according to schedule."

"Excellent Renaud." Marc was really pleased that Paul Renaud was going to stay with him; after five years together as employer and major domo, for lack of a better term, they were used to one another's habits. There was no one whom he trusted more.

In addition to running his home, Renaud frequently ferreted out things, which would otherwise have escaped Marc's notice. Renaud's knowledge of almost everything, from wine to wiring was uncanny. Indeed, he had helped enormously with the research for Marc's most recent novel, set in the Belle Époque. "Renaud, I'd like for you to do me a little favour, if you have some time between now and your leaving."

"Certainly, monsieur." Paul could tell something was afoot. He'd not worked for Balanger for five years without recognizing the nuance implicit in certain types of requests.

"See what you can find out about a Dimitri Karpov. He is a very wealthy Russian businessman. Karpov was in the diplomatic corps in Paris during the seventies. Also check on an artist, Sergei Reisky, also Russian. He lived in Canada during the mid-seventies, and currently resides in Paris."

"Anything else, monsieur?"

"Well, yes, Renaud," Marc added, knowing he was pushing his luck with someone who had his own departure to organize within two days. "See if you can find anything on a Prince Felix Andronikov. He was a Russian émigré who was murdered in Nice sometime in the early twenties. I'll explain it all when I see you."

"Sounds like we have a mystery on our hands, monsieur."

"Very likely, Renaud, very likely," Marc replied. "Call me before boarding the train in Nice, and let me know when you'll be arriving at the station in St Raphael. I'll arrange for someone to drive down and pick you up." He paused for a minute. "If you find out anything that you think I ought to know about your research, before you arrive, call me on my Paris cell, it works anywhere in France."

"As you wish, monsieur."

"And Renaud," Marc added, slightly chastising. "Get some sleep."

"Yes, monsieur."

The driver appeared at his door promptly at eleven. In minutes he was on his way to the Gare du Nord, luggage in the boot, and an arm wrapped protectively around his briefcase and laptop. When they arrived, the driver parked, leaving Marc in the car. The driver entered the station with the traditional placard, which in this case read, "S. Hampstead."

"Marc, cher," Stephen said, stepping into the car. Stephen brushed a wisp of blond–streaked brunette hair from his forehead. In his early forties, he still had that boyish charm and handsome face that had made his reputation on the West End stage. Tanned and toned from his favourite off-stage, screen occupations, the tanning salon and jogging on the Heath, he was the picture of health.

"Beastly trip," he said, settling himself. "The woman across the table chatted endlessly about her female problems, her divorce, and her darling gay son, whom she was certain I must have met since he is currently in school in London."

"American?" Marc stifled a laugh.

"American," Stephen replied flatly. "So, I will only sit next to you if you promise not to discuss your divorce, your female problems or your gay son."

Marc chuckled in spite of himself. "Well, you don't have to worry about the female problems or the gay son…" he paused, sobering up somewhat. "And as for divorce, well, I would just as soon not talk about that. Except to say that I get to keep the house and Renaud."

"Good God, Maude…" Stephen's eyes got rather large. "If I ever get married again, I want the name of your solicitors."

"Done," Marc quipped. Before he could get another word out, his cell phone rang. "Allô?" Marc replied. "Laurent, un instant s'il te plait."

He turned to Stephen. "Hold that thought, Stella dearest."

"Laurent," Marc spoke back into the phone. "What a surprise, where are you?"

"At the airport, waiting for the flight to Nice," Laurent replied. "Where are you?"

"In a car with my friend Stephen, who just arrived on the Eurostar from London. We're on the way to the Gare de Lyon to get the train to Monte Carlo."

"You must tell him hello for me, and say that I hope to meet him soon." Laurent paused a brief moment and braved through his next comment. "And tell him that I am jealous that it is he that is traveling with you and not me."

"Would you like to tell him yourself?" he glared malevolently at Stephen who was making all sorts of strange faces in an attempt to get him to laugh.

"No, no, I just wanted to thank you for having dinner with me last night…and to say how special I think you are…and to ask if we can have dinner together tomorrow night in St. Tropez."

"You're becoming irresistible, you know that," Marc spoke

seductively into the receiver. Stephen made yet another funny face. "Laurent, its really a bit difficult to talk just now. I have a very ill mannered English friend, who is making funny faces, trying to get me to laugh, thereby appearing ridiculous to the person at the other end of the phone. So...let me just say that if you are on the terrace of L'Escale tomorrow evening between 7 and 7:30, you will see a rather tall Frenchman and a somewhat shorter Englishman getting out of an XLS, hunter green. Doubtless the Frenchman will be very happy to dine with you, provided, of course, you don't mind the added company of his ill mannered English friend."

"Marc..." Laurent spoke softly, his words were almost a whisper, "I just called to say..." The hesitation in his voice was genuine. "I mean...I think...I think I may be falling in love with you," he blurted out the last phrase with effort.

The warm smile in Laurent's voice was definitely having its desired effect. "I think I'm glad...see you tomorrow then." Marc pressed the end button, terminating the call.

"Stephen Hampstead," Marc began, shoving his cell phone back into his jacket pocket. "I've only just met Laurent a couple of days ago..."

"Where?" Stephen interjected quickly, before Marc could launch a monologue on funny faces when someone else was on a call.

"On the Eurostar as a matter of fact, and we did not discuss divorce, female problems or his gay son."

"I can well imagine," Stephen replied, insinuating the worst, or the best as the case might be. "Why is it you always have all the luck?"

"Because, dearest S," Marc adopted a playfully sarcastic tone. "I'm the pretty one."

They both laughed. Marc noticed that the driver was smiling too. Funny that, he thought.

"But I promise you this, S," Marc said, turning slightly in his seat to face his friend. "If you ever call me Maude in front of either Laurent or the new help, I'll do what the American woman did at US immigration when asked to prove that she was really an American."

"And what's that dearest M," Stephen quipped, with a grin.
"I'll just pull out my gun and shoot you," he replied with a laugh.
"Good God, what happened?" Stephen asked wide-eyed.
"They let her in, of course." Marc could not help but grin, it was an old joke, but it was still funny, even the driver didn't try to stifle his laugh.

The luggage was on board the train, and they were comfortably settled in their seats. The waiter came for their drink orders and left the luncheon menus. As the train pulled out of the Gare de Lyon and headed for the southern coast, Marc felt a sense of well-being coming over him.

"So," Stephen began with a childish grin. "Now that we're settled, the topics of the day are…the house…and of course, Laurent."

"Well, let's do the house first, assuming that your curiosity about where you will be staying for your holidays, is greater than your vicarious interest in my as yet…and I say this in all seriousness…non-existent love life," Marc replied.

"Your assumption is wrong," Stephen replied. "But we'll do it your way…tell me about the house."

"Well, the location is ideal," Marc began, smiling his thanks as the waiter put their drinks on their table. "It's only 4 kilometres from Lorgues, a charming village built on a hill, with a medieval walled "old town", which is in turn, 40 kilometres north of St Tropez."

The house itself," Marc continued after a sip of his drink. "Is a bit larger than the house in Montréal…eleven bedrooms, instead of seven, five reception rooms instead of three…" He stopped mid- sentence. "Wait a minute, I have the photos that Edward took when he and Chantal went down to sign the papers for me."

Marc reached down between his leg and the wall of the train, where he had carefully placed his briefcase and laptop. He put the briefcase on the table between them and pulled out the envelope marked Chateau de Maure. Taking out the photos, he handed them to Stephen.

"You've outdone yourself M." Stephen emitted a low whistle,

looking at the photo of the entrance front of the house. "...And pink stucco," he added, tongue in cheek.

Marc returned the briefcase to its place.

"What's this?" Stephen turned the envelope towards him, eyeing the writing on its face. "A chateau, aren't we grand?" he added, with a wry grin.

"Enough of that, S," Marc interjected, reaching as if to take away the photos.

"OK, OK." Stephen pulled the photos away from Marc's grasp. "Beautiful entry, the fountain and the gravel court...so many trees, and so green."

"Yes, it is rather nice, isn't it? Look at the interior shots; the dark fruitwood Louis XV wood paneling in the library and the second sitting room...the wonderfully arched French doors everywhere...lots of light. Did Edward take the photos?"

Marc nodded.

Stephen continued flipping through the photographs. "It really is beautiful...Good Lord, the pool is huge!" he organized the photos into a neat stack and handed them back to Marc. "A bit big for Renaud to handle, though."

"Renaud can handle anything," Marc said, putting the photos back into the envelope. "Besides, the housekeeper and caretaker have agreed to stay on, at least for the time being...and there are two cleaning women who come twice a week to help out."

"When was it built?"

"1750 or thereabouts, at least that's what Chantal said."

"Are you sure you can afford the upkeep on this place? I mean what if it needs renovations?"

"Well, it is paid for, no mortgage, that is...and the farm is leased. I do get a percentage of the profits from the crops, so there is some income to cover maintenance...and I have my writing, two projects in the works. With the royalties from the books and films, and my investments, I really don't think there will be a problem. Besides, if push comes to shove, I'll just travel less." Marc replaced the envelope in his briefcase. "As for restorations, there were two lots done by the previous owners, the first in 1917 when they bought it, and again in the '80's. The wiring had to be re-done when they put in the security system."

"Well, sounds like you have it all covered."

"Chantal did, in any case."

"Good on Chantal." He took a sip of his drink, but couldn't hold back any longer. "So, tell me about Laurent."

"There's not a lot to tell…not yet, in any case."

"He's a handsome, younger man…" Stephen began.

"All right, he's younger."

"Please tell me he's not twenty-six, they're *always* twenty-six."

"No, he not twenty-six, he's thirty-four. He is tall, handsome…very handsome, extraordinarily sensual and extremely sexy."

"So, the usual," Stephen quipped.

"He's a successful architect, specializing in residential architecture, renovations and restorations. He has offices on the rue de Rivoli."

"Hmmm," Stephen nodded approvingly. "Rich, well connected, and conveniently located for the occasional afternoon assignation."

"And just because I know *you*," Marc anticipated the next question. "We haven't gone to second base yet."

"Not even to second base and he's already protesting his undying love?" Stephen chuckled. "You know you really need to lower the volume on your cell phone."

"You're in the wrong profession, you know."

"How's that M, dearest?"

"You really should have been a journalist for CNN, the way you can take a simple statement and jump to as yet unfounded conclusions. By tomorrow, I'm sure, you'll have informed everyone in Europe and North America that we're married and living in the south of France."

"Well, M, you know what they say?"

"Do I?"

"The four fastest means of communication; telegraph, telephone, television, and last but not the least, tell-a-queen."

"A little less drama, if you please, Your Majesty."

"Look, I'm just a little concerned, that's all. And don't get how you often get."

"What do you mean?"

"All defensive and huffy." Stephen looked at his friend. "We all know," he began referencing their large circle of friends. "That you're a hopeless romantic, incapable of saying no to a pretty face, particularly when you're vulnerable…and at the moment you are very vulnerable."

"So?"

"Just take it easy. You may be in your mid forties, but you are still a very attractive and desirable man. You're successful, charming…did I say rich…? And you have a family that was on a first name basis with Vercingétorix."

Marc laughed, "I didn't even know you could pronounce Vercingétorix, much less that you knew who he was."

"I'll ignore that little jibe." Stephen feigned injury. "Just go slow, that's all."

"Advice accepted with appreciation," Marc replied, with a smile.

The waiter arrived with their lunch, and the conversation drifted to gossip about their mutual friends, Stephen's wind up of the series, and the upcoming rehearsals for the film he would be doing in the summer. Backgammon followed lunch, and after game number seven, a tiebreaker which Stephen gleefully won, Marc excused himself to find the bar car so he could have a cigarette.

When they traveled together, Marc always took a non-smoking car out of deference to Stephen, who had given up smoking several years previous. Marc took the inventory sheet along with him to try and get an idea of what he would need to purchase, in order to make sure that Maure, as he had come to call it in his mind, was really ready to live in.

He settled into a comfortable club type chair and perused the list. He skipped the furniture section, since Chantal had told him that all the furniture, most of it antique and in good condition, had come with the house, as had all the lamps, lighting fixtures, draperies and linen. Gourmand that he was, he went straight to the section listing the tableware.

There were two Haviland dinner services for twenty-four, as well as a luncheon service and breakfast service for the same number. There was a service for 24 of Christofle flatware in sterling, along with a coffee service and several serving pieces in a matching pattern. There was a Provencal earthenware service, and a set of Provencal wine glasses.

Ridiculous, he suddenly thought. Renaud will sort through all of this when he arrives. He flipped over to the page dealing with the outbuildings and their contents. He looked at the heading labelled garage. There were vehicles that went with the sale, a mid-sized paneled van and a jeep, for the use of the caretaker for gardening and hauling. Good, that was a problem solved. He'd send the caretaker down in the jeep to pick up Renaud on Wednesday. He closed the list and decided he would enjoy his "smoke break".

"Forgive me." The accent was unmistakeably Russian. "Could I trouble you for a cigarette." A man in his late fifties stood in front of him; salt and pepper hair, a full, close-cropped beard, salt and pepper as well. He wore rather thick round glasses.

Marc offered him a cigarette from his pack.

"Thank you." The bespectacled man extended his hand, "Sergei, Sergei Reisky."

"Marc, Marc Balanger." Marc stifled his surprise. He recognized the name immediately.

"Thank you for the cigarette Monsieur Balanger." He enunciated Marc's last name with particular clarity. Then he lit the cigarette with a match from a matchbook, which he held in his hand. "And thank you for the light." He placed the matchbook in Marc's hand, folding Marc's fingers around it. "You will excuse me." Turning, he walked over to the bar and ordered a drink.

The gesture was not lost on Marc. He had just been slipped a message. He put the matchbook in his trouser pocket, stubbed out his cigarette in the ashtray, and quickly returned to his car. Sitting down, he returned the inventory list to the briefcase.

"M?" Stephen eyed him quizzically. "You look as if you've just seen a ghost."

"Worse," Marc replied. "I've just met Laurent's stepfather."

"You can't possibly be serious," Stephen quipped.

"I'm quite serious," Marc replied, reaching into his trouser pocket and extracting the matchbook. "He bummed a cigarette, introduced himself, then he gave me this matchbook, thanking me for a light," Marc said, putting the matchbook on the table.

"You don't use matches," Stephen said, recalling one of Marc's signatures, a gold Dupont lighter that had belonged to his grandfather; he always used it.

"I didn't light his cigarette either." Marc opened the matchbook. There were two words written hastily on the inside of the cover, 'Karpov, danger'. "He passed me a message."

"What, stay away from my son?"

"I wish that's what it said." Marc paused, and wiped his forehead. He was actually perspiring. "It says Karpov, danger," he added, his voice almost a whisper.

"Karpov?"

"Shush," Marc said quickly. Just at that moment his cell phone rang, he almost jumped out of his seat.

"Jesus, M, it's just your cell." Stephen chuckled, a look of amused bewilderment on his face.

"Oui, Allô." Marc spoke into the phone, still somewhat shaken. "Renaud, no, no, it's just that I wasn't expecting a call, and the ring startled me." He paused, listening. "OK, if you find anything else, just call. No, no, I promise, next time I won't jump out of my skin…and Renaud, thanks."

Stephen waited just long enough for Marc to take a deep breath. "Alright M, what's the story, who is Karpov, and is he *in* danger or *a* danger, and what does Laurent's stepfather have to do with this, and what did Renaud have to say that made you look like you're about to fall into a cauldron of boiling oil?"

Marc let out a heavy sigh. "Well, you know I told you that we were going to spend the night in Monte Carlo on the way to the new house because I was doing a favour for Sean,"

"Go on."

"Well the favour is to deliver a letter which Sean bought for one of his clients at Sotheby's in New York last week. The client's name is Karpov. Prince Felix Andronikov wrote the letter."

The rest spilled out like the waters from an opened floodgate.

"The daughter of that self-same Prince Andronikov was the last owner of the house I just bought, a house in which there was supposed to be a fabulous treasure buried by the aforementioned Felix Andronikov, which no one has ever found. Andronikov, by the way was murdered mysteriously in Nice a few years after his arrival in France."

Marc paused a minute to catch his breath, then continued, "Sergei Reisky defected from Russia by fleeing to the Canadian embassy while he was 'on show', as part of a Russian artists' exhibition at the Petit Palais in the seventies. The defection was organized by the same Karpov to whom we are delivering the letter, who was at the time a 'cultural attaché' at the Russian embassy in Paris."

Marc finished with a somewhat forlorn look on his face. "Laurent's father died when he was ten. Two years later, his mother married Reisky."

"Well, now that you've cleared that up," Stephen interjected, with more than a bit of sarcasm. "What did Renaud have to say?"

"I asked him to check on several things, among them Karpov and Reisky. I was trying to see if there was any connection. Seems they are actually related. Karpov's wife Marina Reisky was Sergei's older sister."

"Which makes him Karpov's brother-in-law."

"Former brother-in-law, actually, Marina died of cancer in Leningrad in 1987," Marc continued, "They had one daughter, Irina. Renaud said that Karpov got into a lot of hot water when his brother-in-law defected. He was recalled from Paris, and did not resurface on the international scene again, until after the fall of the communist government in the early nineties. By then he was in the energy ministry and was in charge of negotiating arrangements, for foreign investors in the Russian petroleum industry. His position allowed him to acquire a large number of leases, first in the Caspian Sea, then subsequently in Siberia, and now in the Chukotka region of the Arctic."

"Then he's rich."

"Enormously."

"Then why would he care about a buried treasure; he's already an oil tycoon."

"I don't know," Marc replied. "It doesn't make sense. It makes even less sense that Reisky would try to warn me about Karpov."

"And I thought I was off to the south of France for six weeks of peace and quiet," Stephen said, wryly.

"Look, all I did was buy a house and agree to do a favour for a friend."

"When are we supposed to make the drop?" Stephen asked, purposely using gangster parlance.

"I spoke to Karpov on Saturday," Marc replied pensively. " His driver, Malinkov, is picking us up at the station in Monte Carlo. From there he'll drive us to Karpov's yacht, the Rosenkranz, to have dinner. I'm to give him the letter then."

"Not necessarily a good plan, being on a yacht in the middle of the harbour," Stephen mused. "That is, if Karpov really is dangerous."

"I'd have to agree with you there," Marc said.

"We're driving to Lorgues from Monte Carlo, right?"

"Yes, right." Marc quickly saw what Stephen had in mind. "Too bad about dinner, but as you seem to be a bit unwell," Marc smiled. "It really is best that we pick up the car and drive straight on to our final destination."

"Clever M, but why do I always have to be the one to get sick?"

"Right," Marc ignored the question. "It's about an hour's drive from Monte Carlo to Lorgues, only 4 km more, and we're comfortably settled for the evening. Under an hour and a half, if I don't miss my guess."

"What about getting into the house? You have the keys, the alarm code? It wouldn't do to have the local constabulary show up at 10 o'clock at night. Not the best way to start out as the new owner."

"You're right," Marc agreed. "Ah, but I've got the caretaker's phone number here in my briefcase with the house papers." Marc reached down and took out the envelope marked Chateau de Maure. Flipping through the papers, he found the telephone number. "And I have my trusty cell. What time is it?"

"Five thirty," Stephen said, looking at his watch.

"Good, the caretaker is probably preparing his dinner about now," Marc said, dialling the number. "Allô, Monsieur Doumé, ici Marc Balanger. Je m'excuse de vous déranger à cette heure, mais j'ai voulu vous prévenir que je vais arriver au château ce soir, au lieu de demain matin. Est-ce que vous y seriez?"

"Oui, Monsieur Balanger."

"Bon, je crois que nous y arriverons, Monsieur Hampstead et moi, envers 22 heures, le plus tard."

"Bien sur, Monsieur, j'y serai, mais Madame Trochet…"

"Ne la dérange pas, je sais qu'elle habite Lorgues, nous sommes capables de nous occuper de nous même. Merci, Monsieur Doumé, à ce soir."

"Queen's English, please," Stephen said, as Marc pushed the button ending the call.

"Short version, he's expecting us tonight around 10."

"Very complicated, French," Stephen chuckled. "So many words for such a brief message."

"So," Stephen continued. "Should we telephone Karpov?"

"And give him a chance to prepare something new and different," Marc asked, with a raised eyebrow. "Not a chance. Your sudden *turn* should be sudden, I'll just tell Karpov's driver to deliver our apologies, hand him the letter, and then we'll be off."

Karpov was seated at his desk, writing, when the knock came at the door of his study.

"Come," he replied gruffly, looking up at the tall, well muscled, uniformed man who entered the room. "Malinkov," he said, acknowledging his driver and bodyguard. "Our guests have arrived, have they?"

Malinkov had worked for Karpov for more than 15 years. He had been bodyguard and driver since Karpov's days in the energy ministry before the regime change. He knew his master's temperament well. He walked forward and laid the brown envelope on the desk. "The package you were expecting Mr. Karpov."

"And my guests?"

"Unfortunately, they were unable to come, sir," Malinkov began. "Mr. Hampstead was not feeling well, so they have continued on to Monsieur Balanger's home." He bowed slightly, "Monsieur Balanger sends his regrets and those of Mr. Hampstead."

Quickly, Karpov opened the envelope. The letter was there, sealed in its protective plastic sheet. He looked at it, carefully. This was not going according to plan. His anger was cool, but very present. "Has Reisky arrived?"

"Yes, sir," Malinkov replied quietly. "Sergei Reisky has just come aboard."

"Tell him I will see him at once," Karpov said coldly. "At once, I said," he added, the edge of his voice sharpening.

Silently, Malinkov left the room.

Chapter Four ~
Maure

It was a bright, clear April day. The warmth of the morning sun was rejuvenating after the cold Montréal winter. Marc was an early riser, and had made his way down to the kitchen, where Madame Trochet was already at work. She was steaming a large pottery jug of milk.

"Bon jour Madame," Marc said, greeting his new housekeeper. If first impressions mattered, and often they do, Marc was pleasantly impressed. Madame Trochet was a pleasant looking woman, handsome even, a bit on the full figured side; she seemed at home in the kitchen.

"Bonjour, Altesse," she replied, turning off the steamer. "I have prepared breakfast for you and Monsieur Hampstead." Her accent was rather pronounced, but her English was perfect. "I thought perhaps you would like to eat on the garden terrace, as it is such a beautiful morning."

"Of course, Madame, that's a wonderful idea." He followed behind her as she led the way.

"Doumé saw to everything last night?" she asked.

"Yes, Madame." Marc replied. "He was kind enough to show us to our rooms and bring in the luggage." He was immediately taken by the view as they stepped onto the terrace; a lovely stretch of lawn led to formal gardens, lovely shaped parterres with their flowers already in bloom, the smell of roses and lavender filled the early morning air. Neatly trimmed hedges bordered the carefully laid out patterns. He stopped to drink it all in. Remembering he was not alone, he turned towards Madame Trochet. "He made us feel quite at home. He even had a fire going in the sitting room."

"Monsieur Doumé is quite efficient, as I am certain you will find Altesse."

Just then, he heard Stephen come bounding down the stairs.

"I'm on the terrace out back S," Marc called out.

Stephen stepped out onto the terrace, a picture of British sartorial country house splendour, tan pleated trousers, crisp cotton shirt, cashmere pullover and comfortable looking walking shoes. "Good Lord!" he said, taking in the garden. "Good!" he exclaimed again, looking at the table laden with their breakfast.

Madame Trochet had prepared a wonderful country breakfast for them; cheeses, plump juicy strawberries and slices of sweet orange and green melon, thin slices of ham, boiled eggs and quantities of delicious homemade jams, preserved figs, fresh country butter, sliced baguette, croissants, steaming bowls of café au lait and freshly squeezed orange juice. A small army could have joined them.

Doumé must have phoned her after Marc's call, because the baguette and the croissant were freshly baked that morning. She must have brought them with her from the village on her way to work.

"Madam Trochet." Marc performed the introductions. "This is my very closest friend in all the world, Stephen Hampstead."

"Monsieur Hampstead," she nodded respectfully, flashing a charming smile.

"Stephen," Marc continued. "Madame Trochet, the obviously resourceful and immensely capable woman who will be looking after us. Who," he added, by way of a warning. "Speaks excellent English."

"Thank you, Altesse." She flushed slightly at the compliment. "I try my best."

"Well, Madame." Stephen pulled out his chair, gleefully eyeing the bountiful and beautifully appointed table. A vase, filled with magnificent white roses from the garden, graced the centre of the white wrought-iron table, which was covered by a dusty rust and blue Provencal cloth. "I'm so glad you do, as my French is limited to the simple phrases gleaned from an English middle school."

Marc sat in the other chair. "The table looks beautiful Madame, and the food delicious."

"Merci, Altesse." She was genuinely pleased her efforts had been so greatly appreciated. The princesses Andronikov had always taken everything for granted. For them, perfection was to be expected, not appreciated. The only comments the princesses ever made, were when things were not as they should have been.

Brigitte Trochet was pleased her new employer seemed to have a more contemporary attitude. To be sure, if her new employer were as pleasant as his sister had been, she was certain that she would like the new owner of Maure very much indeed. "Monsieur Doumé thought you and Monsieur Hampstead would like a tour of the grounds and the park after breakfast, Altesse."

"What a wonderful idea, Madame Trochet. Ask him if he could come round in about an hour." he looked questioningly at Stephen, who was already munching on a slice of baguette slathered with butter and homemade strawberry jam.

Stephen nodded his head in agreement.

"I will tell him to come in an hour, I'm certain that will be convenient for him, Monsieur." Madame Trochet smiled at Stephen's obvious appreciation of her strawberry preserves. "If you will excuse me, Altesse, Monsieur."

"Of course," Marc replied. "And thank you again, Madame Trochet, for this wonderful breakfast."

"God," Stephen said, spooning a large helping of preserved figs onto his plate. "The food, the view, and the garden. M, you are the most fortunate man on the planet. This has to be paradise."

They passed their breakfast in complete ignorance of the events of the day before. Their surroundings were far too idyllic to be clouded over by a near miss, so to speak. Mysteries and dangerous men seemed far away as the excitement of discovering his new home mounted. The hour passed quickly amid conversations of future projects and new romance. Doumé arrived precisely as planned to take them around the grounds of the house.

Doumé seemed an interesting type. He was of average height,

about the same as Stephen, but with a much sturdier build, consistent with the heavy work he must do around the house and the grounds. Broad features, with glinting brown eyes beneath a shock of closely cropped brown hair, he had a pleasant smile, and an easygoing manner.

Respectful of his new employer and his guest, Doumé was nevertheless not the cap-in-hand kind of caretaker, which made Marc feel more at ease. He'd always had a more casual kind of relationship with his household help, and was uncomfortable around those who, fortunate like himself, insisted on the formality of another generation when dealing with their domestic staff.

They decided to make the tour of the grounds on foot. They started in the front, where opposite the house and the entrance court, a thickly wooded patch of ground, through which they had driven the evening before, lined a wide gravelled lane, which laid a straight access to the entrance gates and the road to Lorgues beyond.

The trees completely enclosed the gravel covered entrance court with its elegant ornamental pond and fountain. The fountain was turned on; gentle arcs of water shot into the air, landing on the basin below that in turn spilled over in streams to the pond in which it was the central ornament.

To the west of the house was a small, stonewalled kitchen garden filled with herbs and vegetables and bright coloured beds of berries. The beds were neatly laid out, much as they must have been when the gardens were made in the mid eighteenth century, when kitchen gardens were as decorative as they were essential. Narrow crushed-stone paths ensured easy access to the garden's produce. A small stone shed with a bright blue-painted wooden door contained the gardening equipment.

There was a small orchard of fig, pear and apple trees, just beyond the ample kitchen garden's walls. The trees were perfectly grouped, carefully pruned and tended.

On the southern front of the house, the garden front, two small wings enveloped a broad balustraded terrace. Beyond the terrace with its wide sweeping stairs, which led down to a lovely stretch of lawn, were the formal gardens Marc and Stephen had so admired at breakfast; manicured hedges and flowerbeds leading down to the large rectangular pool, with a lovely cottage style pool house.

To the east of the house was a wooded grove, which came almost to the walls of the chateau, itself. They walked through the grove, down a wide, long established lane that led to a small lake surrounded by a vibrant green meadow, dotted with wildflowers.

On the opposite side of the lake, there was an imposing Gothik styled bagatelle, a sort of pavilion made up of three parts. An octagonal tower raised its stone face towards the sky. It was connected to a more traditional, rectangular room by a windowless, stone passage.

The stone walls of both the tower and the large rectangular room were set with gothik arched French doors, arranged in such a way as to fill the rooms with natural light. A flagstone terrace ran across the front of the charming bagatelle.

It was a perfect site for picnics and parties. Doumé had forgotten to get the keys from Madame Trochet, so they decided to come back later for a look inside.

They were back to the house just after one. Madame Trochet had already set the table on the garden terrace. It was a light luncheon menu, at Marc's request, Pissaladière, Salad Niçoise, and a platter of fresh garden vegetables with tapenade, all washed down with several glasses of a good locally produced Cote de Provence.

They were just finishing up dessert; fresh strawberries drizzled with honey and covered in cream, when Doumé came on to the terrace. Rather conveniently, Marc thought, Madame Trochet came from the kitchen to clear away the lunch. The golden opportunity, he thought, two birds with one stone. "Monsieur Doumé," he began.

"Luc, Altesse," Doumé replied.

"Madame Trochet," he nodded to the housekeeper.

"Brigitte, s'il vous plait, Altesse," she replied.

"Bon, Luc, Brigitte, asseyez-vous s'il vous plait," Marc indicated the two chairs opposite him and Stephen. They eyed each other a bit warily, but took the chairs indicated by their new employer, albeit somewhat disconcerted. "Et s'il vous plait, je vous demande de me rendre le service de mettre de côté les titres chez nous. Je préférerai

Monsieur ou Monsieur Balanger, c'est plus de notre époque, n'est ce pas?"

"Comme vous voulez, Monsieur," they replied in chorus.

"I guess I'll just go for a swim," Stephen said, starting to get up.

"No, sit," Marc said, resting his hand on the arm of his friend.

"Next thing you'll be telling me to rollover and play dead," Stephen said, rising out of his chair.

"Stephen, please."

"Monsieur," Brigitte began. "Both Luc and I can speak English if this will make your friend more comfortable." Brigitte displayed that peculiar sense of warmth that seemed to be the birthright of Frenchwomen of all ages, shapes and generations. Her kind smile and bright hazel eyes convinced Stephen that his presence was appreciated.

"Well then," Stephen replied, sitting again. "Just for you Madame."

"Brigitte, please Monsieur." Her smile really was charming.

"I wanted to reassure both of you that your positions are quite secure," Marc began. "As you are both aware, Renaud, who has been with me now for a number of years, is arriving the day after tomorrow. I hope that he will receive the same kind of warm welcome, which you have already extended to me."

Marc was choosing his words very carefully. It was important at this early stage not to tread on anyone's toes. Not only was he dependant on these two people for the day to day running of his home, but they were the continuity with its previous owner, and perhaps an important part of the puzzle that he was trying to piece together out of the loosely connected threads that seemed to have come along with the house and its unsolved mystery.

"Lorgues and the Var are new to Renaud, and though they are not quite so new to me, I am sure that things have changed since last I spent time here. We both will appreciate your advice and council as we get used to our new home." He paused for a moment trying to determine the effect of his words, indeed, to determine if he was making himself clearly understood.

"En tout cas, in any case," he continued. "I don't expect that your duties will change very much. Renaud will be in charge of the house when I go away, and, as a general rule, I will leave much of the day-to-day running of Maure to him. But you should not hesitate to speak with me directly if there are any concerns. Do you have any questions?" he asked, smiling warmly.

"Monsieur Renaud, he is your secrétaire?" Brigitte ventured, somewhat timidly.

Marc thought for a moment. Renaud had run his house for many years now, he supposed that he was due a promotion…and how absolutely perfect that it should be Brigitte who would give it to him. "That is a very good way to express it, Brigitte," Marc replied. "Monsieur Renaud handles all the details of my daily life so that I am free to do my work."

Both Brigitte and Luc seemed happy with this explanation of Renaud and his duties; it seemed to make them feel more secure. They seemed to relax a bit more in their chairs.

"So," Marc continued. "When Renaud arrives on Wednesday, I would be very grateful if you would show him around and explain all the details of what you do to him. This is not to say that I am not interested myself, it's just that if Renaud can take care of something it will allow me to focus on my own work."

"Bien entendu, Monsieur," Luc replied.

"As you wish, Monsieur," Brigitte responded in turn.

"Good." Marc smiled warmly. This was going to work out well, he thought. Trust was important in a relationship such as theirs, and he was beginning to get the feeling that these people could be trusted. "Mr. Hampstead and I will be going down to St Tropez this afternoon to return the rental car." He turned to Luc, "How is the gas in the Jaguar?"

"The tank is full, Monsieur."

"Thank you." Marc continued. "We will have dinner in St Tropez this evening. So Brigitte, if you would care to take the rest of the afternoon off, please feel free to do so."

"Merci, Monsieur," she said, standing. "Vous êtes bien aimable."

Luc stood too, not wishing to be disrespectful. "Monsieur," he began, waiting to be acknowledged.

"Yes, Luc?"

"My niece is being engaged tonight, and there is a party for her at my sister's house in Draguigon. It is not far from here, but well, I think we will drink much to her health…and…"

"I see what you mean, Luc," Marc interrupted. "Perhaps you should stay the night and come back sometime in the morning."

"Monsieur is very kind," he said appreciablytingly.

"Oh, before I forget," Marc added. "Renaud will be arriving at the station in St. Raphael Wednesday. Do you think you will be able to collect him?"

"Of course, Monsieur."

"He will phone on Wednesday morning, before the train leaves Nice, to let me know when he will be arriving. I will let you know the time then."

"Monsieur." Luc nodded his agreement. He paused a moment, selecting his words. "If I may, Monsieur, I will leave after I bring the cars to the front."

"Parfait, et Luc…"

"Oui Monsieur?"

"Mes félicitations à votre nièce et à son fiancé."

"Mine too," Stephen piped in.

"Merci, Messieurs."

It was four o'clock in the afternoon. The sky over St Tropez was a glorious cloudless blue. Marc and Stephen were seated on the terrace of Le Café, on the Place de Lices, sipping Pastis and watching the teams playing pétanque. The rental car had been returned, Marc had officially taken possession of his new house, things were arranged, at least for the moment, so that they could relax and enjoy the afternoon.

"Beautiful, eh," Marc said, lighting a cigarette.

"Life doesn't get much better." Stephen sipped his Pastis.

"Now is the time to make, if I may borrow a phrase from Hercule Poirot, the 'little grey cells work'."

Stephen moaned. "I wish we didn't have to...can't we just watch the game and pretend that Karpov and his minions don't exist. Some of those guys are really horny, look at the one in the white t-shirt."

"OK. I'll think out loud and you can pretend you are hearing a running discourse of the game with the 'horny guy in the white t-shirt'."

Stephen did not respond, he just continued sipping his Pastis and watching the boules roll across the ground.

"What do we know?" Marc began his musings. "Maure was bought by Felix Andronikov in 1917. He moved in with his family sometime that same year. Andronikov was murdered in Nice a few years later; the case remains unsolved to this day. Sometime between taking possession of the house and his death, he is supposed to have secreted a fabulous treasure somewhere in the house or on the grounds. Rumour has it that the treasure was never found."

Stephen continued his preoccupation with his Pastis and the pétanque players.

"The same Felix Andronikov was a intimate of the imperial family. He was also a copious letter writer, and although he lived in St Petersburg, wrote frequently to his cousins in Georgia to keep them abreast of news at the court and in the capital."

Marc, apparently talking to himself, paused again, took a long drag off his cigarette and a sip of his Pastis. "One of these letters was written to his cousin Andrei Barataev. The letter, dated March 1, 1917, found its way to Sotheby's auction block in New York earlier this year, and was purchased by a rare book/document dealer in Boston for his client, a Mr. Karpov, self professed collector of Russian imperial artefacts. This same Karpov says that this letter is a most important part of the Russian imperial legacy, and that he has been searching for this letter for a long time."

Marc continued, slowly attempting to organize, by verbalizing, the loose threads of this intricate tapestry he seemed to have inherited. "The letter, part written in French, a language commonly used among the Russian aristocracy, part in Russian, seems to be a combination of family news and the political events leading to the arrest of the

Imperial family. There is nothing in the letter that we know of, which references a treasure to be brought to France. There is also nothing in the letter which is unknown to historians of the revolutionary period, that would make it important to a collector of artefacts from the period…and…Andronikov, though closely connected to the court, does not appear to have any important connection to the imperial family itself."

"But you haven't translated the Russian passages yet, have you?" Stephen grinned, his eyes still on the game of pétanque.

"You are listening!" Marc said, with surprise.

"Just wanted you to see why I've won a SWEAT, dearest M," he replied.

"Well deserved S, well deserved."

"So when are we going to get that bit translated?" Stephen queried. "Come to think of it, why didn't Sotheby's provide a translation of the document in English?"

"Why didn't I think of that earlier?" Marc said, putting out his cigarette. He reached for his cell phone. "What time is it in Boston?"

Stephen looked at his watch, "Between 9 and 10 pm."

"Great," Marc replied, flipping through the stored numbers on his cell phone. He located Sean's, and pressed the call button.

"Sean Sweeny," the Trinity College lilt of his friend's voice answered.

"Sean, this is Marc."

"Marc, how are you…where are you?"

"St Tropez, actually."

"It's sunny?"

"Sunny and 20 degrees…centigrade."

"Well, we're in the middle of a nor'easter, and the last time I checked, it was around –5." He chuckled. "I think I hate you."

"How nice to know that our relationship is still the same," Marc replied sardonically.

"What's up? By the way, thanks for delivering the letter to Karpov."

"Your quite welcome," Marc replied. "It wasn't really far out of my way." Marc paused long enough to light a cigarette he had pulled from the pack on the table while they were talking. He always smoked more when he was uncomfortable. "Actually that's what I'm calling about. I don't suppose that you had a translation of the letter?"

"Funny, you're the second person who has asked me that," Sean replied, obviously intrigued by the question. "No, Sotheby's didn't provide one. The catalogue just listed it as a letter from Prince Felix Andronikov, officer of the household of Nicolas II to his cousin, relating certain family matters and the events of February 1917. Why do you ask?"

"Idle curiosity." Marc continued, "The house I just bought was owned by the Andronikov family. Quite a coincidence…anyway, I thought maybe there might be something in it about the purchase of the house." He was not really telling his friend the truth, but a little white lie wouldn't really hurt. "You said that I was the second person to ask you the question. Who was the first?"

"Karpov oddly enough," the curiosity in his voice mounting. "I thought that odd, since Karpov obviously speaks Russian, and his French is excellent. Why do you ask?"

"It's not important really," Marc replied, trying to throw him off the scent. "Just trying to piece together a bit of the history of the house."

"M," Sean replied knowingly. "After all these years, you can't fool me. Something's up or I'm a Dutchman…and we both know I'm Irish, Dublin born and bred."

"Really Sean!"

"Doesn't matter though, I know I'll hear from you or Renaud sooner or later, there'll be something obscure you can't live without. Do me a favour though."

"Yes?" Marc replied.

"Try to phone during normal hours, will you? There is a bit of a time difference between your sunny southern paradise, and my snow bound northern clime. By the way, give my best to Stephen. He is there with you now, I believe."

"Right you are, and I'll remember about the time…and Sean…thanks."

"Same old Sean," Stephen said, as Marc ended the call with a push of the button. Stephen could not help but overhear the conversation, since Marc had put the volume up to full, to compensate for the connection.

"So, Karpov couldn't make out the Russian paragraphs either," Marc mused.

"Sean didn't say that," Stephen replied, with a wave to the waiter. "The drinks are on me," he added. "I'll settle the tab."

"I still say it's the Russian he didn't understand, because the French paragraphs are textbook. If you took the language in secondary school, you could read the paragraphs without the aid of a dictionary. Karpov was a cultural attaché at the Russian embassy in Paris. His French would have to have been better than grade school."

"Maybe the Russian isn't really Russian, but some sort of code," Stephen observed thoughtfully.

"S, you're brilliant. That makes sense." Marc patted his friend on the arm. "Sometimes you amaze me."

Stephen rolled his eyes. "I may have been born yesterday, but I, like Mae West, spent the whole day downtown."

"You were born yesterday?" Marc replied, with a smirk.

"Ouch!" Stephen feigned extreme hurt. "Well, now that you have your wits about you again," he said, paying the check. "Let's go meet your new boyfriend and see if we can discover just how much he is in bed with the Karpov clan."

Marc groaned his annoyance with Stephen's analysis of what was to have been a quasi-romantic dinner, watching the boats arrive and depart in the harbour. He had to admit, however, that his friend was right. Laurent did have a part to play in this mystery, unwitting or not. He fervently hoped that it was an unwitting role that this all too attractive and charming young man was playing.

The quai Jean Jaurès was coming alive with the foot traffic of early evening diners. Stephen noted that there were just a few people sitting on the terrace of L'Escale, Only one sat alone. The tall, tawny haired young man had to be Laurent.

Stephen could see Marc's attraction instantly; Marc seemed to take on a bit of a glow when the young man waved to them. The welcoming smile, and the seductive baritone voice that greeted them both only served to clarify the impression. For Marc's sake, he found himself hoping that Laurent was only circumstantially connected to the Karpov clan.

"Pleased to meet you Mr. Hampstead," Laurent said, standing and shaking Stephen's hand.

"Enchanté," Stephen tossed out one of the standard phrases he still remembered from middle school.

"Vous parlez français," Laurent was impressed.

"Sorry," Stephen replied quickly. "That was my phrase for the day."

"But beautifully said," Laurent replied, charming as he spoke. "And how was your day?" Although the question was directed to them both, his gaze was fixed on Marc, whose hand he still held in his own.

"Well, Marc here made a very good start as the new lord of the manor," Stephen quipped, only half jesting. It was clear that this was a job for Stella Goodthighs, and she was about to leap into the fray.

"Gentlemen," he said, separating their hands. "We'll have no arm wrestling at the dinner table…bad form don't you know," Stephen finished, with a quirky grin and a nod of his head. "But soft, what light on yonder horizon breaks, it is the waiter who brings sweet sonnets of love from the chef…better known as menus to you lot."

Laurent was genuinely amused. Marc, on the other hand recognized the sudden appearance of Goodthighs humour. Dame Stella was on, and at least for the moment, would or could not be pulled off centre stage. In truth, Marc thought this was probably the best tack. A person's reaction to wit and humour often revealed more than simple questions and answers.

"Garçon," Stephen said dramatically, taking all three menus from the waiter. "In the interest of time, I hereby declare myself host for the evening. I shall order not only for myself, but for my young friends here as well. Well for my young friend and his old…Ouch!" he exclaimed quietly, responding to the not too gentle kick he felt from underneath the table. "M, you do injure me in your enthusiasm." He turned back to the waiter.

"Besides, I have the distinct feeling that our new friend here, mine not yours," Stephen indicated the waiter with an elegant stage gesture. "Our new friend is quite probably de la famille," he finished with a French expression, purposefully pronounced with an overly British accent.

"Oui, Monsieur, vous avez raison, je le suis," the waiter replied graciously, with a broad grin. He knew that he was in for a very large tip if he played along.

"There," Stephen grinned. "I told you. Here is what we will have." Stephen picked up the menu with a slight flourish. "We will have," and he read off the items from the menu with the decidedly English accent of the West End stage. "Terrine Maison du moment et sa marmelade d'oignons, Épaule d'agneau confite en cocotte, Pommes Matouille, and for dessert, Crème Brûlée à la vanille Bourbon, with Pastis to start, followed by a bottle of Chateau de Berne, cuvee rouge, if you have it."

"I have a '96 Monsieur Hampstead." The waiter's accent was heavy, but he was obviously accustomed to speaking English.

The look of amazement on Stephen's face at having been recognized was such that Marc, Laurent and the waiter had to chuckle.

"Pardon, Monsieur." The waiter was grinning broadly. "You see I have satellite television. I watch the Majors of Tilford every week. It is very funny, and helps me to understand English humour."

"I thank you for your kind words, young sir," he replied, looking the waiter directly in the eye. "Let the feast begin."

The waiter went off to place the order, still smiling.

"You've acquired the slightest rose colour, S." Marc sniggered. "Unusual for you."

"Have a care M," Stephen returned with a playful glance, tinged ever so faintly by a hint of malice. "I might just risk the American woman."

Marc took a deep and audible intake of breath. "Truce S?"

"Truce M." Stephen smiled. "Now to you, dear." He turned his attention to the perplexed looking Laurent. So, you're an architect."

"Yes." Laurent felt as though he were about to step under a close friend's microscope. "Actually that's why I'm here. One of my clients has bought an old house in the town and wants me to remodel the interior."

"Ah, the old 'gut the place but leave the Provencal charm' request."

"I see you know the story well."

"I do, I do." Stephen replied. "Having made the same request once too often regarding Hampstead charm…the village, not the man," he added quickly.

The waiter arrived with their Pastis. "Your drinks, messieurs."

"Ah, what an angel," Stephen quipped.

"So they say Monsieur," the waiter replied with a mischievous grin, serving their drinks.

"Oh, behave," Stephen delivered the phrase with the Austin Powers inflection. "But do leave your number," he added, without batting an eyelash. The waiter was, after all, fun, and the number game just might yield some interesting evenings in St Tropez.

"But of course," the waiter interjected. "Bonsoir, Monsieur, Madame," he said, welcoming an arriving couple coming onto the terrace.

"So," Stephen swallowed a gulp of his drink and turned his attention back to Laurent. "What do your parents think of your new boyfriend?"

"Stephen," Marc said, with a hint of frustration.

"No," Laurent interrupted, placing his hand on Marc's, looking him in the eyes. "I don't mind the question. I'm glad he asked." He turned back to Stephen. "Actually they don't know about Marc yet. My mother is in New York; she's doing an apartment there for a Texas oil heiress. My mother is an interior designer."

"My stepfather, Sergei Reisky, is in Zurich supervising the installation of a mural he just finished for a bank there." He looked back at Marc. "I know they will approve, though…that is if and when you will let me tell them."

GRANNY'S CHIPS

Now it was Marc's turn to blush. He was both embarrassed and relieved. Although they had not known each other for very long, Marc felt that Laurent was telling the truth. Something about the frank and open way Laurent had replied, seemed to assure him that Laurent really did believe that his stepfather was in Zurich.

Dinner was really enjoyable, especially with the waiter thrown into the mix. Quips and quotes with obscure literary and film reference kept the table and their waiter in good humour now that one of the loose threads had been knotted, at least to Marc's satisfaction. Too soon, dinner was finished and the check was on its way.

"What time do you have to be at work in the morning," Stephen asked.

"I don't have to be on site again for a couple of days," Laurent replied. "We took all the measurements yesterday, so I'm finishing up the final drawings…we can go out for some dancing if you'd like. The Cave du Roy is in my hotel; I'm staying at the Byblos."

"Actually, that is not quite what I had in mind," Stephen continued. "If you don't have to be on site for a couple of days, why don't you come back to Marc's place with us. You can draw anywhere, n'est pas?"

Marc's face bore a look of genuine amazement; Laurent looked pleased.

"I must say that I would greatly appreciate the opportunity to spend some quality time with Marc," Laurent replied. "With both of you," he added quickly. "But," he continued looking at Marc. "I would not want to impose."

"Don't be silly," Stephen interjected imperiously. "The house has eleven bedrooms and there's only the two of us, three if you come."

"Stephen's right," Marc said. "It is a big house, there's plenty of places for you to work…it would be nice to spend some time together."

"Well then, it's settled," Stephen said standing. "We'll go and collect the car from the car park and drive you up to the hotel. You can pick up what you need, and we'll be off to the hinterland." He waived to their waiter, occupied another table, as they left. Quite pleased with himself, he fingered the slip of paper in his pocket, a slip of paper with a name and phone number hastily written on it. Hopefully they would solve this little mystery soon and he could really enjoy his vacation.

Chapter Five –
Midnight Mayhem

They knew something was wrong as soon as they saw the lights of the house. As they walked onto the broad terrace that stretched across the entrance front, Marc noticed one of the French doors that led from the terrace into the Green Drawing Room was open; broken glass was scattered on the terrace.

"Get back in the car." Laurent grabbed Marc by the arm, instinctively aware of what was wrong. "Whoever broke in, might still be in the house."

Quickly they went back down the stairs to the courtyard. Marc appeared visibly rattled; his hands trembled as he pulled out a cigarette.

"I'll drive," Laurent said, sensing that Marc was reluctant to get behind the wheel. "Lorgues is just down the road."

They found the prefecture de police without much effort and returned to the house, local constabulary in tow. The police searched the house and as much of the grounds as they could see, but they found no one. There were the usual questions, which Marc and the others answered.

"Monsieur Balanger," the taller of the two gendarmes spoke. "Please try to refrain from moving anything until morning. Inspector Leclerc will want to have the scene of the break-in to remain, as close as possible, the way it was when we found it. The inspector will come with a forensic team to take photographs and fingerprints."

The gendarmes had gone; the house was silent, and a mess. Drawers and cupboards were open; their contents tossed about on the floor. Pictures had been pulled off the walls and left, canvas side up, on the floor. The lighter furniture, tables and chairs, had been upturned. Pieces of broken porcelain, crystal and glass lay scattered about the carpets near the tables on which they had rested.

The library was the worst, all the books had been pulled out from the shelves and were tossed carelessly around the room in complete disarray; some had the end papers pulled from their bindings. Papers were scattered everywhere.

They went upstairs; the bedrooms were not in bad condition. The furniture was too heavy to lift; the cupboards and chests were empty for the most part, in any case. No other windows were broken, so they must have come and gone the same way. They returned to the informal sitting room. The sofas were large, leather-upholstered and heavy, so still upright. Marc sat down; Laurent sat beside him.

"I think drinks are in order," Stephen said, heading for the kitchen. "There's bound to be a bottle of wine we can open without smudging any fingerprints."

"Grab something to use as an ashtray will you," Marc called after him. He reached in his pocket and pulled out his cigarettes and lighter. The packet of matches from the Eurostar was tucked in the cellophane of the cigarette pack. At first sight, he knew what had happened. His hands were shaking with anger as he extracted a cigarette. Laurent lit the cigarette.

"Karpov," Marc said coldly, exhaling a long stream of smoke.

"Karpov?" Laurent made no attempt to hide either his recognition of the name or his bewilderment at its use.

"Do you know him?" Marc asked.

"Only what Sergei has said of him." Laurent looked completely perplexed.

"Laurent, I have some things to tell you," Marc began. "Not the least of which is, that your stepfather is not in Zurich."

Laurent stared back at Marc with unabashed amazement. Marc could tell it was genuine.

"He was on the train from Paris to Monte Carlo yesterday," Marc continued. "He introduced himself to me in the smoking lounge car."

"Oops!" Stephen, entering the room, wine bottle and glasses in hand, half turned as if to exit again.

"Stephen," Marc called him back. "You're a part of this too, besides, I think we all need that drink."

"I didn't tell you about your father at dinner, because I had to know if you were part of this *thing*," he almost spat out the word, "or not." He finished with a heavy sigh. He paused and took Laurent's hand. "I believe you're not."

"I second that," Stephen interjected, straining as he removed the cork from the bottle.

"I don't know how Sergei is involved, but he tried to warn me against Karpov." Marc let go of Laurent's hand and removed the matchbook from the cellophane of his cigarette pack. "He gave me this." Opening the cover, he showed it to Laurent.

Laurent gazed at the message. He recognized his stepfather's handwriting instantly.

"I don't know what to say." He looked at the hastily written words again.

"I'm at rather a loss for words myself."

"Drinks, anyone?" Stephen handed each of them a glass of wine. "Thank heaven for heavy crystal." He retrieved an upturned, unbroken bowl from the carpet. "I don't think my prints on this bowl will matter much, do you?" he said, placing it under Marc's rapidly elongating ash.

"No," Marc replied, half grinning.

Over the wine and the better part of his pack of cigarettes, Marc told Laurent about the letter, its connection with the house and Karpov, everything that he and Stephen either knew or surmised, the mysterious buried treasure, and the unsolved murder of Prince Felix Andronikov.

"It still doesn't make any sense to me," Marc said, finishing his tale. "There are a great many questions and so far no answers, but Renaud will be here on Wednesday. Maybe he'll have found something new by then."

"There is, however, one thing of which I am certain," he paused, lighting his last cigarette. "My uninvited visitors were associates of Karpov, and they were looking for something…and whatever it is they didn't find it."

"Why do you say that?" Laurent asked.

"Call it a gut feeling for want of a better reason," Marc said quietly. "But I know."

"So." Stephen, as always, rose to the occasion. "We'd best be off to our beds. You two go on up. I'll just leave a note for Brigitte, apologizing for the mess, and letting her know we don't intend to have this kind of get together often." He smiled, amused by his own thoughts. "It would be a shame to loose such a dependable housekeeper over a silly surprise party."

Marc grinned, and squeezed his friend's arm affectionately. "I'm glad you're here S."

"Me too, M."

There was no sleeping in. Marc had set his travel alarm for 7 a.m., half an hour before Brigitte was due to arrive. At the first sound of its always-annoying buzzer, he depressed the off switch. He slipped out of bed as gently as possible. Marc was determined to let Laurent sleep as late as he wanted.

He couldn't say if Laurent snored or not, he was exhausted. When they'd finally gone to bed, his sleep had been immediate and profound. Marc could only hope he had not kept Laurent awake. Stephen, a light sleeper, had once told him that he could be heard in the next county.

It had been a while since he'd slept with anyone and he still basked in the afterglow. Marc and Francois had separated six months before the divorce, thinking that maybe the separation might help. Life is full of little delusions, that was just one of them.

He looked at his face in the mirror; good features, strong, classic yet refined, not too many wrinkles. Thanks mummy, he mumbled. His loosened hair fell in gentle waves just below his shoulders. As he looked at his reflection more closely, he recognized a distant ancestor whose portrait still hung in his family's home near Aix. He was a baroque man, and proud of it.

He pulled his hair back into a ponytail to get it out of the way while shaving. With his hair back, the steel blue of his eyes became even more pronounced. Maybe he could afford to wait a few more years before…a knock at the door interrupted his searching self-analysis, something that usually plagued him at the beginning or the end of a relationship.

"Marc." It was Laurent's voice.

"Entrez…come in," he replied.

Laurent opened the door and came up behind him, encircling Marc's waist with strong well-defined arms. Laurent planted a light kiss on his shoulder, pulling him close.

"I thought you might want to sleep a little later…hope I didn't wake you," Marc said, trying to keep his mind on the mess downstairs.

"No," he said, punctuating his response with another light kiss, this time on the neck. "I'm a morning person, myself."

"That's a plus."

"Pardon?"

"Francois was often going to bed when I was getting up. Just one of many incongruities."

"Want to take a shower…together?"

"Don't tempt me…*please*," Marc pleaded, wanting to forget the mess downstairs. "Brigitte will be here any minute, and the last thing I want, is for her to get the same fright, that we got last night."

"You're right, of course, I'll get back in bed and wait till you've finished. Then I'll take my turn."

Laurent went back to the bed, propped himself up on the pillows, and stretched out on top of the covers; he left the door open. Marc focused with effort. He shaved and brushed his teeth. Laurent shaved while Marc was showering. Marc was dressed in record time, and slipping on his shoes as Laurent, dry, towel wrapped around his waist, came out of their bathroom.

They both heard the alarmed cry from a female voice at the bottom of the stairs. "Mon dieu! Qu'est-ce que c'est passé ici, Monsieur Balanger! Monsieur Balanger répondez-moi!"

"J'arrive, Brigitte," Marc called back, hurrying toward the door. "I'm coming Brigitte." Stephen's note had obviously been left in a not very visible location.

"I'm right behind you," Laurent said, as Marc scurried out of the door and down the stairs.

Brigitte stood, a look of unqualified horror on her face as she stared at the disarray around her. "Monsieur, what has happened? Are you all right? What has happened here?"

"I'm fine Brigitte, really, I'm fine."

"Oh Monsieur, who did this?"

"We don't know Brigitte, the police will be back this morning to try to sort it all out." He put his arm through hers to manoeuvre her through the hall to the garden terrace.

At that moment, Laurent descended the staircase at a brisk clip, a vision in a pale blue cashmere sweater, tan light wool, full-cut pleated Armani trousers, and a pair of black Bally slip-ons. Marc stopped in rapt admiration; Laurent truly was a beautiful man. He couldn't help himself; he gave an audible sigh of appreciation.

"Brigitte, I would like to present Monsieur Laurent Teyssier, an architect friend of mine from Paris." He paused a moment, then with a slight smile that mingled perplexity with amusement he said, "Would you care for a cup of coffee, Brigitte?"

Laurent came towards them, his pace slowed. He extended his hand to Brigitte who, still bewildered by her sudden shock, shook it politely.

"Vous êtes bienvenu, Monsieur," she said quietly.

"Look," Laurent said, releasing Brigitte's hand. "I know my way around a kitchen, if you will permit me Madame, I will prepare some coffee while Monsieur Balanger brings you up to date." He took the baguettes and the bag of croissants from her other hand. "I'll take care of these."

"Please Brigitte," Marc entreated gently. "Let's go onto the terrace."

"No, Monsieur, there is no time. I must call the housemaids. Normally they come on Mondays and Thursdays, but this…this." The sight of the dining room through the open doors, on the other side of the corridor had rendered her speechless.

"Brigitte," Marc continued. "Please, the police have asked us not to touch anything until they have taken photographs and fingerprints. They said they would come first thing this morning." He spoke as he guided her down the central hall towards the arched French doors leading to the garden terrace. "You can telephone the housemaids after we've had our coffee." Marc nodded gratefully to Laurent who, as they were going onto the terrace, went off in the direction he hoped was the kitchen.

Happily, the morning was glorious. The sun was bright and warming. Marc brought Brigitte up to date on all of the germane points of the previous evening. Although she had gotten beyond her initial reaction of horror, she was still in a state of disbelief.

"I cannot understand, Monsieur," she said, clasping her hands. "My mother was the housekeeper for Princess Elena, and her mother before her, I have been in service in this house since I was a young woman, and never have we had such a thing happen." She paused, searching for the words. "It is, how you say, incroyable, c'est incroyable Monsieur."

"Well Brigitte, these things do happen, and unfortunately they have happened to us," Marc sighed. "So we must just put things back in order and go on."

"Of course you are right, Monsieur."

"Now…" Marc hesitated and then decided to plunge ahead. He might as well get all the surprises over at one time,. "About Monsieur Teyssier."

"Monsieur," she interrupted gently. "Your sister informed me of your orientation." She used the French pronunciation of the word. "She said that if that was a problem for either of us, Luc or myself, we might wish to consider looking for other positions. She was of course very kind in the way she said it."

Brigitte shrugged her shoulders lightly. "For my part, Monsieur, my brother Lucien, he is gay, he and his partner have a lovely little boutique in St Tropez….They have been together for many years…perhaps I should let Luc speak for himself, but I can assure you, Monsieur that it is not a problem for him either."

Marc breathed a sigh of relief. Chantal really did think of everything.

"Monsieur Balanger, Monsieur Teyssier…he is your…*friend?*"
"Yes, Brigitte, he is my *friend.*"
"I think he is very nice, a real gentleman, Monsieur. He has a very kind face…and, if I may say so, Monsieur…he is very handsome."
"Yes, you may say so." Marc smiled appreciatively. "Thank you Brigitte."

Just at that moment, Laurent appeared at the doorway leading onto the terrace with an enormous wooden tray on which were cups and plates, a large pot of coffee, a steaming jug of milk, sugar, croissants, butter and a pot of jam. "Shall I pour," he said, placing the tray on the table at which they were sitting.

"Please," Marc said, with a look of complete relief on his face.
"Oh no, Monsieur, that is my duty."
"Please Madame." Laurent looked at Marc as if to ask his approval. Marc gave an almost imperceptible nod. "We have a great deal of work to do today," he continued. "You most of all, since you are the only one who will know what is missing or broken. So, I would consider it a privilege, if you would allow me to serve you this morning."

Brigitte seemed almost to blush at the attention. "Comme vous voulez, Monsieur."

God that man is charming, Marc thought. He forced himself to censor the rest of that thought and turned back to the matters at hand. "The police will have questions for you and Luc," Marc continued. "But I want to reassure you…as I told them last night…I am absolutely certain, neither you nor Luc, had anything to do with this unpleasant affair."

"Thank you, Monsieur," Brigitte replied gratefully. She was glad that Monsieur Balanger had bought the chateau; there was no doubt in her mind that he was a real gentleman, kind and considerate. Although the Princesses Andronikov had been kind enough, they were both very stiff and formal. It would be nice to have a little modern informality around the house.

GRANNY'S CHIPS

Karpov sat in a comfortable chair on his private deck aboard the Rosenkranz. Under other circumstances he would have enjoyed the view of the beautiful village in the distance, and the harbour his yacht was berthed in. St Tropez, playground of the wealthy and famous.

He could almost imagine what it must have been like, in the days before the revolution against the tsars. The Russian aristocracy had roamed up and down the French Riviera on their yachts and their gleaming white private trains. Now it was Dimitri Pavolovich Karpov, great-grandson of servants, who themselves were grandsons of serfs, Dimitri Karpov, who sat on the grand yacht, in the tranquil harbour of this charming village, on the coast of the still renowned French Rivera.

Enjoyment was not to be his on this day. Instead, he was struggling to contain his anger at the clumsy manner in which his orders had been carried out. Malinkov had told them of his search of the chateau, and how they had tried to cover it up, by making it look as though thieves had broken in and ransacked the place, looking for valuables.

The description of broken china and upturned furniture had practically sent him into a rage. To make matters even worse, they had not found Felix Andronikov's codebook. A codebook without which, he might never decipher the passages he so desperately needed.

But he was in a place where he could be overheard, his daughter Irina and her fiancé Prince Michael Alexander Romanovsky were having breakfast with Reisky on the deck below. So he controlled his anger, just as he had when exiled to that backwater diplomatic post in Afghanistan after Reisky's defection. He was lucky he had an uncle in the energy department or he might never have overcome his "disgrace."

"This is not our old Russia, Malinkov," he began coldly. "The clumsy techniques of the KGB will not be tolerated in a country like France. This matter must be handled with delicacy. Not, as you have done, thrashing about like a bull in a china shop." He was still angry, but he was cautious. "You are certain that these helpers of yours are reliable?"

"Yes, Mr. Karpov. As far as they are concerned, I was their employer. I was very careful not to involve you in anyway."

"You are a wise man, Malinkov…remember a wise man lives a

long and healthy life…a foolish one dies young." Karpov relied on Malinkov for special tasks, things with which he could trust no other. But sometimes, sometimes Malinkov forgot where and when they lived. He would need to find a way to remind him, a way that would bring the point home to Malinkov and still keep his secrets safe; for Karpov was a man with many secrets, and Malinkov knew them all.

"You are certain that you saw this Balanger with Reisky's stepson, Teyssier?"

"Yes, Mr. Karpov. The three of them, Balanger, Teyssier and the Englishman, this Hampstead…they were all having dinner at a restaurant on the quai last night. I had just returned from the chateau. I had gone to wait on the quai as we had arranged. I saw the three of them sitting on the terrace. Fortunately it was already dark, I was careful to move into the shadow as I passed. I ducked into the café next to theirs and took a table under the awning. I am certain they did not notice me, they were too absorbed in their own conversation."

"And this Teyssier, you say he and Balanger were *close*?"

"There were being openly affectionate with each other; touching in a familiar manner. They left together, Mr. Karpov."

"Perhaps we must change out strategy. Perhaps we will play a game of *queens*, eh Malinkov?" Karpov chuckled at his own innuendo. "Yes," he said, his anger subsiding quickly as a new plan formed in his mind. "A game of queens…and Reisky is just the pawn for the game."

"You see, Malinkov, Reisky owes me a debt, one which I think he is now in a position to repay, with say, a codebook." Karpov grinned malevolently.

Suddenly he felt good again, the outline of his plan was completed. Sergei could be trusted to handle the matter with tact, and finesse. He was not tainted by Malinkov's KGB enthusiasm. Besides, Reisky had a reputation to protect.

"I think I will join our guests for breakfast now, Malinkov. I must begin to put this new plan into action." Karpov rose from his chair and walked towards the stairs leading to the deck below. "I will send for you when I have need of you," he said, descending the staircase.

Chapter Six—
A Gothik Revival

Marc, Laurent and Brigitte were still on the terrace. Stephen had just joined them. He was wearing a pair of tan shorts, a t-shirt with "Don't ask and I won't tell" printed across the back in bold lavender script, and sandals; his housecleaning uniform he called it. They heard a car pull up to the front of the house. Marc glanced at his watch; it was a few minutes after nine.

"Stephen," Marc looked at his friend. "It's probably Luc. Do me a favour and head him off at the pass, as it were…you know explain things…the Readers Digest abridged version."

As Stephen was going into the house, they heard several other cars coming to a stop on the gravelled entrance courtyard.

"That would be the police, I'll warrant," Marc said. "It never rains but it pours."

"I'll make more coffee," Laurent said, getting out of his chair.

"Monsieur," Brigitte rose from her chair at the same time. "I will go to help Monsieur Laurent, besides I need to call the housemaids, if I am to get them to come today."

"Yes, of course Brigitte, thank you," Marc replied appreciatively. "And Brigitte…"

"Yes, Monsieur?"

"I'm very glad you are going to stay on."

"So am I, Monsieur, so am I."

Brigitte and Laurent had no sooner disappeared into the house than Stephen returned with Luc and a rather stocky, moustached man in a suit that seemed a bit too large for the frame that was wearing it.

"Marc, this is Inspector Leclerc," Stephen said, performing the necessary introduction. "Inspector Leclerc, Marc Balanger."

"Monsieur Inspecteur." Marc stood. "Asseyez-vous s'il vous plait," he indicated the empty chair opposite him.

"Luc," Marc turned his attention to his caretaker. "I guess Stephen has put you in the picture?"

"Yes, Monsieur."

"Please see what you can do to help the police with their inspection of the grounds."

"Yes, Monsieur."

"When you have a minute, do what you can do to arrange for the repair of the broken window panes," Marc continued. "Brigitte is calling the housemaids to see if they can come to help us put the place back in order, when the police have finished their investigation. Will you have time to help?"

"Yes, Monsieur."

"Thank you Luc." Marc sat down and turned towards Inspector Leclerc, who was now sitting, loading his pipe. "Inspector Leclerc, I'm sorry that we have to meet under such circumstances."

"As am I Monsieur," the inspector paused, lighting his pipe. "However, I assure you that we will do our best to find out who has broken into your home."

"I am certain that you will, Monsieur." At that moment Laurent and Brigitte returned with the coffee and fresh cups. "Inspector Leclerc, I would like to introduce you to one of my guests, Monsieur Laurent Teyssier."

"Inspecteur Leclerc."

"Monsieur Teyssier."

"You have already met my other guest, Mr. Hampstead?" Stephen was already seated in the chair next to him.

"Yes, Monsieur Balanger, we met in the hall."

"And this is my housekeeper, Brigitte Trochet."

"Madame," he said, nodding politely to Brigitte. "It is a pleasure to see you again."

"May I offer you some coffee, Inspector?" Laurent said, taking the fourth chair.

"Yes, thank you."

"Brigitte, a word…" Marc stood. He walked over to her. "Please see if the other officers would like some coffee. Luc is going to attend to the repair of the broken glass, and he said he will be able to help us this afternoon."

"I have already started more coffee, Monsieur, and I managed to find enough in the pantry to offer them some little sandwiches. I have spoken to Marie and Suzanne, they will come at one o'clock."

"Merci, Brigitte," Marc said, giving her arm a gentle squeeze. "You really are an angel."

Leclerc had already begun his questioning when Marc returned to the table. Laurent was giving an account of the evening of the break in.

"I don't think there is anything more that I can tell you, Monsieur Inspecteur. When the gendarmes left we all retired for the evening."

"Monsieur Hampstead?" Leclerc turned his attention to Stephen.

"I certainly can't think of anything else." Stephen took a sip of his coffee. "After they went up, I wrote a note for Brigitte, locked up and went to bed, myself."

"I have a theory, myself, Inspector," Marc said, pouring himself another cup of coffee. "As you know, I just arrived yesterday…very few people know that I am here, my household goods won't even arrive from Montréal for another month."

He paused, taking a cigarette from the package on the table. Lighting it, he continued. "In reality, I don't think the break-in has anything to do with me. Whoever forced their way in last night was looking for something that was here before I purchased the house."

"I believe you are correct, Monsieur Balanger," Leclerc replied. "I believe that we will also find that the intruders were professionals. I doubt we shall find any fingerprints other than your own." He paused to relight his pipe. "Do you know what was taken?"

"Not yet," Marc replied. "I haven't been in the house long enough to know what was here before I came. They did not quite manage to break into the silver vault, although they did give it a try. My assistant, Paul Renaud, arrives from Montréal tomorrow, so I will give him the inventory lists and have Brigitte go over the lists with him to determine what is missing."

"I suppose there is little else one can do for the moment," Inspector Leclerc said, standing.

"Monsieur Inspecteur," Marc added thoughtfully. "I am certain that neither Brigitte nor Luc had anything to do with this."

"I would agree, Monsieur." Leclerc flashed his first smile. "In a village as small as our own, you get to know your neighbours, as I am sure we will get to know you…over time. I have always known Brigitte and Luc to be most trustworthy, Monsieur Balanger. It speaks well of you that you have already recognized this."

"Thank you Inspector," Marc said, rising from his chair. "Now where should we go to be fingerprinted?"

"Sergeant Riviera is in the Green Drawing Room."

The police left around eleven, so the five of them had a quick lunch together on the terrace. Brigitte and Luc were quickly becoming accustomed to Marc's free wheeling sense of democracy in dealing with his staff. They made their plans for the afternoon.

The men on the "clean-up team", as they decided to call themselves, would upright the furniture, and put it back in place, re-hang the pictures on the walls, and in general do anything which required heavy lifting. The women's team would clear away the broken things, clear up any debris or mess left behind, return the unbroken decorative objects back on their respective tables and shelves, and generally tidy up the rooms.

Once the heavy jobs had been done, Stephen and Luc would drive to Lorgues and provision the larder for the next week, while Laurent and Marc would clean up the library.

Marie and Suzanne, the housemaids, arrived around one. With seven people hard at work, things went quicker than was hoped, and by three, Stephen and Luc were in the jeep headed for the village. Brigitte and her crew had cleared away the debris. Brigitte was already making the list of things that had been broken. From memory, she was also making a list of what she thought had been taken, preparing for her session with Renaud on Wednesday.

Marc was most particular about the way he and Laurent would approach the clean up of the library. This room had been the one most impacted by their trespassers' intrusion. It was here Marc hoped to find a clue as to what they had been searching for. Once the furniture was righted, all the loose papers would be placed on the desk in neat piles.

The books, open to exactly the places they were found, would be laid out one on top of the other in piles of three or four, depending on their size and weight, and on the available open space on the library table and the surrounding floor.

Once everything was organized, they would examine the books themselves. Perhaps the positioning, the pages to which the books had been left open, or the titles of the books with ripped endpapers, would provide them a clue as to what the intruders were searching for.

The organizing did not take more than an hour or so, but the examination of the books would take a bit longer. Marc hoped that with Stephen's help, the three of them might be through by dinnertime.

"So what are we looking for?" Laurent glanced up from the last pile of books he was assembling on the floor.

"I don't really know." Marc was finishing up the organization of the loose papers on the desk. "Anything that looks like it could be related to the Andronikov family." He reached into his pocket and pulled out a pack of cigarettes and his lighter. "Is there a dish or something around here that could double as an ashtray?"

"How about this saucer?" Laurent retrieved an unbroken plate from the pile of, as yet un-catalogued, broken porcelain Brigitte had assembled earlier on the large console table, between the pair of French doors that led to the garden terrace.

"Perfect." Marc exhaled a puff of smoke. "I keep thinking back to something that Stephen said yesterday afternoon." Briefly Marc told him of his call to Sean Sweeney in Boston, and Sean's comment of his call from Karpov subsequent to the letter's delivery. A call asking if there were a translation from Sotheby's that accompanied the letter. "Stephen said that maybe Karpov wanted a translation because the Russian paragraphs were in code. Maybe what we're looking for...and what they were looking for, is a code book of some kind."

"Did I hear my name?" Stephen poked his head through the door to the library.

"That was fast." Marc smiled broadly.

"Check your watch, M." Stephen looked down at the face of his Bulgari chronograph as he walked into the library. "It's after five...five twenty-two to be precise." He stopped beside Laurent. "You'll get used to that, once you've known him for awhile. Give him a pile of musty old books and he'll loose all track of time."

"What a glorious village." Stephen was in holiday mode. "Lorgues is a miracle. I thought places like this really had gone the way of the dinosaur. Sheer picture post card charm...the market is phenomenal...fresh everything, and I do mean fresh, as in picked this morning...and all grown in the neighbourhood. I counted over 150 varieties of cheese, and the breads, and the fresh fruits. Marc, we're in a gourmand's paradise!"

"That's why I moved here, remember." Marc looked down at a piece of folded yellowed paper somewhat larger than the others. "...Close enough to the Mediterranean to benefit from the climate but far enough away to avoid the tourists." His voice trailed off as he opened the folded paper. It was an architectural rendering of the bagatelle next to the lake. The Gothik pavilion they had seen when touring the grounds yesterday morning.

"What did you find?" Laurent stood up from his pile of books.

"Hello," Stephen said, looking over Marc's shoulder. "That's the plan for that little summer house we saw by the lake yesterday."

"Yes," Marc said distantly, "and it's dated 1918."

"I thought it was one of those Victorian follies." Stephen said.

"It is Victorian," Laurent said. "Look at the scribbled note in the bottom left corner."

"Ah, yes," Stephen quipped. "How could I have missed it, it's as plain as the nose on Diaghelev's face, and that my dears was quite a nose. Is there a translator in the house? My Russian is not as good as it used to be."

Marc looked at his friend with one eyebrow raised. Stephen's Russian was non-existent. "As a matter of fact, there is." Marc turned the plan around so that Laurent could see the note right side up.

Laurent looked at the inscription carefully. Quickly he made a mental translation, from Russian to French, then French to English. "It says, 'plans for the restoration and enlargement of the Gothik folly, approved, F Andronikov.'"

"Now why do you suppose that Karpov's cronies would have overlooked this little bit of Andronikoviana?" Stephen said, doing his best to coin a new phrase.

"Well," Marc replied. "We know that Karpov would not have come here himself, and if the hired boys were looking for a code book…"

"That's *exactly* what they would have looked for," Laurent finished Marc's sentence. "Even if they were supervised, as it were, by one of Karpov's agents, it is doubtful that an architectural rendering would have attracted his or her attention."

Stephen stepped back a bit and looked at the two of them. "If you two start making a habit of finishing each other's sentences, I might just get a little intimidated."

"Pardon Monsieur." Brigitte stood in the open doorway. "I have prepared a little supper on the garden terrace from some of the things Monsieur Stephen picked up at the market today."

"Thank you Brigitte." Marc came round the desk and walked towards her.

"Marie and Suzanne have gone, everything is back in order…except for the library," she added, with a gentle smile. "I've made a list of all the things which were broken and those I believe to be missing…except for the library." She smiled again.

"Thank you Brigitte," Marc replied warmly, catching her delicate hint about the library's condition. "I cannot tell you how much I appreciate your help today."

"Monsieur, I have worked in this house for over 30 years, and this is the most excitement we have ever had." She was now smiling broadly. "And something tells me that this won't be the last time we have excitement in this house....But please sir," she added, almost as an aside. "Can we have a bit less chaos the next time?"

Marc chuckled in spite of himself, competent and with a sense of humour; this woman was a keeper, as they say in the States. "I promise, Brigitte."

"Why don't you go along home," he added. "We'll do the washing up...and if you should see Luc, please ask if he would care to join us for supper. There are things I would like to discuss with him regarding the security system."

"Of course, Monsieur." She nodded to Stephen and Laurent, "Bon soir Messieurs, à demain."

"Bon soir, Brigitte," the three replied in chorus.

"Ummm, supper." Stephen was really hungry after the day's activities. "Shall we proceed to the terrace?"

"Sounds like a good idea," Laurent added, folding the drawing and tucking it under his arm.

"What can I say, I've been outvoted."

As the stepped onto the terrace, they found Luc waiting. The early evening was pleasantly warm, just a gentle breeze, such a change from the frozen north that Marc had left behind him! Renaud was going to love it here. Renaud, he'd be here tomorrow...Marc had almost forgotten in the swarm of events of the past twenty-four hours.

"Please everybody, sit." Marc said casually.

The dinner was delicious; a tapenade, chevre tarts with onion, rabbit pâté, a prossito salad, made with smoked ham, green beans, and sun-dried tomatoes, eaten with an ample quantity of baguette, and a lemon tart for afters, all washed down with a Cuvée Château Roubine Rouge millésime 1999. One could almost forget Karpov and the Andronikov mystery, if it weren't for the uncertainty of those still nagging questions. What does he want, and what will he do next to try to get it?

"You wanted to ask about the security alarm, Monsieur?" Luc

was the first to broach the subject.

"Yes, Luc." Marc poured another glass of wine. "Did he come today?"

"Yes, Monsieur," Luc replied. "Mercier, the technician, reconnected the alarm this afternoon."

"What did he have to say?" Marc could see the euros flying out of his pockets.

"The system is very basic, Monsieur, it is not connected to the company's security monitoring network. It's a local alarm only." Luc nodded as Stephen offered another glass of wine. "Of course he thinks we should upgrade the security. Mercier said that if we added some lighting around the grounds, it would be an added deterrent. He said the best solution is to update the system completely, making sure that it is part of their monitoring network."

"Security systems have changed a lot since the '80's," Marc agreed. "Paul arranged for the system we have in Montréal. Why don't you and he see what you can do about replacing the old system with something more up to date?"

"Of course, Monsieur."

"And Luc, I want to thank you for all the help you've been today. I don't know how you managed to get a repairman on such short notice, but he did an excellent job on the repairs to the broken glass."

"Well, Monsieur." Luc grinned his cheeks a little rosy from the wine. "Things are much easier to arrange when one's employer is a celebrity."

"I have another big favour to ask," Marc said sheepishly.

"Of course Monsieur."

"Renaud's flight is arriving in Nice tomorrow morning around nine. Would you mind terribly driving down to pick him up, instead of waiting until he takes the train to St Raphael?"

"Actually, Monsieur, I was going to suggest that. It's only an hour to the airport, if the traffic is not too heavy. It is the least we can do to welcome him to his new home after such a long journey…provided of course you will not need me in the morning."

"You know your day far better than I, Luc."

"In that case, Monsieur, I will be off to my bed, it was a late night last night, and I want to leave early to make certain that I am there a little ahead of the arrival time." He stood up from the table. "I have orders," he said, with a slightly emphasis on the last word. "From Brigitte."

"Orders?" Marc asked, somewhat entertained by the fact that the caretaker accepted orders from the housekeeper.

"Yes, Monsieur, orders," he repeated, standing beside his chair. "Brigitte said although she will accept your kind offer to clear away the supper things, you should please not do the washing up, or she will have to become quite cross with you for not allowing her to do her job."

Marc chuckled. "Well, I would not want Brigitte to be cross with me for any reason." Secretly he was relieved, although he had intended to be as good as his word, he, too, was getting tired. "I'll leave Renaud's flight information on the table in the hall. I'll phone Air France in the morning and leave a message for him about the change of plan."

"Do not worry, Monsieur," he said. "I'll find him."

"Somehow, I have no doubt of that."

"Good night Messieurs."

Marc had avoided any mention of Karpov and his suspicions at dinner. He thought it best that the fewer people who knew the better. He waited until he was sure Luc was out of earshot, before he brought up the question. "Well Laurent, what was so interesting about those plans that you brought them out with you?"

"I've been waiting all evening for you to ask." He moved the plates out of the way and unfolded the paper he had kept in his lap throughout the supper. "The original structure is an octagonal tower; a single room with stonewalls. In the centre of each wall, a pair of gothik pointed, arched French doors provides access to the pavilion. This was not changed from the original plan for the walls on the north and south sides of the structure.

"The west wall of the hexagon is a sort of monumental style fireplace, which according to these plans, was kept in the original state. The east wall of the pavilion was originally a set of arched windows like the north and south faces, but these plans call for the French doors replaced with a set of wooden ones." Laurent used his finger as a makeshift pointer as he spoke.

"The new structure incorporated the original tower design, adding a passage between the tower and a new, much larger rectangular room, to be added at the opposite end. The passage has very thick walls. Judging from the scale of this drawing, I'd say the walls are about two meters thick on either side of the passage

"The overall length of connecting structure is about six meters. The interior is around three meters wide. It seems that the passageway was conceived more as a gallery than a simple corridor…perhaps a gallery to exhibit a collection of some kind.

"You're saying that it's around 20 feet long and ten feet wide." Stephen converted the measurement into the old British standard of measure.

"That's the interior dimensions," Laurent continued. "The overall width, including that from exterior wall to exterior wall, is around 17 feet. The plans indicate a thickness of six and one half feet, 2 meters for each of the exterior walls

"What I find incredibly curious is that there are no external openings in the design, there are no windows to light this gallery, nor is there an indication of sky lights. And the drawing does not indicate that any niches were built on the interior of the gallery, if I may call it that. There is certainly no structural reason for the walls to be that thick."

Marc and Stephen looked at each other. Secret room was the first thought that came to both their minds. Narrow, to be sure, but two meters wide by six meters long was still large enough to hide quite a few things.

"Have either of you been in the pavilion?" Laurent asked.

"No. It was locked when Luc took us on a tour of the grounds yesterday," Stephen said, intrigued. "Remember M? He said that he had forgotten to get the key from Brigitte."

"It seems odd that the caretaker shouldn't have keys to all the buildings on the property."

"Actually, not…with all that's been going on, I'd forgotten." Marc paused for a minute recalling the events of yesterday afternoon. "They're in the library." He started collecting the plates and glasses. "Come on, let's get these things to the kitchen."

While they cleared the table Marc related, what at the time, had been a puzzling event. When they returned from their tour of the grounds the day before, he'd gone into the library to 'get the feel' of the room in which he would be finishing his new book. Brigitte had come in with an ornate silver box.

She'd apologized for forgetting to give the keys to Luc before he took them on their tour of the grounds. Princess Aleksandra had apparently used the pavilion as a sort of 'fortress of solitude', his own words, Marc interjected, not Brigitte's. Brigitte told him that Aleksandra used to go there every Saturday to have tea with her father.

"Apparently it was a sanctum sanctorum, a memorial to her dead father. No one, including the staff, was allowed to enter the building except for Friday afternoons. It was a ritual. Brigitte would get the keys from Princess Aleksandra, and she would take the tea things down to the pavilion with one of the housemaids. They would do any cleaning that was required. They would come back to the house, and return the keys to the princess."

"You know M," Stephen said, as they walked back into the library. "This is getting stranger by the minute. Now we have a woman who, every Saturday, had tea with a ghost; a man murdered when she herself was little more than an infant."

"I don't think our uninvited guests found the keys," Marc said, only half listening. "They were rather large, old fashioned keys, three of them strung together on a piece of faded black velvet ribbon."

Marc walked over to the desk and sat in the chair behind it. The desk was a beautiful fruitwood bureau plat, Louis XV provincial cabinetwork with gilt bronze mounts where the legs joined the elegantly paneled apron, a fine piece of furniture by any standards.

"They emptied the drawers of their contents, but they didn't examine the furniture very carefully. Watch the apron panels on your side of the desk." Marc opened the drawer and reached in, finding a tiny lever. He pulled it. "Brigitte showed me this little trick while you were changing for dinner, yesterday." The left side panel on the front side of the desk apron swung open. There was a small compartment behind the panel; in it was the silver box, precisely where he had put it the day before.

"Bingo," Stephen exclaimed quietly.

Marc looked at Laurent, "And you are thinking that the walls of the passage between the old and new parts of the pavilion…"

"Might just contain something similar." Laurent confirmed the thought.

"A secret room hidden in the walls."

"There you go again," Stephen said. "Completing each other's sentences."

Marc reached into his trouser pockets, searching.

Laurent pulled the cigarettes and lighter out of his own trouser pocket. "You left them on the table on the terrace."

"Thanks," Marc replied gratefully, accepting the cigarette and the light. "She said the princess gave her very specific instructions to give the keys *only* to the new owner of the house."

Carefully turning the box upside down Stephen looked for the hallmarks. He collected little silver 'objets de vertu' as the French called them. His knowledge of hallmarks was extensive. On the base of the box he found what he was looking for. "It's Fabergé, from the St Petersburg workshop, there's a date stamp…1905."

"Thought so," Marc said. "Open it please."

Stephen opened the box. Inside, resting on a padded dark blue velvet lining were the three keys. "Contents present and accounted for, M." Stephen pulled the keys from the box jangling them.

"Well, what do you say to a treasure hunt tomorrow…say, after breakfast?"

"I agree," Laurent replied enthusiastically.

"All for one…"

Reisky paced the floor of Karpov's study aboard the Rosenkranz. "I don't know what else I can do," he said, puffing furiously on his cigarette. "I've left messages at his office in Paris, at his hotel in St Tropez, on his cell phone."

"You must find a way to get into that house and get that codebook," Karpov said coldly. "Sergei, you know that I am a determined man, I would not have survived the changes that have come to my career," he said pointedly, "and to Russia, if I were not."

Karpov took a cigar from the humidor on his desk, clipped the end, and slowly lit it. "I have succeeded where others have failed because I took action. People think that I am a cruel man, some think that I am dangerous, and they are right, Sergei." He exhaled a long stream of smoke, enjoying the flavour of the Cuban tobacco. "But I have adapted to the changes. In another time, I would have arranged an accident for our friends, taken the place apart stone by stone if necessary. I would have what I wanted by now."

"I know, Dimitri," Sergei said, sitting on the sofa.

"But I have not taken such actions. Malinkov was excessive in his zeal to assist me, and he has been reigned in." Karpov continued. "But I will have those Andronikov documents Sergei. When the old princess contacted me about them, I agreed to pay her price, but she died before I could complete the transaction."

"Dimitri." Reisky stopped his pacing and sat in the chair beside his former brother-in-law. "What is so important about these documents? Why do you care about what happened in 1917? That is almost a century ago."

"I want to tell you something, Sergei," Karpov leaned forward. "I know you never really liked me. I was part of a government, a system you hated because it did not permit you to be the artist you believe yourself to be. And..." He got up from his seat and walked over to the liquor cabinet, over which one of Sergei paintings hung. "In truth, you were right to feel the way you did. You were too good for those cultural dictators who once controlled your life."

Karpov poured them both a cognac. "I was very angry that you used your position as my brother- in- law to grab your first opportunity to flee to the West. It made my life difficult for some time."

Karpov sat on the sofa, placing the glasses of cognac on the coffee table. "And not just for me, for your sister Marina and our little Irina as well. They suffered more than I, outcasts from Soviet official and private life, while I was exiled to the Afghanistan embassy.

"I recovered, landed on my feet in the ministry of energy, thanks to the help of my mother's brother. But with no social outlets, no life outside the party, my family, or my work...I became the petroleum expert, then the petroleum advisor to the energy minister, himself. In a way, I suppose I owe all this to you," Karpov waived his cigar around the room, gesturing at its contents. "It is my contacts in the ministry that enabled me to profit when the foreign investors came in."

Reisky sipped his cognac. He sat quietly waiting.

"I loved Marina." Karpov tone mellowed. "I still miss her. I know you think I had something to do with her death, but it is not true. She may have been your sister, but she was my wife, and Irina's mother." He began to be irritated again. "Whatever sins I may be guilty of, that was not one of them. I know she had nothing to do with your flight, although she was glad you were free."

"Dimitri..."

"Sergei," Karpov interrupted. "Irina is all I have left, and her happiness is the only thing I care about now." He downed his cognac and went back to the liquor cabinet for another. He returned with the decanter and set it on the table between them.

"The Andronikov documents would reveal that a Karpov was involved in the killing of the Tsar Nicolas and his family. Although for me, I don't care. Why should I care what a bunch of royalists think? I am a rich and powerful man...but Irina, she is in love...and I believe that Michael genuinely loves her as well. Unfortunately the young man is a Romanovsky. Not a Romanov, to be sure, but a member of the clan. What do you think would happen to their wedding plans, if it were to become known that her great great grandfather was involved in the deaths of the Imperial family?"

"So what does this letter have to do with these other documents?"

Sergei was loosing his fear. But he still did not trust Karpov, he had many reasons not to, and to do what he was being asked, no, told to do, would put his relationship with Laurent in great jeopardy. "This letter was written before the murder of the Romanovs."

"The letter was a blind, an attempt to delay Balanger from arriving at the chateau long enough, to allow Malinkov time to search the place. I thought I could convince him to allow me to take him from Monte Carlo to St Tropez on the Rosenkranz."

"And the codebook?"

"The codebook is important, very important." Karpov walked back to his desk. He took a small key from his vest pocket and unlocked the desk drawer. From it he withdrew a book, bound in faded red Moroccan leather. The binding was stamped in gold with two initials, FA, in the Cyrillic alphabet, surmounted by a prince's crown.

"You see I have this," Karpov turned it around carefully, so that Sergei could see it clearly. "It is the diary of Prince Felix Andronikov, written in his own hand, in his own code, sent to me by the Princess Aleksandra, his daughter."

"What?" Sergei was visibly astonished.

"It was part of our deal." Karpov picked up the diary and returned it to the desk drawer, which he closed and locked. He put the key back in his pocket. "She told me that the location of the documents' hiding place was in the diary. She said that she would supply the codebook when the second part of the payment was made."

"She died two days after the diary was delivered…a fact of which I was unaware, until I sent Malinkov with the second payment." Karpov returned to his place on the sofa. "He returned, sans codebook, with the news of her death."

"What was the payment, Dimitri?"

"The first instalment was the return of the Alastani diamond, which was taken from her family by the Bolsheviks in 1918. The second instalment was the death of the great-grandson of her father's assassin, a Pavel Uriatkin."

"You killed a man and stole a diamond?" Sergei said, shaking his head in disbelief.

"No, I bought the diamond, Sergei," Dimitri said, pouring himself another cognac. "Fifteen million in US currency," he added, shaking his head. "As for the death, Pavel Uriatkin was a gangster, and ex-KGB hood. The princess was not the only one who wanted him dead. An *accident* was easily arranged. He will not be missed."

Karpov relit his cigar. "Now you know the whole story. You know what I want and why, and what I have done to try to get it."

Sergei leaned forward; with an unsteady hand he poured himself another cognac. "You are a dangerous man, Dimitri." He took a deep drink of the cognac to steady his nerves. "Why did you not just buy the estate after the princess' death?"

"Princess Aleksandra Andronikov was no saint, Sergei. She was a cold woman bent on revenge. Why do you think that she wanted Pavel's death? He was the last of the line, and she wanted the ultimate payment for the crimes committed against her; the end of a line for the end of a line, an eye for an eye.

"The princess was a Russian, Sergei, a bitter woman bent on revenge, and that revenge was not only directed at the Russian state and the assassin of her father. It was directed at her own heirs, for what reason I do not know, and at me, the descendant of a murderer of the Tsar and his family.

"After she died, I contacted the executor of her estate, a Monsieur Legalais. He told me of the codicil, no Russian or person of Russian descent was allowed to purchase the property. So, I contacted one of her heirs, Arakcheev, Baron Stephane Arakcheev."

Karpov poured another cognac. "Arakcheev was not a happy man. He told me that Princess Aleksandra's will stipulated that the estate and all its contents, excepting those items specifically mentioned as bequests, were to be sold and the proceeds distributed equally among the members of her family. No member of the family was to inherit the property. Even the jewels, which had belonged to her and her mother; she ordered them sent to Paris to be sold and the proceeds given to the church in Alastani, in Georgia, for the rebuilding of the family chapel, an everlasting and fitting monument to her father. She had her revenge on all of us.

"Arakcheev and his mother contested the will. They moved into the chateau. But after a two-year battle they lost. They returned to Hungary." Karpov stood up; it was late and he was tired. "I am not asking this for myself. I am asking it for Irina, for the happiness of your sister's only child. Sergei, please, get me the codebook, and if the documents are on that estate, get me the documents…you have as much reason as I, for wanting to avoid any further *incidents*." He stressed the last word; Laurent's presence on the estate was implicit in its underlying meaning.

"I will do as you ask, Dimitri; not for you, but for Irina and for Marina's memory." He stood up; he too was feeling tired, and suddenly very old. "I will go to Laurent's hotel tomorrow and wait for him to contact me there. His office said that he has appointments with workmen on Thursday. He will return to St Tropez before then. But you must promise me, on Marina's memory and on your love for Irina, that you will do nothing else until I call you."

"I promise," Dimitri replied.

Chapter Seven – A Daughter's Grief

"So this is where you two are hiding!" Stephen walked into the library, bright and chipper. "I thought to find you on the garden terrace."

"No rest for the weary." Laurent smiled slightly, looking up from the last of the books he was returning to the shelves.

"Not a lot of sleep last night, M?" Stephen flashed an impish grin.

"Let's just say I tossed and turned a lot." Marc raised an eyebrow, looking across the now cleared desk where he was sitting.

"Now there's an image I could have lived without," Stephen quipped, feigning a shudder. "It's nice to see you've gotten everything cleaned up in here." He plopped himself down in one of the comfortable wing chairs that flanked the carved red marble mantle of the fireplace. "Brigitte cracking the whip?" He noticed that all the breakage had been cleared away, and the still intact bibelots had been returned to tables and shelves.

"You might say that." Marc flashed a somewhat fatigued smile.

"Find anything new?" Stephen queried.

"Nope, nothing…at least nothing to do with a codebook or Andronikov's mystery," Marc replied, sitting back in his chair. "The papers were mostly old bills, receipts, that sort of thing. We did find a number of papers and inventories from the Andronikov purchase. It would appear most of the contents of the house belonged to the family that built it, the ones from whom Prince Felix purchased the estate."

"Which means?" Stephen queried.

"That most of the furniture and paintings were in the house when Andronikov's agent acquired the property for Prince Felix. The bills pre-dating the Andronikov possession would seem to verify it. There were a lot of papers dealing with the house before the Andronikov time. Once we have Karpov off our backs, I'll have to go through them more carefully. The documents regarding the house are phenomenal, we found the original plans for the house, and the original invoices for the furnishings and the decorations. It's really a treasure trove. If I'm correct, the entire history of this house is here just waiting to be pieced together."

"It's unusual for a house of this age to have so much detail of its history just sitting here waiting to be read," Laurent added, placing the last books on the shelves.

"What about the books?" Stephen asked, poking at the logs in the fireplace.

"There aren't many Russian ones," Laurent replied. "Between forty and fifty titles. They are mostly literary classics or genealogies. The rest are French, books which predate the Andronikov ownership of the place.

"The Andronikov princesses appear to have wanted little change. Aside from some bills for repairs to either the structure or the furniture, little seems to have been changed from the original structure or its contents. Prince Felix made the most changes during the three years before his death. He updated the wiring, the plumbing, and the heating. There are bills from this period for tableware; silver, china and crystal, a few pieces of furniture for the guest rooms, and the linens and such."

"I thought you said the place was restored during the eighties," Stephen interrupted.

"Yes, we did find bills and receipts for some extensive renovations at that time. The wiring had to be re-done when the alarm system was installed. The architect convinced the princess to update the plumbing and heating," Laurent said, taking the chair opposite Stephen. "A section of the roof was replaced at the same time…oddly enough," he added, "the architect said he found no structural problems that needed to be fixed. Unusual in a house this old."

"So, you have a solidly built house, in pretty much its original state, and no new clues." Stephen said, summarizing the results of the search.

"That's about the size of it," Marc replied. "We've not had

breakfast yet," he anticipated Stephen's next question. "I knew you'd want to sleep in, and so I asked Brigitte to prepare a light brunch for around eleven."

"So, light brunch at eleven and treasure hunt to follow?"

"No, the treasure hunt will have to wait, perhaps Laurent should fill you in."

"You remember that I turned my cell phone off when we were having dinner in St Tropez the other evening."

Stephen nodded.

"Well I forgot to turn it back on yesterday," Laurent continued. "I had some appointments with some contractors today, and I was going to call to reschedule. So this morning I went to make my calls and I noticed it was still off. When I turned it on, the message light was flashing. I checked the messages, there were two from Sergei."

"Your stepfather?" Stephen asked.

"Yes…apparently, he is in St Tropez…said he'd be arriving this morning and that he'd be at the Byblos. I checked my messages at the hotel, and discovered he left a message there as well, yesterday. There was also a message from my office in Paris, saying that he had phoned them."

"Sounds like he's anxious to reach you," Stephen interjected. "Got any ideas as to why?"

"We think we do," Laurent said, looking at Marc. "The message that I left at the hotel, in the event anyone phoned…you know, contractors, the office, that sort of thing, was that I was staying with some friends for a few days, and that I could be reached on my cell…Sergei's second message said that he was anxious to meet my friends."

"We think that since Karpov's *associates* failed to find the codebook, he's sending in the second wave." Marc stood up. "We decided to bring Sergei here."

"So how about lunch in St Tropez this afternoon?" Laurent grinned.

"Revised itinerary." Stephen stood up from his chair and in a pseudo tour guide voice continued. "Light brunch on the garden terrace followed by an excursion to St Tropez and lunch."

"Just so." Marc chuckled at his imitation. At that moment, Brigitte appeared at the door with Renaud. Marc smiled broadly at the sight of him. This tall jet-haired Quebecois with his refined features and deep-set brown eyes was more than his employee; over time he had become his friend and confidant as well.

"You asked me to bring Monsieur Renaud to the library when he arrived, Monsieur."

"Yes, thank you Brigitte," Marc said appreciatively. "Is the brunch ready?"

"Yes Monsieur," Brigitte replied. "I'm just preparing the coffee…Messieurs," she excused herself. "Monsieur Renaud, bienvenu au Château de Maure," she added with a smile.

"Welcome to France, Renaud, and congratulations." Stephen flashed a warm smile. "Don't let the idyllic surroundings fool you, this place is hotter that the Heath on a warm summer night."

Still grinning, he followed Brigitte out the door to the hallway. Stephen had been a frequent visitor to the house in Montréal. He had developed an easy familiarity with the man, who, if the truth were known, he found to be quite sexy.

"Paul," Marc put his arm around Laurent's shoulder, clearly establishing their relationship. "This is Laurent."

"Laurent Teyssier," Laurent said warmly, extending his free hand.

"Renaud," he replied, shaking Laurent's outstretched hand. "Paul Renaud."

"I'll be out in a few minutes." Marc gave Laurent's shoulder a tight squeeze, and then let go.

Laurent, as if to underscore Marc's point regarding their relationship, leaned over and kissed Marc lightly on the lips. "A bientôt." He made his way out of the library, closing the door behind him.

"So, now you've met Laurent." Marc could feel the flushed colour of his face. "Paul, please…have a seat," he indicated the chair that Stephen had just vacated.

Renaud seemed a little perplexed. As Marc's houseman, cook, and all around jack-of-all-trades of almost six years, he was more properly called by his last name. Now the staff was calling him Monsieur Renaud, and his employer was calling him by his Christian name. He took the offered seat and waited.

Marc sat in the chair opposite him. "I am so glad you're here," he said, with a sigh of relief. "I suppose Luc brought you up to speed on the break in?"

"Yes, Monsieur."

"Well, I'll get to that in a minute." Marc fumbled in his pocket, and took out his cigarettes and lighter. He lit a cigarette. "Any first impressions, about Brigitte and Luc that is?"

"Luc seems very capable. He talked quite a bit on the way here from the airport. He seems to have the running of the grounds well in hand."

"And Brigitte?"

"Monsieur Balanger." Renaud smiled, emitting a little chuckle. "We've only just met, but judging from the condition of what I have seen of the house, she must be very capable, particularly as Luc says it was in shambles yesterday."

"Well." Marc exhaled a long thing stream of smoke. "I think you'll find them both to be good people, loyal, and…I guess I should get to the point."

"That's probably best, Monsieur."

"Actually it was Brigitte that gave me the idea," he continued. "I was telling her that you would be in charge of the house when I was away, and she asked if you were my private secretary. And not knowing what else to say, well…of course I said yes…I believe I said you handled the details of my day to day life so that I could concentrate on my own work, or words to that effect."

"So does that mean I get a raise to go with the promotion?"

"I just gave you a raise a month ago when you agreed to come with me."

"No harm in trying." He grinned.

"So, you think you'll get used to the staff calling you Monsieur Renaud, and the rest of us calling you Paul?"

"I think I can live with that." Paul grinned.

"They'll be other changes too," Marc continued. "You'll be taking your meals with me and whoever else is visiting…when there are guests," Marc paused a moment trying to think of the next thing to say. "You know that I have come to rely on you over the years we've been together. You've become a member of the family."

"Monsieur," Renaud leaned forward. "People may come and go, but Renaud, he will always be there." He leaned back in his chair and smiled broadly, his voice taking a lighter tone. "So when do I start? The new duties, that is."

"Now." Marc breathed a sigh of relief. "And you've got a lot to do." Marc put out his cigarette, running over the list quickly. "I'd like for you to check the inventory with Brigitte to see what, if anything is missing from the break in. I've promised Inspector Leclerc that we would have a list of anything missing by the end of the week. We'll need it for the insurance, as well. And I want you to work with Luc and the security company to update the alarm system, maybe add some exterior lighting. Get a handle on what everyone does around here and see if there is anything we can do to streamline the running of the house."

"Would you like a report on Reisky and Karpov?" Renaud said, turning the conversation back to the mystery at hand.

"You've found out something new?"

"Not much, but enough perhaps to provide you a little more light on the subject," Paul replied. "Karpov's biography in the 'International Who's Who' provided some revealing insight. He is a widower with a daughter, Irina, who is 22. His late wife, deceased in December of 1990, was one Marina Reisky, but you knew most of that already.

"Your issue of 'Point de Vue' arrived the day before I left. In the sections with the parties, there is a series of photographs taken aboard the Rosenkranz, Count Dimitri Karpov's yacht, in the harbour of Monte Carlo. It was a party to announce the engagement of his daughter Countess Irina to Prince Michael Alexander Romanovsky. Among the guests was Grand Duchess Tatiana Feodorovna, the Head of the Russian Imperial House."

"Count Dimitri Karpov?"

"Since 1996," Paul said, with a self-satisfied smile. "I checked with a friend of mine in the Canadian branch of the Assembly of Russian Nobility. It appears that Grand Duchess Tatiana Feodorovna, in March of 1996, ennobled several people in 'recompense for their special services rendered to the motherland'. Among them Dimitri Pavolovich Karpov, who apparently has given substantial donations to the assembly's charities."

"I'm beginning to catch the scent of blackmail in the air," Marc said. "Two questions come to mind. What did the Princess Andronikov have on Karpov, and why, two years after Princess Andronikov's death, is Karpov still on the hunt?"

"You think that Karpov was responsible for the break in?"

"Yes, I do, especially now."

"I fear you're right." Paul nodded. "As for Sergei Reisky, he's a successful painter known mostly for his portraits and murals. The examples I saw on the gallery site I checked out reminded me a lot of Marc Chagall. Born in St Petersburg, he attended the State Academy of Art and Design and the Russian Academy of Fine Art. He defected in 1975 and moved to Montréal. He married Andrea de la Barre Dumont in 1981 in Paris, where he now lives. He has no children. His parents' are deceased, as is his only sibling, a sister, Marina Reisky," Renaud paused before delivering the endnote, "died of cancer in St Petersburg in 1990…Reisky is Karpov's brother-in-law."

"Sergei Reisky is Laurent's stepfather," Marc said quietly, reaching into his pocket. "He was on the train from Paris to Monte Carlo, and he gave me this." Marc opened the matchbook cover, and handed it to Renaud, who read the warning.

"And Monsieur Teyssier?" Paul asked.

"Laurent's only involvement in this is his relationship with me." Marc's reply was defensive.

"You're sure?"

"I'm certain of that," Marc said, with conviction.

"I hope you're right."

"Reisky has been trying to reach Laurent since yesterday," Marc continued. "Reisky's message said that he was arriving in St Tropez this morning. Supposedly, he was in Zurich, supervising the installation of a mural he has just finished for a bank there."

"But you think he's been with Karpov."

"I'm sure of it," Marc said.

"And you think he's being sent by Karpov?"

Marc nodded, lighting another cigarette.

"What do you plan to do?"

"Reisky's second message said he was anxious to meet Laurent's friends, so Laurent and I decided to invite him here. You remember the old adage; 'keep your friends close, keep your enemies closer'."

Paul nodded.

"Although Reisky tried to warn me, he's still working for Karpov, as it were. We need to know what he knows, and I think that if we have him here at Maure, we might just stand a chance of finding out what that is. Judging from the message on the matchbook cover, he doesn't seem overly fond of Karpov, himself."

"So you'll need a guest room prepared."

"Yes, have Brigitte give him one next to Stephen's. Stephen is a light sleeper, if there are any sleep walking activities, Stephen will hear them, and rouse the rest of us."

"So." Marc extinguished his cigarette, and stood up. "How about some brunch?"

"Sounds great." Paul stood in his turn. "I haven't eaten since breakfast on the plane this morning."

It was such a beautiful day. Stephen decided to remain behind when Marc and Laurent drove down to meet Reisky in St Tropez. If the treasure hunt was off, then vacation time was on, and sun maven that he was, he was going to soak up some real sun's rays.

Shortly after Marc and Laurent left, he went up to his room, changed into his bathing suit, a loose comfortable terrycloth robe, and grabbed one of the big thirsty cotton towels that fortunately had come with the house.

He walked down the stairs, across the terrace, then down to the lawn and through the manicured flowerbeds of the garden to the pool. He was a bit surprised to find a couple of canvas chaise lounge chairs set up on the wide flagstone apron that surrounded the pool. He stretched out on one and found them to be quite comfortable; a perfect place to spend some time working on his tan. He was lying there, soaking up the early afternoon sun when Luc arrived to clean the pool.

"Bonjour Monsieur," Luc said cheerily, stooping down to check the chemical levels in the pool.

"Bonjour Luc," Stephen replied, looking over the rim of his sunglasses. "Pool cleaning day?"

"Yes, Monsieur," he replied, eyeing the colour of the water in the test container as he added the drops of chemicals to the samples of pool water. "I check the chemicals once a week."

"These chairs are quite comfortable."

"Baron Arakcheev bought them while he and his mother were staying here." Luc stood up. "The princess didn't have any pool furniture." He flashed a broad smile. "When Brigitte said you would not be going into St. Tropez, I thought you'd probably want to profit from the sun."

Stephen smiled at the way his phrases translated so literally from French to English. "Tell me something Luc." He shifted to a more upright position in his chaise lounge. "How long have you been caretaker?"

"Three years." He poured the water onto the wide flagstone apron that surrounded the pool. "But I've worked here for over thirteen years, since I was 19. I spent five years as a gardener, then five more as head gardener. When old Franck, the caretaker before me, retired…it was the year before Princess Aleksandra died…she made me caretaker." He closed the chemical kit.

"Did Princess Aleksandra ever use the pool?"

"No, Monsieur, not that I know of," Luc replied. "She was a very solitary person, didn't like the staff around when she was in the garden. She used to take tea here in the afternoons, so we had to have the work in the garden and the pool finished before her tea time." He paused a moment, "Will you be swimming this afternoon, Monsieur?"

"Not for a while. Why?"

"I need to add some chemicals to the water and backwash the pool. I could always come back if you want to have a swim."

"No, please go ahead. I'm not disturbing you, am I?"

"No, Monsieur." He smiled again. "I was just about to ask you the same question."

"Unlike the princess," Stephen replied grinning. "I like having people around. Does it bother you to have someone bending your ear while you're trying to work?"

"Bending my ear?" The image of Stephen trying to bend his ears while he was trying to work flashed through his mind. It made him chuckle.

"Talking to you," Stephen explained, making a mental note to try to avoid obviously idiomatic phrases when talking with Luc or Brigitte.

"Not at all, Monsieur, it helps to pass the time." He paused a moment. "But, you must excuse me for a moment. I need to get the chemicals from the pool house."

"I'll walk along with you." Stephen got up from his chair, and slipped on his robe. "The pool house looks like a little cottage."

"Yes," Luc agreed, as they walked across to the pool house on the south end of the pool. "Franck told me that the princess' father built it in the Russian style to remind him of their estate in Georgia. He put in the pool, too. Franck said the prince was quite an athletic man."

Luc opened the door to the utility room, a narrow door on the outside of the building.

"I think I'll just have a look around the pool house, if you don't mind," Stephen said, as Luc was disappearing into the utility room in search of chemicals and the pool strainer.

"As you wish, Monsieur," he replied, from inside the utility room.

Stephen walked into the pool house. He and Marc had gone through the little cottage on their first tour of the property. The main room was substantial in size and comfortably furnished. Large windows were set in the north and south facing walls, a feature which allowed the room to be filled with natural light.

The eastern wall was almost completely covered by an outsized fireplace, the entire face of which was constructed of natural shaped stones. A hefty wooden beam served as the mantle. On either side of the fireplace, there were doors that led to changing rooms and showers; one for the men and one for the women. On the opposite side of the common room was a door to a small kitchen.

Stephen looked about with a new sense of interest. The ceiling was open from the top of its heavy exposed wood beams, to the top of the high-pitched roof. A wrought iron chandelier hung in the centre of the room. A large tapestry of the Andronikov coat of arms hung over the fireplace.

The décor: overstuffed leather, stone, heavy wood and iron, and the size of the room resembled a hunting lodge in the Balkan forest, more than a pool house in the Var. Must have been some estate, Stephen thought.

He tried to put himself in the place of the builder. If he were going to construct a hiding place, where would he put it? The only place he could think of was the rock-faced wall of the fireplace.

Stephen walked over and started to examine the stones. They were uneven in size; small boulders worn smooth by water and wind. It seemed as if they had been randomly collected, like the stones used for walls in the fields. Yet they fit together almost seamlessly.

Stephen was so intent on their examination that he jumped when a knock came at the open door. He almost fell off the stool on which he was standing.

"Pardon Monsieur," Luc ventured timidly. "I didn't mean to startle you."

"Oh that's alright, in fact you've done me a service," he replied, somewhat breathlessly. "You've just scared ten years off me." He flashed a grin, "That would make me a year or so younger than you."

Luc chuckled. He got the joke.

"Luc," Stephen said, stepping down off the stool. "You said that Prince Felix built the pool house."

"Yes, Monsieur."

"Have there ever been any repairs that you know of?"

"Odd you should ask that, Monsieur," Luc replied, walking into the pool house. "The year the princess died, she had some restoration done to the fireplace. She noticed some loose stones behind the tapestry when it was taken down to be cleaned."

"She used local stone masons, of course."

"No, Monsieur. She had men come from Paris."

"From Paris?" Stephen did a quick calculation. "You were caretaker then, weren't you?"

"Yes, Monsieur."

"Do you remember the section of the wall that was repaired?"

"Yes, Monsieur." He pointed to the tapestry. "It was just above the mantel. It's covered by the bottom of the tapestry."

Stephen thought for a moment. How plausible was it that a frail woman in her eighties, would hide something behind a heavy tapestry, in a wall built of stone boulders. She would have to use a chair to climb up to access the compartment; she'd have to have a very good latch mechanism, one that moved the stone for her. He decided it was just as plausible, as anything else that had transpired, since his arrival in the south of France.

"Have you ever been on a treasure hunt?" Stephen asked.

"A treasure hunt, Monsieur?"

"Yes, a treasure hunt…you know, where you search for a hidden treasure."

"You mean we're going to look for the princess' missing jewels? That's what the burglars were looking for when they broke in…wasn't it?"

"What missing jewels might those be?" Stephen asked, barely able to conceal his curiousity.

"When the princess died, her jewels were sold and the money given to restore a church in Russia. Yvonne, her personal maid, said that only the princess' ordinary jewels were found. She swore that the family had found the princess' special jewels, and kept them for themselves. The family denied it."

"The princess had a lady's maid?"

"Yes, Monsieur. Yvonne retired after the princess' death. When the princess was alive, Yvonne looked after the princess' personal things, her clothes and jewels. She was one of the few people to receive a personal bequest from the princess. She received many of the princess' personal things and an income for the rest of her life."

"Where does Yvonne live now?"

"In Lorgues, Monsieur. She has a house in the old town, inside the city walls."

"Can you arrange for me to visit her?"

"Yes, Monsieur," Luc replied, somewhat puzzled. "Brigitte and I go to see her once a week. You see, Yvonne was an orphan; we were the only family she had. Brigitte and I look after her now. She is a very kind, very gentle person, and she was devoted to the princess; I think the princess cared for her a great deal."

"In fact," he continued. "I am going to see her today. On Wednesdays I leave at 2:00 and go to the village to do her weekly marketing for her."

"Can you arrange for me to go with you?"

"I can telephone to see if it is alright."

"Well, it's 1:30 now," Stephen said. "I can be changed by the time you're ready to leave."

"Very well, I'll telephone as soon as we get back to the house." Luc paused a moment. "I suppose that means no treasure hunt?"

"Tomorrow, Luc, tomorrow."

They walked through the narrow streets of the old town, past the houses built of pale stone, brightened by vivid blue painted doors and shutters. Here and there the vibrant green of a solitary tree accented the ancient buildings with the colour of nature. They walked past the arches of the old fortifications, till they arrived at a small street near the summit of the hill, too narrow for a car to pass.

Both Luc and Stephen carried mesh shopping bags filled with Yvonne's provisions. Stephen had bought a box of special pastries for their tea. They paused before the only bright yellow door on the street. Luc knocked.

After a short wait, a small, delicate featured woman appeared at the door. Though she was in her seventies, traces of her youthful beauty remained. Stephen could tell that she had, indeed, been a beautiful young woman. Her fine, straight hair was pulled back tightly and gathered into a bun at the base of her neck. Its fine silver was streaked with strands of chestnut, which had once been its colour.

"Luc!" her face beamed with the pleasure of seeing him. "Monsieur," she added shyly, nodding at Stephen. "Entrez, entrez."

Stephen was facing a real challenge, Yvonne spoke only French, and Luc was going to have to serve as his translator. Perhaps it would have been more appropriate for Marc to make this visit. However, the "tale of the missing jewels" was his discovery, and he wanted to get to the bottom of it himself.

The house was small. A narrow entry hall led to the kitchen in the back. There was a pleasant sitting room to the left, and a steep narrow staircase led up to the bedroom and bath on the floor above. The sitting room was furnished simply with simple Provencal furnishings.

A small sofa and two comfortable chairs faced the small fireplace. To the left of the simple stone mantle, a small television rested on a cabinet. A small, round dining table with four chairs, and a matching corner cabinet, which displayed plates, glasses, and serving pieces on its upper shelves, completed the room's furnishings.

The table had already been laid out for tea. A Provencal patterned cloth covered the table; terra cotta strawberries on a field of muted yellow. The tea service was an antique, the finest white porcelain. Its only decoration was the letter "A", in a deep rust colour, surmounted by a gold prince's crown. The flatware was an old pattern, silver, and similarly monogrammed. A crystal vase, filled with flowers, sat in the centre of the table. The princess had been generous to her companion.

"Asseyez-vous, Monsieur." She smiled sweetly at Stephen, indicating one of the dining chairs. With a polite smile, she took the mesh shopping bag and the box of pastries from his hands. "Merci pour les pâtisseries, Monsieur, il est très gentil de votre part."

Luc, still laden with his shopping bags, followed her into the kitchen. Stephen sat in his chair and drank in the simple elegance of the room's décor. Here and there, scattered around the room, Stephen noticed other mementos from her years of service; a pair of silver candlesticks on the narrow stone mantel, a little silver box on the coffee table in front of the sofa, photographs in small ornate silver frames scattered on tables and on the mantelpiece. All the little treasures of her life in the chateau, carefully placed, shinning in the filtered light of the Provencal sun, which filtered through the small lace-draped windows opening to the street.

They returned, Yvonne with a steaming pot of tea, and Luc carrying the pastries artfully arranged on a footed cake-stand.

Late afternoon turned into early evening as they sipped tea and ate delicate pastries; Yvonne recounting stories of her years with the princesses in her soft lilting voice, Luc translating in his smooth heavily accented baritone. It was almost hypnotic. Stephen felt as though he had gone through a door into the past, to a time long disappeared. Stephen learned much about the family that had lived at Maure before Marc bought the place.

Yvonne was orphaned at birth. Her father drowned in a boating accident, and her mother in childbirth. She spent her childhood in an orphanage. It was there that the Princess Elena had found her, a young adolescent with a pretty face and a talent for needlework. She was, by her own admission, not a clever girl, but she was honest and hardworking. She went into the service of the princesses as a young girl of fourteen.

The two women were lonely, aloof, they lived looking to the past, seeing only what was lost, alienated from the time in which they lived. Their relationship with their relatives, the Germans and the Hungarians, was strange. The Germans had little time for two women who lived in seclusion, mourning their loss of the past. The Hungarians were treated with enmity, as though some secret betrayal lay hidden in the shrouded mists of the past. Though they never spoke of the reason, the Hungarians were somehow linked to the events that had forever changed the character of their lives.

They were not unkind to the people who served them, who helped them remain isolated from a world they chose not to face. In the case of Yvonne, a bond grew between them that spoke of the gentleness that must have been inherent in their characters. Yet, the desire for revenge, for what had been taken from the lonely princesses, was never far from the surface. Princess Elena maintained her widow's seclusion until her death. Princess Aleksandra forsook the mourning, in which she passed her entire life, only once.

Shortly before her death she gave a grand ball in honour of the new head of the Russian Imperial House who was visiting Monte Carlo at the time. On that evening, the Chateau de Maure blazed with light, glittered with diamonds, jewelled decorations, and Paris gowns. Gold plates and crystal covered the buffet tables, champagne and vodka toasted the hope for a new Russia. The ballroom of the Gothik pavilion was filled with music from the orchestra, hired for the occasion. The princess' guests danced late into the night.

For the only time in her life, the Princess Aleksandra wore her 'special jewels'; jewels that from Yvonne's description were worth a king's ransom, jewels to which only the Princess Aleksandra had had access, jewels that were now missing.

Yvonne told him too, of the Princess Aleksandra's death, in itself, a strange tale. After the ball, she had become brighter, some secret energy seemed to burn inside of her, and she became consumed with a strange sense of purpose; something concealed, hidden, something she did not even share with Yvonne.

She began to spend long hours in the pavilion, sometimes not returning until after dark. Then, shortly before her death, a Russian man had come to visit her. He brought her a package. The princess seemed almost happy. For the first time in all the years Yvonne had known her, the princess seemed to be almost serene.

Then suddenly, inexplicably, she became ill, first the fever, then she could not eat. The doctors did the best they could do, for she refused to go to hospital. Yvonne did the best she could to nurse her dear princess, but to no avail. On her last day, the fever seemed to subside. She was weak, terribly frail. She smiled meekly, and for the first time in all the years they had know one another, thanked her long-time companion for her gentle patience, assuring her that she would be cared for.

"I go to join my father and mother," the princess said. "I go happily…for Papa will be avenged."

Yvonne was deeply moved as she recounted the end of her tale, her eyes moist. She told Stephen how the princess took her hand…and then she died, quietly, peacefully…and the Russian man came again…the day after her death.

It was a quarter to six when they left. Stephen was anxious to return to Maure. Marc and Laurent would have returned by now. He made a mental note to ask Renaud to check on just how solvent Karpov really was.

Chapter Eight –
Revelations and a Plan

The dining room was magnificent. Brigitte had laid the table with the best china and crystal. The china was Grand Apparat from Haviland. Its wide cobalt rim was encrusted with gold, an elaborate gold medallion decorated the centre of the plate. The vermeil flatware, from Christofle, was monogrammed with an "A" surmounted by a prince's crown. The crystal was Irish, Waterford's Lismore.

The centrepiece was an eighteenth century silver fantasy around which cherubs, sculpted in three dimensions, played with animals in a Dionysian garden. It was filled with an elegant mass of flowers from the garden, blue irises, white and salmon coloured roses, and tulips, brilliant yellow and soft pink.

Matching pairs of silver candlesticks flanked the centrepiece, shedding the light of their white candles on the table's elegant arrangement. Candles in the silver wall sconces, and in the large silver-gilt candelabrum on the sideboard, provided the lighting for the rest of the room.

The dinner had been prepared and placed in elegant serving dishes, some silver, some porcelain; all were covered to keep the food warm. They waited on the sideboard for each course to be served in turn; rabbit pâté, followed by filet of roast duck in a honey sauce, caviar d'aubergines, garlic puree of potato, finishing with chocolate mousse filled meringues. The wines, except for the champagne to be served with dessert, were in silver coasters, uncorked and ready. The champagne was chilling in its chased silver bucket of cracked ice.

In the absence of a footman, Luc, who had often performed these duties for the princess, agreed to serve the dinner. Marc counted himself lucky, but resolved to find another addition to his household staff for such duties, as Luc, now caretaker and gardener, already had a full plate, and Renaud was now above stairs staff, as they say in Britain.

They had dressed for dinner, black tie. There was a point to the formality. It was to serve as a reminder of the Andronikov legacy, a legacy that refused to leave any of them in peace.

Mark was resolved to get to the bottom of this mystery, to bury the ghosts. This was his home now, and he was determined to clear out the last of the vestiges of a bitter exile, and the nemesis she had somehow created in the person of Karpov...and he was determined to start the housecleaning this very evening.

Marc sat at the head of the table, Laurent on his right. Sergei Reisky sat next to his stepson. Stephen sat on Marc's left; Paul Renaud was seated next to him. The foot of the table remained empty.

Luc served the rabbit pâté and the wine, a '96 Chateau Barbazan. Marc had asked him to remain in the room as much as possible. His pool house conversation and afternoon visit to Lorgues with Stephen had brought him into their little band.

"Gentlemen, I should like to offer a toast," Marc began, lifting his glass. "Welcome to the Chateau de Maure, now under new management." He smiled slightly and lifted his glass to his lips, taking a small sip. Then he raised his glass again. "And I should also like to offer a toast to Luc, who was kind enough to give up his evening and serve the dinner." Marc drank again, this time a little more deeply.

"Sergei." Marc turned to his newest guest. "Perhaps you would care to enlighten everyone as to why Karpov sent you here." The change of subject was sudden, abrupt, but Marc could think of no other way to begin, and begin they must.

Sergei swallowed a large gulp of wine. He had already made his confession, as it were, to Marc and Laurent on the way back from St Tropez. He knew of the relationships of the rest of the company, so now he repeated the details for their benefit, his last conversation with Karpov aboard the Rosenkranz, Princess Aleksandra's blackmail, and her price...a price Karpov had paid. He clarified his relationship to the Russian oil tycoon and his daughter; former brother-in-law to Karpov, uncle to Irina.

"Laurent was unaware of my connection to Karpov," Sergei added, for Laurent's benefit. "My relationship with Karpov was strained because of the circumstances of my leaving Russia. With my sister dead, Karpov saw no reason to include me in his *circle*," he pronounced the word with something akin to disdain, "until last week."

By the time Karpov had finished his story, the plates and cutlery from the first course had been cleared away, and the second course served and half eaten. Luc listened intently, containing his surprise as each new twist of the story unfolded. If his former employer had been distant, he would never have imagined her a murderess. In truth, she had not pulled a trigger; yet, her hands were still stained with blood. Mafia or no, the murdered man was innocent of the death of the princess' father.

Marc finished the last bite of duck, and placed the knife and fork across his plate. "So, we still are left with a reason as to why Karpov was willing to pay a blackmailer. Although he told Sergei it was because of his daughter's engagement…"

"Obviously a sympathy ploy," Stephen interjected.

"His daughter was only recently engaged to Prince Michael," Marc continued. "Princess Aleksandra has been dead for two years. Both the blackmail and the death of Princess Aleksandra pre-date the engagement."

"Why didn't Karpov search for the codebook earlier," Laurent asked. "Even though, as Sergei said, he could not purchase the property, there must have been ample opportunity to enter the house during the past two years."

"Perhaps I can answer that, Monsieur," Luc interrupted respectfully.

"Please, Luc, go on," Marc said.

"Princess Aleksandra had two heirs, cousins on her mother's side. The Countess Apraskin, and the Baroness Arakcheev. They contested the will. The Countess is a wealthy woman, who lives in Germany; they say she wanted the Princess' jewels. The Baroness lived in

Hungary. The Arakcheev were, as Yvonne once said to me, the poor relations."

"The Baroness wanted the chateau." He continued. "She and her grandson, Stephane. They came to Lorgues for the princess' funeral. Their lawyer obtained permission for them to live in the chateau until a decision was reached regarding the princess' will. They lived here for almost two years, until the will was finally upheld, and the jewels and estate ordered sold. They only moved when the house was purchased, by you, Monsieur, a month ago."

The rest of the company listened with interest as Luc told his tale.

"The Baroness is a year older than the princess, and very frail," Luc added, as he served the dessert. "She never left the house...the house was never empty."

"No opportunity, no search," Stephen summed up the story.

"As for the matter of the jewels." Marc took a sip of his champagne. "We have a double mystery. There are the princess' 'special jewels,' which you found out about today, Stephen, and there is the missing Alastani diamond; Karpov's first blackmail payment, which according to Karpov was delivered, and is now unaccounted for."

"And it just keeps getting better," Stephen muttered.

Marc leaned back in his chair. "Perhaps you and Luc would tell us about your tea with Yvonne."

Over dessert and champagne, Stephen told the story of his afternoon, with Luc filling in the finer points Stephen had missed due to the language difficulty.

Marc finished the last bite of his mousse. "So, we have a number of things to find before we can really air out this place; the Andronikov codebook and documents, and the missing jewels.

"I suggest that we retire to the drawing room for cognac and liqueurs. Perhaps between the six of us we can come up with a strategy." He got up from the table. "Luc, why don't you take the rest of the night off and join us for a drink in the drawing room." He grinned. "We are perhaps a motley crew of amateur detectives, but I assure you the company is good."

"Je n'en doute pas, Monsieur," Luc said, with a chuckle. "I'll join you as soon as I have cleared away the dining room."

"I'll help," Paul said, getting up from his chair. "It will go more quickly."

"Ah no, Monsieur Renaud," Luc protested quickly.

"Paul," he said, with a warm smile. "And I insist."

The main sitting room of the chateau faced the entrance courtyard. Its tall, wide French doors opened onto the front terrace. It was called the Green Drawing Room because of the principal colours used in the decoration. The Green Drawing Room was the larger of the two sitting rooms in the chateau.

Wainscoting covered the lower third of the walls. It was painted a rich apple green. The remaining two thirds of the wall above the elegant paneling was papered with a celadon-coloured striped silk. The draperies were rich emerald green velvet. They were hung by gilded rings suspended on black wrought iron rods, with fleur-de-lis finials.

It was a pleasant night, with just a slight breeze; Marc had opened the doors when they'd come into the room, pulling back the draperies to let in the night air. A soft light filled the room from the twelve branches of its electrified crystal chandelier, which was suspended from an elegant medallion in the centre of the ceiling.

The light was reflected in the large rectangular gilt-wood mirrors placed strategically around the room; over the fireplace, between the two sets of French doors leading to the terrace, and over an elegant fruitwood Louis XV commode, on which was placed a large Waterford crystal vase filled with roses.

The commode had been set up as a bar. Two silver trays rested on its green marble top; one with liqueurs, the other with Lismore snifters and liqueur glasses.

By one set of the French doors, at an angle to the wall, there was an ebony game table, with an inlaid backgammon board on top. The game was set up; round tiles of rose quartz and jade, and matching coloured-ivory dice, were ready for the players' arrival.

On either side of the elegant little table was placed one of a matching pair of medallion-back Louis XV gilt-wood armchairs. They were upholstered in a fine tapestry fabric; a Watteauesque garden scene in pale rose and green on a beige ground.

The fireplace mantel was pale green marble, carved in the Louis XV style. Facing it was a seating area. There were four large, walnut, French Regency fauteuils, upholstered in the same tapestry as the chairs at the backgammon table. They were arranged in a conversational grouping, flanking an emerald green leather sofa. The grouping formed an intimate "u" shape, facing the mantelpiece. Small occasional tables were conveniently placed to hold drinks and ashtrays.

There was a pair of faded green, velvet-upholstered, beech wood bergères in front of the second set of French doors, and behind the sofa was a Louis XV beech wood card table with cabriole legs in a verde gris finish, and four matching chairs.

Marc found his way to the sofa, pulled a cigarette from a small crystal urn on the table in front of it, and made himself comfortable. Sergei took one of the chairs closest to the fireplace. His choice of seating reinforced the distance he felt from the rest of the group.

"Would you like a drink, Sergei?" Laurent asked, heading for the bar.

"Grand Marnier?" he ventured quietly.

"Make that two," Marc added.

"Make that three," Stephen said, taking the chair to Marc's right.

"That makes it unanimous." Laurent grinned.

"I guess I should help," Stephen said, getting of his chair.

They served the drinks, and were just sitting down, Laurent on the sofa next to Marc, and Stephen in his place, when Paul and Luc appeared at the door.

"Name your poison." Stephen stood as they came into the room. "I'll be mother." He delighted in using that old English expression, generally reserved for serving tea. He waived them to the empty chairs. "Sit, sit."

"I'll have a Grand Marnier," Paul spoke first.

"A Calvados for me, Monsieur Hampstead," Luc replied, sitting.
"So, here we are," Stephen quipped, returning with the drinks.
"All dressed up and no place to go."
"Ah, but you're wrong," Marc said. "I can think of at least one place we could go."
Paul flashed a wry smile. "This evening's entertainment will be a tribute to the genre films of the thirties, a re-enactment of the assault on Frankenstein's castle."
"I can see it now," Stephen joined in. "Six men in formal attire, heading through the forest, across the meadow, around the lake to batter down the doors to the Gothik pavilion; pick axes, shovels, and blazing torches in hand. They emerge from the pavilion some time later, covered in dust, carrying a secret codebook, a portfolio of documents, and a heavy chest overflowing with treasure. Just as the last of the adventurers exits the blazing tower, the building collapses, covering their clothes in dust and debris."
Laurent chuckled. "We should definitely change first."
"And loose the comedic effect?" Stephen stood up. "I think not!"
"Perhaps we should wait until tomorrow." Paul remained seated; taking a leisurely sip of his Grand Marnier. His manner became more serious. "This evening might be better spent getting this 'motley group of amateur detectives' organized."
"Right you are Paul." Marc took a cigarette from the silver urn on the coffee table. Lighting it, he spoke through a long stream of exhaled smoke. "I want this Karpov cretin out of my life…yesterday. So, let's organize. What do we have to do to get him what he wants?"
"We find the code book," Sergei said quietly.
"And then give him the run of my home to find the damn papers he wants?" Marc was beginning to get angry.
"He is right, Marc," Stephen agreed. "After all, Karpov did send him here to find the code book."
"He already has the diary." Sergei continued, "Karpov said the key to the documents' hiding place is in it. If we find the codebook, I could take it to him. He can tell *me* the hiding place; I can come back, retrieve the documents and take them to him. With Laurent staying

here, it is natural that I would return."

"Why not just go to the police?" Luc asked.

"And tell them what?" Paul softened the question with a smile. "We cannot prove it was Karpov's people who broke into the house. As for Monsieur Reisky's conversation with him, that is hearsay. Karpov can deny it. Lest we forget, Karpov is an extremely rich man…he could simply feign offence and leave the country."

"We must also keep in mind that Karpov is a determined man. He has already arranged one *accident*, to get his hands on the Andronikov documents," Sergei added. "He will not stop there if he feels that another would guarantee their delivery." He paused and took a deep drink of his Grand Marnier. "After all, Monsieur Balanger has no codicil in his will prohibiting Russians from purchasing his property."

"So what would you tell Karpov?" Laurent asked, looking intently at his stepfather.

"I will call him in the morning and tell him that I managed to get myself invited to the chateau. That I am here, and that I will find the code book."

"And if he starts to ask questions as to how or where you will look?"

"I'll tell him I have free reign of the house…because of Marc and Laurent's close relationship." Sergei was inventing his story as he spoke. "I will say…the housekeeper told me of work Princess Aleksandra had done the year before she died…changes to the library; a hidden compartment…I'll tell him that I'm certain this must be where the princess hid the code book."

"And if he asks you how long it will take?" Laurent played devil's advocate.

"No more than a day or two." Sergei smiled slightly. "I'll tell him that Marc and his guests are often out, visiting the local sites…I am staying behind because my host has asked me to look at the Russian books in the library, to determine if there are any of value. I'll say that the servants leave me in peace to do my 'work'."

"Well done," Stephen said. "Believable yet nebulous. Are you sure you're not a writer?"

"A painter must also tell a story when he applies his colour to the canvas," Sergei replied.

"How right you are, Sergei." Marc took a sip of his Grand Marnier. "Now that we have a plausible story for stalling Karpov, where do we search?"

"That's the easy part." Stephen jumped in. "There were only two major changes made to the property…that we know of…during the time the Andronikov's owned the chateau. The restoration and extension of the Gothik pavilion by Prince Felix, and the changes made to the pool house by Princess Aleksandra the year before she died. The code book has to be in one place or the other."

"I think he's right," Paul said, getting up and going over to the bar. "Can I freshen anyone's drink?"

"Yes, I'll have another." Sergei pulled a cigar case from his inside pocket. "We must assume that we are being watched."

He extracted a cigar from the case, clipped the end with a small tool that he took out of his waistcoat pocket. "I think it's a safe bet that Malinkov was sent to keep an eye on things."

"Malinkov?" Stephen went back to the bar to refill his own glass.

"Karpov's body guard." Reisky paused, lighting the cigar. "He handles all of Karpov's more delicate arrangements." He emphasized the word delicate. "I feel certain he is lurking in the village…we must be very careful."

"As you say," Marc responded. "We must be careful…so tomorrow morning, Stephen, you and Paul will go for a swim. Luc will, of course, need to check on the plumbing in the pool house. As for me and Laurent, we will take his stepfather on a tour of the grounds and the Gothik pavilion beside the lake."

"Clever, M." Stephen quipped, refilling his glass.

"And just to make certain that we have no difficulty with this Malinkov," Marc continued. "Tomorrow I will phone Monsieur Karpov myself…I still have the number."

"Good God M!" Stephen almost dropped his glass. "What are you up to?"

"Just a slight modification of Sergei's plan. Actually, it's Sergei who gave me the idea." Marc lifted his glass as if in a toast in Reisky's direction. "The Russian books...as Karpov professed to be such an avid collector, I shall offer them to him."

Marc put his glass down and reached for a cigarette. "I will reinforce Sergei's 'previous call'...a call unknown to me, of course...I'll let Karpov know that I have decided to sell the Russian books, that a Monsieur Reisky, the step father of one of my guests, who is himself a guest, is looking at them for me...that I thought he might like first choice of any 'Imperial' related manuscripts."

"Isn't that dangerous?" Laurent was genuinely concerned. "Perhaps he will think that you are picking up where Princess Aleksandra left off."

"I think it will be safe enough. I shall simply tell Monsieur Karpov that my sister and her family are joining us for the weekend...from Paris...that he, his daughter and her fiancé are invited to join us for the weekend, to round out the party."

"Wait a minute M," Stephen said. "How are you supposed to know about them being on the yacht?"

"I will simply blame it on Point de Vue. When was that picture taken, Paul?"

"Two weeks ago, Monsieur," he replied, taking the decanter of Grand Marnier from the bar. "The caption did say that the couple were off on a Mediterranean cruise on Count Karpov's yacht, the Rosenkranz."

"What about Chantal?" Stephen walked over to the backgammon table, admiring its workmanship.

"No problem there." Marc grinned, somewhat mischievously, glancing at Laurent. "I'll tell her that there is someone I need for her to meet."

"Our theme for the weekend," Stephen looked up from the game, "will be drawn from that age-old contest of wills...poker."

Paul caught the allusion. "Does a full house beat three of a kind?" He smiled, refilling Reisky's glass.

"Indeed," Marc said, standing.

"Anyone for a game of backgammon?" Stephen was admiring

the board. "Now that we're organized, we might as well have a little fun."

"No, I think I'm ready to turn in," Laurent looked at Marc.

"I'm with you," Marc replied.

"Well, we all know that," Stephen quipped, in a tone of mock disgust.

"I'll take you up on that game," Sergei said, crossing over to the table.

"Stephen, I'll leave it to you then." Marc stood up. "Please lock up and set the alarm before you turn in."

"Will do, M."

"I think I'll turn in too," Paul said. "It's been a very long day for me."

"For me too, Messieurs," Luc said, rising.

"One last thing," Marc said, pausing in the doorway. "Tomorrow, every one have your cell phones on you. We exchange numbers at breakfast. We stay in touch…and if you see anyone on the grounds who is unknown to you, phone the police."

Malinkov walked quickly up Avenue Auguste Grangeon. The small black sedan was waiting, carefully parked in the shadow of the hotel. He got in on the passenger side, and quietly closed the door. "It's all arranged," he said, warming to the sensation of the black-gloved hand as it expertly slid up his inner thigh.

"What did you tell them?"

"That I had a family emergency…in St Petersburg." He spread his legs further apart, relishing the sensation of sexual energy that was beginning to course through his body as the hand continued its exploration. "I left in time to catch the bus for Nice."

"If all goes well, we will soon be on our way to South America."

The hand, teasing, pulled away and turned the key in the ignition. The black sedan headed for north for Lorgues.

Chapter Nine – A Princely Icon

It took three tries to get the right key for the exterior door of the tower, but finally they entered the tower room of the Gothik Pavilion. It was exactly as the plans had shown; gothik-pointed arched French doors formed three walls of the octagonal north and south walls of the building.

The western wall's monumental stone fireplace was surmounted by a coat of arms carved into the stone over the mantel. The blazon was different from the tapestry in the pool house. It was probably that of the silk-merchant family that originally built the chateau. Each side of the octagonal tower was six meters in length. Laurent estimated the diameter of the room to be around twelve meters.

The walls, into which the French doors were set, were evenly divided; two meters on either side of a door, each door panel a meter wide. The interior walls, between the multi-paned French doors, were decorated with slender elegant columns, carved stone bundles in the gothik style. The effect was a pure faux gothik sophistication of the sort that only the Victorians could produce.

The vaulted ceiling rose to a height of thirteen meters. It was painted deep blue, with gold stars glittering here and there across its surface. The main source of artificial lighting was suspended from the centre of the ceiling by a heavy black iron chain. It was a large electrified chandelier, forged like the chain from black wrought iron, with traces of gilding.

The room was sparsely furnished. Centred under the chandelier, was a single large rectangular dinning table in the gothik style surrounded by eight matching chairs. A pair of large gothik styled console tables and several tall multi-branched, floor-standing candelabrum of black iron, with traces of gilt, completed the tower room's furnishings.

The candelabrums were not electrified. The wide, iron bobeche terminals of their branches were filled with tall, white pillar candles. The floor was bare stone, grey like the walls and columns. The only exception was a large rust and blue Persian carpet that had been placed, artfully, under the dinning table and chairs.

The east wall led to the gallery, connecting the tower room with the Prince Felix's addition—the ballroom, as Yvonne had called it. The door to the passage was solid oak, banded with black wrought iron. In the centre of each door, a black metal lion's head, with a ring in its mouth, was meant to serve as a handle for the door. The door on the right contained the keyhole, an open-mouthed gargoyle waiting for its meal.

Marc repeated the exercise with the keys. Finding the correct one, he and Laurent opened the doors to the passage. The reverse side of the open doors were but the first of the amazing revelations they were to discover, as they began the search of the mysterious connecting gallery.

The doors on the tower room side were a simple gothik confection of oak banded with black iron; the insides were completely gilded. The morning light streaming in through the French doors brought a new life to the heavy gold leaf.

Each door was divided into three panels by heavily carved wooden moulding. Inside each of the carved and burnished gilt wood panels, inset icons of Russian Saints stared out at them with their sad and distant eyes. Each icon retained its original frame; gold inset with pearls and jewels. The effect was breathtaking. They stood a long moment, drinking in the Byzantine splendour.

The gallery was dark, except for a small pool of pale blue light, which seemed to be coming from high above the centre of the room's barely visible domed ceiling. The blue light illuminated an ornate gold lantern suspended from a chain, descending from its domed centre. From what they could see, Laurent's approximation of the room's size appeared correct; six meters long and three meters wide.

"We'll need some light." Laurent entered the gallery and walked over to one of the torchères near the door. He grabbed three pillar candles, pulling them from the spikes that held them in place on their gilt metal bobeches.

"Got your lighter handy?" he grinned, knowing the answer. Laurent returned to the doorway. He handed a candle to Marc and one to Sergei. Marc took his lighter from his pocket and lit the candles. They were amazed at what they saw as they entered the passageway, from every direction, the gleam of burnished gold reflected the glow of their candles.

The gallery was divided into three parts; an eastern entry passage, with an arched ceiling; the centre section, with its interior dome; and a western entry passage, the one that led to the ballroom. The ceiling of the western entry passage, like that of the eastern one, was arched.

The gallery was decorated in the Old Russian style. Rounded vaults supported the interior dome of the centre section, a two-meter square. The section's twisted columns, which provided the support for the vaults, were spaced two meters apart. A pale blue glow filtered down from the ceiling. It seemed to come from a hidden skylight, which allowed the daylight to pass through the roof and then through the blue-stained glass centre of the dome.

As they walked further into the gallery, they noticed that it had been meticulously laid out. Triple branch torchères of gilded metal were placed between each column, along the eastern and western entry passages of the gallery. There were pillar- candles in the each one. They could just make out the pair of candelabrum on a console table, placed against the north wall of the central section.

"Shall we shed a little light on the subject?" Marc approached the closest torchère and began to light its candles from his own. Laurent and Sergei followed suit until all the candles were lit.

The effect was breath taking. The soft light of the pillars and the diffused blue light from the ceiling gave the room an enchanting aspect. The walls and the ceilings were painted a soft deep shade of sky blue; gold leaf had been applied to the twisted columns. The floor was laid out in tiles of pale blue, veined marble. It was as if the three of them had been lifted out of reality, and inserted onto the page of an ancient illuminated manuscript, depicting a Russian Gothik image of heaven.

The golden lantern, suspended from the centre of the dome, was pierced and worked in the Old Russian style. It, too, contained white candles.

"Here's the chain for lowering and raising the lantern." Sergei stood near the doors to the ballroom. He pulled gently on the chain, lowering the lantern to an easy-to-reach height.

Marc opened the gilded lantern door and lit the three candles. "You can raise it back now," he said, closing the door.

Sergei returned the lantern to its original height. The room was now bathed in the warm glow of candles. The burnished gold of the decorations, the torchères and the lantern gleamed in the soft light. The doors leading to Prince Felix's ballroom were still closed. They, too, were carved and gilded wood, inset with jewelled icons of saints.

The room was sparsely furnished, but the furniture was as superb as the decoration that served as their backdrop. Under the lantern was a round table. Three gilt bronze sphinxes formed its legs. They supported a round top of solid lapis lazuli, the rim of which was decorated with ormolu appliqué.

In the centre of the table was a vase. Marc ran his fingers around its wide rim in silent appreciation. It was a solid piece of rock crystal, carved in the shape of an urn, with mounted ormolu handles and a square ormolu base.

Arranged around the table were four chairs, in the same Russian Empire style. The legs were carved griffins, whose claws encircled golden orbs. The griffin's wings formed the arms of the chairs. In the middle of the back chair was a carved sunburst, with the face of the sun in its centre.

The griffins' heads and wings, the orbs and the sunburst, were all gold-leafed, but the rest of the chairs' frames were painted a deep rich lapis lazuli blue. The cushions were dark blue velvet, edged with gold braid.

The table and chairs were centred on a fine Persian carpet, silk threads woven in shades of blue on a fawn background. The only other furniture in the gallery was a console table. It, too, was in the Russian Empire style. From its design, it appeared to have been made to match the table. The frame was a rich mahogany, the apron inset with matching ormolu mounts identical to those of the table, the front legs of the console were the same gilt-bronze winged sphinxes, the top a thick slab of lapis lazuli.

The console table was long and deep. It was centred on the north wall of the centre section. On it were a small golden samovar with its teapot, and six pierced gilt-metal teacups in the Russian style, with crystal liners. There were six metal dessert plates, also gilt, and a gilt-metal cake tray all in the same pattern as the teacups. Gilt cutlery; knives, forks and spoons, was laid out as if the guests for tea would arrive at any moment.

On either side of the samovar, was one of a pair of Russian gilt bronze urns, on lapis bases with ormolu mounts. At each end of the console was placed one of a matching pair of candelabrum, the figure of an Egyptian male figure carved in lapis, standing on a lapis lazuli base with classical ormolu mounts. The five branches of the gilt bronze candelabrum were mounted atop his Egyptian headdress.

The splendour of the gallery was awe-inspiring. Marc could not believe that he was now the owner of such a room. If this were an example of how the Andronikov lived in pre-revolutionary Russia, they must have been extraordinarily wealthy. He forced himself to ignore the opulence around him and got back to the reason for which they had actually come to the pavilion.

Carefully, he examined the cushions of the chairs, only two of them displayed any real wear; one showed more use than the other. "This is her chair, it's the one which shows the most real wear on the cushion…first the mother, then the daughter."

He pulled out the chair and sat in it, his back to the console. The only thing before him was a blank wall. "Why would she stare at a blank wall?" he mused.

"Because the wall was not blank," Laurent replied, carefully running his hands across the wall, trying to find a seam in its smooth surface. "The hidden compartment has to be behind this wall." Just as he was speaking, his fingers brushed across a hairline seam. "I'm right, there is a seam just here, next to the column. It's so fine you almost cannot detect it."

Marc got out of the chair and crossed over to where Laurent stood. Laurent took his hand and positioned it over the fine hairline seam in the wall.

"There, you see," Laurent said. "I'd bet money there's another seam in the shadow of the column to the left."

"That's a bet I wouldn't take," Marc replied.

"How does it open?" Marc wondered out loud.

"The way the side seam fits so closely against the adjoining wall, it can't slide sideways. It has to go up or down…there's not enough height to the ceiling for it to slide up…" Laurent's voice trailed off, as he bent down on one knee, running his hand along the floor. He found another hairline seam between the wall and the marble tiles.

"Does this mean you're going to propose," Marc said, stepping back, leaning against the column behind him. "Merde!" he exclaimed, loosing his balance.

Laurent reached up to steady him.

"This column is loose."

"Loose?" Laurent queried.

"Yes," Marc said, rotating the column gingerly. "It rotates a quarter turn to the right."

"Like a cylinder lock," Laurent said.

"But nothing happened." Marc rotated the column back to its original position, then twisted the column its quarter turn again. "Still nothing."

"Perhaps other columns turn too," Laurent interjected. "Let's check them out."

There were 12 columns, six on either side of the gallery. The first one of each set of six, was placed next to the wall of the adjoining room. They were evenly spaced a meter apart; a gap of two meters was left in the middle of the gallery to form its centre-domed section.

Laurent and Marc checked each column. Only the original one and the column to its right rotated. They tried rotating both columns, first the left, then the right. Nothing happened.

"Maybe they have to be rotated at the same time," Laurent posited.

"No," Marc replied. "They're two meters apart, too great a distance for someone like the princess to manage."

"Yes, but Prince Felix designed the addition."

"I know, but Brigitte said that Princess Aleksandra had tea alone." Marc paused a moment. "The two princesses could perhaps have managed together, but your theory would require that Princess Aleksandra have help after her mother's death."

"I think I have the answer," Sergei said, standing in front of one of the doors. Quietly, intently, he had been studying the icons set in the doors panels. "There are twelve icons, and twelve columns." He paused. "The icons are of the twelve apostles."

"You think there's a correlation, father?"

"Yes, Laurent." He smiled at the sign of affection from his stepson. One of the greatest concerns he had, was how this affair was going to impact his relationship with his own family. He truly loved his wife, and Laurent was the only son they would ever have.

"When these doors are open, there are only six apostles in heaven." Sergei moved to close one of the doors to the tower. "Laurent, close the other door."

Laurent closed the door to Sergei's left. They walked back to join Marc beside the rotating columns.

"Now we have twelve apostles and twelve columns," Sergei said. "Let's see if this is what Prince Felix had in mind."

Marc turned the left column its quarter turn. Laurent rotated the right. Again nothing.

"Maybe you're right," Marc said. "Maybe they must be turned simultaneously."

"No," Sergei interjected. "Twelve apostles, twelve columns. I am standing between Judas and John." He gave a name to each of the columns. "In the Roman church you cross yourself left to right. In the Russian church it's right to left. Turn the columns back to their original position."

Marc and Laurent did as Sergei instructed.

"Now, Laurent you turn yours."

Laurent turned the right column its quarter turn.

"Now, Monsieur Balanger…"

"Marc…please, Sergei," Marc replied, rotating his column its quarter turn.

There was a sudden soft grinding of gears. The three men stepped back, as the wall in front of them started its slow descent.

The first thing to appear was the top of a carved gilt wood frame, surmounted by a prince's crown. As the wall continued its descent, a portrait of Prince Felix in his uniform appeared. He was standing in front of a chair draped with an ermine trimmed red velvet robe. A table on his right held a prince's crown made of diamonds; around his neck he wore the diamond chain and badge of the order of St Andrew. It was an "official" portrait, as Marc often called such paintings.

Then, as the wall continued its slow descent, came the brilliance of jewels flashing in the light of the candles. First, a diamond crown…then jewel studded golden crowns each resting on pedestals of solid malachite. The blocks were encased in gold mounts with lion's feet serving as a base.

As the opening between the ceiling and the floor widened, the top of the console on which the pedestals rested came into view; more jewels, a chalice, and jewelled objects, lovingly laid in place on the console that was a mate to the one behind them.

None of them were prepared for the magnificence of what they saw; treasures that had been hidden from any view, except the Princesses Andronikov, for almost one hundred years.

Beneath the portrait there was another pair of Egyptian style candelabrum, twins of the pair on the console opposite. The candles in them had never been lit. Their replacement was undoubtedly the final act of the princess, before she closed the secret panel for the very last time.

Marc stepped forward tentatively, as if afraid to approach what was obviously an altar to the princesses' memories. He lit the candles carefully, and the light they emitted was reflected a thousand fold in the brilliance of the gems.

"My god!" he said softly. "I don't know which amazes me more, the care with which this has all been assembled, or the opulence of its parts."

"For me it is both," Serge murmured, motionless.

The entire alcove was lined with deep emerald silk velvet, which served as the backdrop for the memorial so tenderly constructed. The largest pedestal was placed directly beneath the portrait. Gold mounts with roman motifs decorated its sides. Upon it rested a prince's crown, so completely covered in diamonds that the metal in which they were set was not visible.

To the right and left of the prince's crown, on malachite blocks of identical design, of a lesser height, were two other crowns. One was obviously a man's; the other, equally obviously, a woman's.

"The wedding crowns," Sergei said, reverently touching the pearl and diamond encrusted woman's crown.

Marc could not resist. Carefully he ran his fingers across the centre stone in the man's crown, a great square cut emerald; it must have been forty carats. The other stones mounted on the crown's gold frame; diamonds, emeralds, rubies and pearls, were equally impressive, if not as large.

A Faberge frame was positioned just in front of the princely crown, perfectly centred between the wedding crowns. It was in emerald green enamel. Centred on the top was a prince's crown set with little diamonds. In it was a photograph of Prince Felix and his bride on their wedding day.

Just centimetres in front of the wedding photograph, on either side, right and left, were the wedding chalice and a plate for the bread. They were exquisite examples of the goldsmith's art. On the left side the cup; it was gold, set with diamonds, emeralds and rubies. On the right side was the plate. The outer rim was ringed with perfectly matched pearls; the inner rim was set with square cut diamonds.

Centred with precision, one in front of each of the wedding crown pedestals, was a box. The two were a perfect match, identical in every way; emeralds mounted in gold wire frames. The stones were so perfectly fitted together that no setting was visible.

Marc opened the box under the man's crown. It contained a square locket attached to a chain of small diamonds. Gently, Marc took it from the case; the front of the locket was set with a pair of initials, "EA", in emeralds. He turned the locket over to look at the back. An inscription had been engraved. It was in French. Marc read it aloud, "To my dearest love on our wedding day, EA, May 1, 1913."

With great care, he opened the locket. On one side was a photograph of a young woman; her long hair cascading down her shoulders, on the other, under a fitted piece of glass, was a lock of fine ash blonde hair. The sheer emotion of the contents of the small box almost brought tears to his eyes. "What is in the other box, Serge?" he asked, gently returning the locket to its box and closing the lid.

Sergei opened the box and removed another locket from it, identical in shape. The initials on the second locket, however, were in diamonds; and the diamond chain was made of larger stones. "The initials are Felix Andronikov's," Sergei said, turning the locket over. "There is a similar inscription, also in French."

"To my own beloved heart on our wedding day, FA, May 1, 1913." Sergei read the inscription. He opened the locket gently. Inside was a photograph of Felix Andronikov; under glass on the opposite side was a locket of fine jet-black hair. As carefully as Marc had done, he returned the locket to its box.

"Their love for each other must have been very great," Laurent said, giving Marc a meaningful glance. Laurent approached closer to the console. As meticulously placed as all the other articles on the console, laid carefully on a green cushion of silk velvet, were the chain and badge of the Order of St Andrew, made entirely of diamonds. Resting in the middle of the cushion, centred in the middle of the chain, was a jewelled coffer, gold studded with precious gems,: diamonds, emeralds and pearls. Laurent opened the lid of the jewelled box. He gasped when he saw the contents.

Inside, resting on a velvet cloth was the largest diamond he had ever seen. He was not a jeweller, but he was certain that it had to be over two hundred carats.

"The Alastani diamond," Sergei uttered, barely audibly.

Marc looked at the enormous Mogul cut stone. "It must be over two hundred carats," Marc said, in abject amazement.

"Two hundred and eight-six carats," Sergei countered.

Marc reached into the box to touch the stone. He felt something underneath. Gingerly he tugged at the deep blue velvet cloth on which it rested. The corner of the cloth was loose, and its movement revealed the corner of a flat enamelled object.

Carefully, Marc pulled the corners of the fabric over the diamond and removed it from its box. Underneath was a small book, a type of souvenir book made by Faberge in the early 20th century. The covers, front and back, were a vibrant canary yellow.

"Those are Felix Andronikov's initials in Cyrillic," Sergei said, pointing to the diamond initials surmounted by a crown.

Marc and Laurent stood patiently while Sergei removed the little book from its jewelled resting place. A fine gold chain looped through a small key rested on the silk lining underneath the book. He removed that as well.

"This will be safer here for the time being," Marc said, replacing the diamond in the jewelled coffer and closing the lid. "Is that what I hope it is?" he asked, looking at Sergei.

Sergei pushed aside the emerald studded latch cover and inserted the key. It fit. He turned it and the lock opened. Quickly he scanned the pages, written in small letters with a fine hand. "This is it," he said. "This is Prince Andronikov's codebook."

Marc breathed an audible sigh of relief. For a moment he was speechless. The sight before him was dazzling, the sentiment behind it almost heart wrenching. A wife and a daughter had kept their vigil for so long. Yet, the little enamelled notebook in Sergei's hand reminded him of the real cost of this window into the past, this carefully preserved portrait of a family's sorrow.

"How do you suppose we close this then?" Marc began to

extinguish the candles on the alcove's console with a feeling of sadness.

"The reverse of the way we opened it," Laurent replied, almost reverently, blowing out the candles on his side of the console. "You want to go first."

"Gladly." Marc smiled, turning the column on the left to its original position.

"My turn." Laurent rotated his column in turn.

The soft subtle working of the gears confirmed Laurent's guess.

"I believe that this is yours," Sergei said, handing the codebook and the key to Marc.

"Thank you," Marc replied, accepting them.

"What do we do now?" Laurent looked at the wall as it made its slow ascent.

"Well, when the alcove is sealed, I suggest we take a look at the other room."

"Maybe we should phone Stephen and the others," Laurent suggested.

"Yeah, ET phone home," Sergei quipped, chuckling.

Marc and Laurent were a little surprised at Sergei's use of an American popular culture icon to inject a little humour and they sniggered, the humour being lost on neither of them. They walked to the western end of the gallery to unlocked doors. Marc found the correct key, and he and Laurent pushed open the doors.

The room was filled with light from the arched gothik windows, evenly spaced on the north and south sides of the room. It was a large rectangle, a good twenty odd meters long, and 12 or so meters wide. Opposite the entrance from the gallery, four massive carved and gilded wooden columns, twisted spirals like the columns in the gallery, supported a balcony with an Old Russian style railing of carved and gilded wood. The balcony ran the width of the ballroom's western wall. The balcony above was a good three meters deep.

Two large crystal chandeliers were suspended from the high ceilings by green velvet sheathed chains, equally spaced between the entrance to the room and the balcony.

The room was painted with a faux marble finish; the columns that supported the rounded vaults of the high ceiling were, however, actually marble; a soft pale green. There were small gilt wood chairs lining the walls of the room. On the south wall, a pair of large, gothik arched French doors provided access to the flagstone terrace, which ran along the southern lake-facing façade of the pavilion.

"Now this is what I call a ballroom." Laurent grinned.

"I wonder if Prince Felix ever used it," Sergei mused out loud.

"There's a small door under the balcony on the left," Marc said, walking towards it.

"Probably leads to a kitchen," Laurent said, following behind.

They opened the door. It was unlocked. Laurent was partially right; it was a galley style pantry. Built into the wall was a china cupboard, which ran the length of the room. Half of it was filled with crystal champagne flutes, the other half with a porcelain supper service with matching serving pieces, enough for at least a hundred people. There was a pair of refrigerators, four large warming ovens, and triple sinks on the back wall, with a large island counter in between them, obviously for arranging platters or plates.

Marc smiled as he looked at the sinks. They were made of wood so as not to chip the china or the crystal during the washing. The island was wood, as well.

On the north side there was a small door, the service entrance. It was locked. Just beside it was a narrow spiral staircase, leading to the balcony in the ballroom.

"So when are you giving your first ball?" Laurent asked with an impish smirk. "You've got everything you need."

"When we become engaged." Marc flashed a mischievous grin.

Laurent leaned over and gave him a peck on the cheek. "That won't be long if I have anything to say about it."

Sergei was standing next to the lakeside window. He caught sight of a movement outside the window, just at the edge of the terrace. "There's someone outside," he said, pulling back.

"Can you see who it is, Sergei?" Marc asked, pulling out his cell phone.

"It could be Malinkov," he replied, staying close to the window jam.

"Laurent, call Stephen, let them know we have an uninvited guest by the lake." Quickly he was cycling through the address book on his cell phone. He had entered Leclerc's number in his cell, the morning of the inspector's visit. He found it and pressed the autodial button. He waited a moment for someone to pick up at the other end.

"Inspector Leclerc, this is Marc Balanger, we have a prowler on the grounds at Maure."

"Yes, Inspector," Marc replied. "Thank you Inspector."

"Stephen said they haven't found anything," Laurent said, pressing the button and ending his call. "They're coming here."

"The Inspector is on his way…call Stephen back," Marc said. Thinking on his feet was beginning to become a necessity. "Tell him to send Luc back to the house. Tell him not to alarm Brigitte nor the housemaids, but to let her know that we have an intruder, and that Leclerc has dispatched a patrol car and will be following behind. Tell Luc to bring Leclerc and the police here as soon as they arrive."

Laurent pressed the redial button on his cell.

"Sergei." Marc reached in his pocket. "Do you have Karpov's number handy?"

"Yes Marc."

"Then call him," Marc said, pulling out his cigarettes and lighter. He was becoming very angry, and it showed in his voice. "Tell him you have found the codebook. Tell him that you'll slip it to him tomorrow night…you know a walk in the garden after dinner, whatever…and tell him that he'd better call off Malinkov. Say you saw him in the garden…tell him that I am very cautious since the break in, and that I've called in the police."

Sergei knew the anger was not directed at him, but he felt its sting none the less. "Anything else?" he asked sheepishly.

Marc lit his cigarette and took a long deep drag, exhaling slowly, forcing himself to calm down. "Yes." He took another deep drag off his cigarette. His reply was cold, his tone chilling. "Find a way to let him know that this is no simple writer of books and plays he's dealing with, but Marc-Antoine de Balanger, Prince de Jonville, son of Louis-Charles Duc de Beaucour, Prince de La Fonde, and a former minister of the French republic. If he values his reputation and his ability to come and go in Western Europe, he'd best not screw with me. And make it clear that the presence of his daughter and future son in law will assure me that he understands. I don't want him to get clever and decide to come on his own."

Sergei searched for the number in the phone's address book. He walked back into the ballroom to make the call.

Laurent walked over to Marc and slipped his arm around Marc's shoulders. "You're trembling."

"Sorry," Marc said, inhaling another puff of smoke. "When I get angry, really angry...Well, I guess you've just seen my worst side...Still think I'm..."

"Yes." Laurent stroked Marc's cheek with his free hand. "Yes, I do. Come on." He took Marc by the hand and led him to the refrigerators. "Let's see if there's anything to drink in this place. I think we could all use one."

They were in luck. There were four bottles of champagne chilling on a shelf of one of the refrigerators. Marc turned one, to better see the label, Moët et Chandon, 1952. "Wonder how long these have been in here?"

"It's been at least two years since the last party," Laurent said, with a smile.

"Get some glasses off the shelf will you?" Marc grabbed two bottles of the champagne; he pushed the door closed with his shoulder.

Laurent placed a couple of flutes on the wooden counter, and a small crystal dish. "Look, an actual ashtray." He turned around and grabbed four more glasses.

"Can I help you with that?" Stephen offered, walking through the door.

"I see you found your way S."

"Indeed we did," Paul added, walking in with Sergei.

"I've delivered your message," Sergei said quietly. "I have Dimitri's assurance that there will be no further incidents."

"Sergei." Marc walked over to him, leaving the serving of the champagne to the others. "I'm really sorry, you know I wasn't angry with you...all you've ever done is try to help."

"I understand." Sergei put his hand on Marc's shoulder and gave it a fatherly squeeze. "Since Karpov got me involved in this mess, he's been holding Laurent and his mother's safety over my head. Sometimes I think he believes he's God."

He took the glass of champagne Laurent brought him. "I've been hoping that someone would come along and remind him that he's a mere mortal, just like the rest of us." He lifted his glass to Marc. "I believe you're just the man to do it."

"Your right there," Stephen said, handing Marc a glass of champagne. "I've only seen M with his back up once." Stephen thought back to a time, years before; he and Marc had just met. "The unfortunate one, who shall remain nameless, was lucky to get out in one piece. Rumour has it he is still hiding out somewhere in the Australian outback."

Marc had to laugh. He remembered that evening too. Although he no longer remembered exactly what was said, he did remember telling the poor unfortunate that he should find a corner of the world, where Marc de Balanger was least likely to go...and remain there for the foreseeable future.

"About Malinkov," Sergei added. "Karpov swore that he sent no one...he told me that he had not seen Malinkov since last evening," he paused. "He said that Malinkov took a flight to St. Petersburg this morning, from Nice, a family matter."

"Do you think Malinkov is playing his own game?" Stephen continued pouring the champagne. "Maybe he wants to take the princess' place, M."

"That's a possibility." Sergei began to be concerned. If Malinkov was operating independently of Karpov, things could become very unpredictable. "Malinkov does know where all Dimitri's skeleton's are buried."

"What are we going to tell the police? They'll be here any minute." Paul turned the conversation back to the matter at hand.

"Well." Marc sipped a bit of his champagne. "We are not going to tell them anything about the codebook…which we found," he added as an aside. "I'm going to show Leclerc Princess Aleksandra's shrine, and tell him that this is what I think the thieves were after, and why they are still around."

"Believe me," he said, stubbing his cigarette out in the ashtray on the island counter. "When you see it, you'll understand why."

"So, M, do we wait in the kitchen?" Stephen asked. "It's a homely touch."

"No," Marc replied. "I need to sit down. I think we'd best wait in the tower room, there're enough chairs in there."

"Sitting is good." Stephen grabbed the second bottle of champagne. "Off we go then."

They were standing in the gallery; Marc, Leclerc and the others. The doors were closed, the candles still lit. Laurent and Sergei had turned their respective columns the quarter turn, and the panel was descending into the floor with a soft subtle grinding of gears. The prince's crown was visible before Marc spoke.

"Inspector," he began. "I believe this is what the thieves were trying to find when they broke in to the house. I believe it is also why their ring leader dared to show his face on the property again."

"I think you are correct, Monsieur Balanger," the inspector replied. Staring with abject amazement at the display in the hidden alcove, now open to view. "I don't think I've ever seen such a memorial of a child for its parents."

"A wife for her husband, Inspector," Sergei interjected, as he and Laurent lit the candles on the console. "I believe that it was Princess Elena who put this memorial together."

Inspector Leclerc was not the only person amazed at what was being revealed in the velvet-lined alcove. Renaud and Luc gazed at the display, captivated by the sheer magnificence of it. Stephen, somewhat bolder, approached the console and picked up one of the emerald boxes.

Turning the box over, he found a hallmark on the bottom right-hand corner. "If this hallmark on this box is any indication, I'd say that you were correct, Sergei. It is stamped with Cartier's hallmark, and the date, 1924. Since Prince Felix was dead by then, it would seem reasonable that they were made to order for Princess Elena." Stephen looked at Marc questioningly, as if to ask if he should continue his investigation. Marc nodded his assent. Stephen carefully examined the boxes, returning them with the precision of a curator to their original positions.

"What is in the boxes?" Leclerc asked.

"The small emerald boxes contain lockets on diamond chains. Lockets which, judging from the inscriptions, were exchanged by the prince and princess on their wedding day. The contents are far less valuable in terms of worth than the containers in which they are placed," Marc replied. "Stephen, hand me the box from the cushion."

"This is of Russian manufacture, I'd say, probably 15th or 16th century judging from the workmanship." He handed the box to Marc.

"The contents of this casket, however, are a different story." Marc opened the lid to reveal the large diamond resting on its cloth of blue velvet.

"This is real?" Leclerc's question held a note of disbelief.

"Quite real," Sergei said. "This is the Alastani diamond, inspector, two hundred and eight-six carats of perfection. I know this stone. It was part of the Diamond Fund on display in the Armoury in Moscow when I was a boy."

"You saw it there?"

"Yes, Inspector. As you can imagine it was a memorable experience. Supposedly, it was a gift from the Emperor of Byzantium, Andronicus IV when his daughter married the Prince Gregor Ivanovich Andronikov of Alastani."

"How do you suppose it came to be here?"

"I heard...from friends," Sergei invented the little white lie as he went along. "That it was purchased from the government several years ago by an agent of the Princess. As I am certain you are aware, Inspector, this would not be the first time the government sold part of the Diamond Fund to pay its bills."

"Monsieur Hampstead, have you any idea as to the value of what Monsieur Balanger has found here?"

Stephen shook his head. "I would say that we are looking at a collection of gems that would fetch conservatively 10 to 15 million euros. The Alastani diamond, however, considering the history associated with the stone...well...on it's own, it could fetch two to three times that much at auction."

"Well, Monsieur Balanger, I think we can safely assume that we have the reason for the sudden interest in your home. I think that I shall have to question the members of the family of the late Princess."

"That could prove to be difficult, Monsieur Inspecteur," Luc interjected.

"And why would that be Monsieur Doumé?"

"The Countess Apraskin lives near Heidelberg," Luc replied. "The Baroness Arakcheev and her grandson, Stephan, are no longer in France, Monsieur. They returned to Hungary after the chateau was sold."

"Perhaps...perhaps not," Inspector Leclerc replied. "Do you know where to reach them?"

"No, Monsieur, but Maitre Langevin in Lorgues, he was their representative in the hearing about the will; he would know how to contact them."

"Good man, Doumé."

"Now as for these jewels, Monsieur Balanger, what are your plans," Leclerc continued. "As long as they are here, I think you will continue to have difficulties."

"Until I can arrange for them to be securely transferred to my bank in Monte Carlo, I will move them into the house," Marc said. "They've already searched it. I have more guests arriving this weekend...the house will be full. It would be difficult to stage a robbery with so many people around."

"Then I will take my leave, Monsieur. Please do not hesitate to call if you have any further difficulties."

"Paul, would you see the inspector back to the house?"

"Yes, Monsieur Balanger."

Once they had gone, Marc turned to Luc. "These are not the 'special jewels' are they?"

"No, Monsieur, they are not." Luc was amazed; he had never seen anything like this. He had no idea that his former employers had possessed such wealth.

"We'd better get these things back to the house." Marc wrapped the large diamond in its velvet cloth. Casually he slipped the stone in his trouser pocket.

"Might I suggest, Monsieur," Luc volunteered.

"Yes, Luc?"

"There are packing cases for the china and crystal in the kitchen, you know, the cloth and zipper things. We can bundle the jewels in those, then I can go for the jeep to bring everything up to the house."

"We'd best take this tea service too." Stephen was standing by the console on the north wall. He had been quietly examining the hallmarks on the cups. "These are solid gold...Faberge's St. Petersburg workshop, 1880."

Marc nodded his assent. He was really speechless; the value of the things that had been found today far exceeded the value of the house. He could understand why the princess had kept this memorial to her past, to her parents. But he could not understand why she had not left them to her cousins, why she had left them here for any stranger, who would become the new owner of Maure and its secrets.

Malinkov was packing his bags when the knock came at the door. He walked over to the door; it could not be the police, not yet. "What do you want?"

"I saw you come back."

Malinkov recognized the voice. He opened the door and returned to shoving his few clothes into a leather tote. "Close the door behind you," he barked.

The tall trench coat enveloped man did as he was ordered.

"What are you doing?"

"What does it look like? I'm packing?"

"Why?"

"Reisky saw me through the window...they called the police. I barely got away before the car pulled into the gates. I'm sure that they have a description of me by now." He zipped up the bag.

"Where are you going?"

"I though I would drive across the border to Spain. We can work from there."

"You think they found something then."

"I'm certain of it. They were in the pavilion for almost two hours."

"Malinkov?"

"What?" he turned around, the irritation and stress in his voice was all too apparent.

His visitor had a gun, pointed directly at his heart. The gun was fitted with a silencer. He didn't have a chance to defend himself; the other man pulled the trigger as soon as he turned. Two shots were fired; both hit their mark. Malinkov fell to the ground.

"Too bad." The man knelt on one knee feeling for a pulse at Malinkov's neck. "You know," he said still kneeling, "I rather liked you...in spite of your rough ways...or maybe because of them. But, you have become much too much of a liability." Malinkov was still alive, but just barely. "Besides, I don't think I really want a partner after all." He put the gun to Malinkov's forehead. "Au revoir Malinkov," he said, pulling the trigger and putting a bullet through his head.

The man wiped the blood off the end of the silencer with Malinkov's shirt, put the gun back in his pocket and stood up. He rummaged through Malinkov's bag and pulled out a little black book. Information of which, he was certain, he could make a profitable use. He walked out the door, closing it quietly behind him.

Chapter Ten – The Arrival

It was still early, Brigitte had arrived, but no one was stirring as yet. Marc had been up since very early in the morning. He had not slept well.

Laurent was still asleep. He had been up late the previous evening, trying to catch up on the drawings for his project in St Tropez. Marc sat in the library, examining the jewelled coffer that had contained the Alastani diamond and the codebook.

The diamond and the two emerald boxes were stuffed between the mattress and the box spring of his bed, for want of a better place. He didn't want to trust them to the silver vault; too many people would have access during the course of the weekend.

Brigitte, like any good general before a battle, had appeared with a tray of coffee and croissants shortly after her arrival. "Monsieur did not sleep well?"

"No, Brigitte." Marc looked up as she sat the tray on the console under the portrait of a 16th century gentleman. "Too many goings on yesterday."

Brigitte poured him a cup of coffee, adding sugar and cream. In the past few days she had come to learn how he liked it.

"Did you bring a cup for yourself?" Marc asked, as she sat the cup on the desk.

"Yes, Monsieur." She had anticipated his desire for company, and this made an excellent opportunity for them to finalize the arrangements for the weekend.

"Let's sit by the fireplace shall we?" Marc got up and brought his coffee over to one of the comfortable, emerald velvet upholstered wing chairs flanking the red marble mantle.

GRANNY'S CHIPS

Brigitte poured her coffee and returned, taking the seat opposite him. "Everything is arranged, Monsieur," she began, sitting down. "Count Dimitri Karpov will have the Maréchal's bedroom, next to Monsieur Reisky's. The Prince Romanovsky will be in the Green bedroom, next to Monsieur Stephen's. Countess Irina Karpov will have the Rose toile bedroom, and your sister, Madame Chantal, and her husband will be in the Chinese suite across from you and Monsieur Laurent. Their little boy will be in the adjoining Cavalier room."

"Sounds like you've got everyone settled." Marc took a welcoming sip of his coffee.

"Monsieur Renaud will go in with Luc for the weekend," she continued, pausing briefly to take a sip of her own coffee. "To make room for Monsieur Karpov's chauffeur."

"Suzanne and Marie will be arriving in another hour. The bedrooms are already prepared, but I wanted to wait until this morning to put the flowers in the guest rooms. I wanted them to be fresh."

"Luc will attend to the flowers in the reception rooms this morning, Monsieur Renaud has kindly offered to help."

"You really are a wonder, Brigitte."

"Lunch will be ready at one; buffet on the garden terrace as requested. Suzanne and Marie will assist. That should give your sister and her husband time to settle in, perhaps even have a swim, before luncheon. Provided, of course their flight arrives on time." She continued through the schedule. "Suzanne and Marie will serve the lunches on the weekend. I have arranged for the breakfasts to be buffet, in the English fashion, as you requested."

Marc drained his cup, got up and walked over to the console to refill it. Brigitte really did think of everything. There were three additional cups, in the event that the others should come down while they were talking.

"I should add that Marie and Suzanne are very pleased with the extra work, Monsieur. They have said that they are available for your weekends, with notice of course, whenever you should need them."

"Thank you, Brigitte." Marc walked back to his chair and sat.

"Luc, Suzanne and Marie will serve the dinners. Luc has agreed to take the role of butler for the weekend, so everything is arranged." She finished her coffee and placed the cup back in its saucer. "Unless of course, there are any last minute changes."

"None that I'm aware of." Marc was concerned. He was wondering about the advisability of this plan of his.

Leclerc had come back yesterday afternoon. He informed them of a murder in the village. Reisky went into Lorgues with the inspector to see if the murdered man was the same person he had seen on the grounds earlier that day.

Sergei confirmed that indeed the murdered man was the intruder, but claimed ignorance as to the man's identity. Had Karpov's comment on the phone been to cover the tracks of Malinkov's murder?

"Everyone is talking about the murder in the village, Monsieur," Brigitte ventured, guessing what was on his mind. "I overheard a woman this morning at the bakery, saying how poor Monsieur Balanger must regret having bought the Chateau. Another called the murder a part of the curse of the Andronikov." She paused a moment, trying to think of the right thing to say. "You don't regret buying the chateau do you, Monsieur?"

"No, Brigitte." Marc flashed a tired smile. "No, I don't. I just hope that this mess is resolved soon, so we can get back to a normal life." He chuckled in spite of himself. "Whatever that is."

"Morning M." Stephen poked his head in the open door, sounding more chipper than usual for this time of the morning.

"Are we interrupting anything?" Laurent stood beside Stephen, in the doorway.

"No, Messieurs," Brigitte said, standing, picking up her cup and saucer.

"We were just finishing." Marc motioned for them to come in. "There's coffee on the console."

"Thank you Brigitte." Marc turned his attention back to his housekeeper. "Everything seems in order. Breakfast on the terrace this morning?"

"Yes, Monsieur." Brigitte turned to leave. "In half an hour."

"Merci," he said, as she left, closing the door behind her. Marc walked back over to the desk. Sitting, he resumed his examination of the casket.

"More coffee?" Laurent picked up his cup from the table beside the fireplace.

"Please," Marc responded abstractly, examining the bottom section of the casket more carefully.

"What's the puzzle M?" Stephen walked over to the desk, coffee and croissant in hand.

"The jewel casket, S." Marc looked up. "The codebook was here, the 1st instalment of the payment for the codebook was here."

"Hum." Stephen moved to pick up the box. "You're thinking the documents might be here as well," he added, stating what to him was the obvious.

"Another secret compartment?" Laurent put Marc's coffee on the desk.

"I think so. I measured it this morning."

"What did you find M?"

"Well, S...the overall dimensions, in centimetres; 23 long, 12¾ wide, by 23 from the top of the lid to the bottom of the box itself. The depth of the box is roughly 14 centimetres when measured from the outside, but only 10 centimetres when the depth is measured from the inside."

"That's a difference of about 1½ inches." Stephen stooped down to look more closely.

"False bottom?" Laurent queried.

"That's my guess," Marc replied. "But I can't for the life of me find a trigger mechanism for releasing the bottom of the box."

"What do we know about the box itself?" Laurent asked.

"Well," Stephen began. "On the face of it, it appears to be of Russian manufacture, 15th or 16th century. The materials are genuine...that's gold, not vermeil," he added, as an afterthought. He picked up the box and carefully examined the bottom. There were no seams. It was as if the jeweller had taken a rectangular sheet of gold and fashioned the bottom and sides of the box by hammering it into shape. The lion's paw feet that supported the casket had been moulded, cast and soldered in place.

Stephen placed the coffer back on the desk and opened the lid. The box had no fabric lining. Twisted thick gold rods, fashioned into rope, ringed the edge of the bottom where it joined the coffer's sides. They were soldered to the bottom, but not to the sides.

"Here's the answer then." Stephen set the box down on the desk. He pointed to a keyhole in the front of the jewelled coffer. "You put the key in the box and turn it and the catches holding the false bottom are released."

"But S, that would mean when you opened the box the false bottom would be revealed as well."

"Not necessarily," Laurent interrupted. "It could be like the alcove in the gallery. If you turn the columns when a door is open, nothing happens. Perhaps in this case, if the lid is closed, and the casket locked, you simply unlock the casket. If the lid is opened you would unlock the false bottom."

"Makes perfect sense M." Stephen polished off his croissant and the last of his coffee. "One would not ordinarily turn the key in an open box…so, where's the key?"

"I don't know."

"The coffer was open when we found it," Laurent said.

"How about a round of the question game M?"

"OK."

"The lockets?"

"Too small."

"Stuck to the bottom of a pedestal or box?"

"Already checked."

"Cutlery handle?"

"Wrong shape"

"The third key," Stephen referenced the keys to the pavilion. "We still don't know what it's for."

"Too big, besides the key would be gold."

"OK."

"The samovar," Laurent jumped into the game.

"Beg pardon?"

"Hang on, I'll be right back." Laurent darted out of the door.

Laurent was only gone for a short time. He reappeared with a smile on his face and his hand in his pocket. He closed the door behind him. "I was lucky, Brigitte just opened the silver vault." He was still somewhat breathless; he had run all the way.

Laurent walked over to the desk and pulled his hand out of his pocket. He opened the palm of his hand in the centre of which was a golden key. At a glance it appeared to be the correct size to fit the keyhole.

"That's not a samovar," Stephen quipped, with a grin.

"No," Laurent paused, still a bit breathless. "When I packed the samovar yesterday, I heard a bit of rattling as I was putting it into the cloth wrapper I used to pack it. I thought that a piece must have come loose inside." He looked at Stephen. "You said you thought it was probably 18th century, so I thought it must be time for some repairs...I just took a wild guess that the rattle might be our key, since the samovar and the teapot were the only things we did not open."

"Looks like it was a lucky guess," Marc said.

"How do you suppose it got in there M?"

"I'll let you two figure that one out." Laurent handed the key to Marc. "Try it, see if it fits" he said anxiously.

Marc opened the lid of the jewelled coffer and inserted the key into the keyhole. "It fits."

"Well don't just stand there M, turn the key."

Marc turned the key in the latch. It was the coffer's key. Carefully he reached into the coffer's interior. Using the rope border of the false bottom, he lifted it out of the box. There, bundled with an emerald silk ribbon, were some photographs and a carefully folded piece of paper; underneath them was an envelope.

A knock at the door made them all jump. Marc almost dropped the false bottom, still in his hands. He quickly put it back into the coffer. "Entrez."

Sergei opened the door and walked into the library. "Brigitte asked me to tell you that breakfast was ready."

"Thanks, Sergei," Stephen said. "I'm famished."

"A moment Sergei?" Marc said. "We've found something that I'd like you to see."

Sergei closed the door and walked over to the three men who were still standing around the desk. "What is it?"

"I think we've found what Karpov is looking for." Marc removed the false bottom from the coffer and pulled out the bundled photographs and paper, and the envelope that lay beneath them. He handed them to Sergei. "Take a look at these."

Sergei laid the documents on the desk. Carefully he untied the ribbon and picked up the photographs. There were two of them, yellowed with age. But the faces were still plainly visible. A look of disgust clouded his face as he examined them. The first was a photograph of a group of men dressed in the military uniforms of Bolshevik solders. The second showed one of the men in the first photograph standing above the body of a woman, the bayonet end of his rifle protruding from her stomach. He had posed as if he were a hunter standing over his prey, the bayonet still in the dead beast.

"Disgusting Bolsheviks," Sergei spat out the words. He turned the photographs over, noticed the handwriting on the back, and quickly read the legends. On the first were written the names of the soldiers. On the back of the second was scribbled 'P. Karpov with trophy'. He unfolded the paper; it was actually two pages, folded together.

The first was a report from Yakov Yurovsky, the commissar charged with carrying out the order of execution, to Yakov Sverdlov, member of the central committee who had signed the order. It described in detail the execution and burial of the Czar and the Imperial Family.

The second page was a personal letter from Yurovsky to Sverdlov, commending the particular zeal of Pavel Karpov, a last minute volunteer replacement for one of the soldiers who had refused to participate in the execution of the women. Yurovsky spoke of Karpov's particular enthusiasm in the use of his bayonet to ensure the death of those Romanov daughters, who had not been killed by the bullets from their rifles.

"These photographs and the documents proved, without a shadow of doubt, that Dimitri's great-grandfather was one of the murderers of the Czar and his family. The handwriting on the back of the photographs is the same as that of the writer of the letters, Yakov Yurovsky." Sergei handed the documents to Laurent. "You can see for yourself the cruelty of which the Karpov are capable."

"What guarantee do we have that he will leave us alone once he has the documents?" Marc asked.

"None," Sergei replied. "If he killed Malinkov to protect his other secrets, he is capable of killing others to do the same."

"You think he killed Malinkov, father?" Laurent looked up from the second document.

"Not personally, no," Sergei replied. "But who else could have been responsible?"

Chantal had arrived, she was settling in, unpacking. Edward had taken Marc-Édouard down to the pool, Sergei acting as their guide. Marc was glad to hear the sound of a child's laughter around the house. It lessened the tension under which they had lived since their arrival earlier in the week.

Stephen was taking advantage of the lull to read over the script of the film he would be starting in June. Laurent was on the garden terrace with his laptop, enjoying the sun and finishing up the drawings for his project in St Tropez. Marc and Renaud were in the library. Marc was finally getting an account of the damage of the break-in. It was an account that he had continuously delayed in light of the events of the past days.

"That much?" Marc exclaimed quietly. "I had no idea the porcelain collection was so valuable."

"It's not just the porcelain, Monsieur, but the crystal as well...and several pieces of the jade collection. There is also a matter of the lamps, several smaller pieces of furniture will need repairs, and two of the portraits in the music room were damaged as well."

"One hundred fifty thousand is a substantial loss." Marc looked over the list of the damaged items.

"Plus another ten to twelve thousand for repairs."

"Ouch!" he muttered. "What about the insurance?"

"There will be a deductible of around 10%."

Marc shook his head. "Well, with all the things that I have coming from Montréal, I think I'll not replace any of the damaged items. We'll repair what can be repaired, and toss the rest."

"Toss the rest?" Chantal walked into the room, her ample, ankle-length silk dress caught the breeze from the open windows which gave access to the garden terrace. She was a picture of grace; Paris come to the countryside, elegance without the ostentation. The large white Polynesian flowers on their pale blue background, made the elegant couture cut of her dress completely apropos to the country environment, in which she now found herself.

"Madame." Renaud stood, ever the gentleman's gentleman.

"What a pleasure to see you, Paul!" she walked up to him and gave him a kiss on each cheek. He was now above stairs, as the English would say, a member of the family, and quite frankly she was very glad. She knew him well from her annual visits to Canada, and she felt his promotion was truly deserved. "Congratulations on you promotion."

"Thank you, Madame."

"Forgive me for interrupting," she said, with her usual charm. "But I thought we might catch up before your other guests arrive. I can come back later."

"No, please." Marc stood up and walked round the desk. "I'm ready for a break in any case."

"Is that one of your found treasures?" Chantal asked, touching the top of the lid of the jewelled coffer.

"Yes, what do you think?"

"Exceptional," she murmured. "I should not be concerned about the loss of the porcelain. This coffer will go a long way towards making up for it."

"Come on." Marc took her by the hand. "There's someone I want you to get to know a little better."

"Paul, when you finish in here, will you lock the doors to the library, please."

"Yes, Monsieur."

"And Paul…thanks for taking care of everything."

"Let's go get to know this new man of yours," she said, entwining her finger in his, a smile in her voice.

Chantal and Marc walked onto the terrace, hand in hand. Together they were a picture of restrained elegance; he in Armani, his shoulderlength hair falling loose to his shoulders, she in flowing flowered silk, her pale ivory skin shaded by a broad brimmed straw hat, the brim turned up just the slightest bit in the front, trimmed with the same fabric as her dress.

Laurent looked up from his laptop, emitting a low whistle. "Que vous êtes beau et belle, vous deux! You are both so beautiful. Your mother must have been Aphrodite."

"Then surely you are the child of Apollo to speak such delightful poetry," Chantal returned the compliment, with a warm sultry laugh. "I am beginning to see why you are so smitten by this handsome Adonis," she leaned forward to exchange the customary *bisous*. "May we join you?"

"Yes, please, I've just finished the last of the drawings. All I need to do now is to email them to the office."

"Then you're all mine for the rest of the weekend?"

"Pour l'éternité." Laurent leaned forward and kissed Marc on the cheek.

"Ah, the lovebirds."

"Pay no attention to him." Marc grinned. "Someone just dropped a house on his sister."

"I'll get you for that my pretty." Stephen quickly slipped into the voice of the Wicked Witch of the West. "And your little dog, too."

Chantal laughed. "Stephen, so good to see you again. I see you brought your wit with you."

Stephen bent down for his bisous. "Thank God you've arrived, fifth wheel is not my favourite role."

"How are the drawings coming?" Stephen asked, sitting down opposite Chantal.

"Finished," Laurent replied. "And the script."

"I don't know why I let my agent talk me into this," Stephen groaned. "I'm to play the antique dealer side kick of a relic hunter, searching for the lost treasure of Amenophis I, Pharaoh of Egypt. It's a cross between 'The Mummy' and 'Death on the Nile' with a little Indiana Jones thrown in for good measure."

"The adventure?" Laurent offered.

"The challenge?" Chantal suppressed a giggle.

"The money?" Marc countered, with a broad smile.

"Hum," Stephen waited, inserting a stage pause. "Let me think…I would have to say…the money."

His comment was greeted with general laughter.

"Maman, maman." Marc-Édouard came running towards the terrace followed by his father and Sergei.

Marc-Édouard bolted up the stairs to his mother. "The pool is wonderful, maman, you must come for a swim; the pool is so big."

"Tomorrow, dearest, I'll come swimming with you tomorrow." Chantal took the towel from around his shoulders and dried his hair a bit more; it was still very damp from the pool. "Right now, you need to go up with Papa and change for luncheon."

Edward came up behind his son, leaning down he gave his wife a kiss. "We won't be long. Come along M.E.," he said, using his son's pet name. He took his son by the hand and led him into the house.

"A charming family, Madame." Sergei, the last to arrive, took Chantal's hand and kissed it. "I feel lucky to be in such company…so many talented artists from so many disciplines, it is rare these days."

"I am certain it will not be so rare in the future." Chantal smiled warmly. "After all," she cast a quick glance in Marc and Laurent direction. "You're practically family." She looked back to Sergei. "Or soon will be if I'm any judge."

"Madame is as kind as she is beautiful."

"Monsieur Reisky, I think your wife must be a lucky woman."

"I hope so…I think so." Reisky reddened slightly, avoiding

Laurent's gaze. "Well, if you will excuse me," he said to the company in general. "I think I, too, will go and change."

Brigitte had prepared a perfect buffet of Provencal dishes, elegantly served on trays and bowls of local pottery. A grouping of earthenware pitchers of various sizes, filled to overflowing with flowers from the garden, formed the centrepiece around which the menu; Pâté de fois gras au truffe, Caviar d'aubergine, Tapenade, Escalope de saumon grillée aux herbes, Cœur de filet de bœuf à l'ail doux, Médaillons de lapin rôti aux pignons, Légumes grillés, Vinaigrette balsamique, and Cœur d'artichauts Provençal competed with each other in colour and fragrance.

A separate table was set up for desserts. More flowers crowded the pressed glass vases and floated gracefully in shallow bowls. Glass plates, trays, bowls and cake stands displayed the selection; Pêches glacées au sirop de lavande, Figues rôties au Porto, Petit baba au rhum, Fraises des bois, Tarte pignons, Tarte au citron, and Croustillant au chocolat.

Bottles of wine, Pastis and water were spaced along the table on which they were eating, so that self-service of one's favourite beverage was effortless. Suzanne and Marie kept the beverage pitchers full, and removed the soiled plates, replacing them with clean ones.

The guests sat on both sides of the table, four to a side, making conversation easier. Marc's nephew, Marc-Édouard sat at the end of the table, a parent at each elbow.

One big happy family, Marc thought, laughing and joking, exchanging anecdotes of the past and present, plans and projects, discussing all the things that made life special. He was hopeful that soon this would be the only thing that intruded on his newly-found sanctuary. No more Karpov, no more murders or mysteries; just laughter, work and enjoying the pleasures, the sights and sounds and smells of his beloved southern France. Marc had just finished his main course when Luc appeared on the terrace.

"Pardon, Monsieur, you have a visitor." He paused, to give

emphasis to the name, "Baron Arakcheev...Baron Stephane Arakcheev."

Marc recognized the name immediately, as did most of the people at the table. Quick glances were exchanged. "Ask him to wait in the Green Drawing Room, I'll join him in a moment...and Luc..."

"Yes Monsieur?"

"It's show time."

"Yes, Highness."

Chantal looked across the table at her brother. He never used a title; with him it was a matter of principal to be known for himself and his work, not for his family's past glories. The only exception he made to that rule was when there was an example to be made or a lesson to be taught. She wondered who this Baron Arakcheev could be that he warranted such a lesson.

Marc saw the look on her face and read it correctly. "Stephen," he said, getting up from the table. "Perhaps you'd be good enough to explain Inspector Leclerc's theory, and why I think it's time to establish with all these Russians that I am the master in my own house." His voice had a slight edge to it. "Forgive me Sergei," he added, his tone softening a bit. "You know I do not include you in that bunch of émigrés and pseudo aristocrats."

"I know," Sergei replied with an understanding smile.

"Go get him tiger." Stephen flashed an impish grin.

"His Serene Highness, Marc-Antoine, Prince de Jonville," Luc announced, as Marc entered the drawing room.

"Your highness." Luc bowed slightly to Marc. "Baron Stephane Arakcheev."

"Baron," Marc nodded, extending his hand. "I'm sorry to have kept you waiting, but I have guests down from Paris for the weekend. We were just having lunch." The baron's handshake was firm, the hand soft, well manicured, the hand of a gentleman. He looked the man over, wondering if Leclerc could remotely be correct about his involvement in the break in.

The baron was tall, dark-haired, with large deep-set blue eyes and aristocratic features. He was elegantly dressed, and obviously at ease. Marc could not easily imagine him breaking into a house in the dead of night, tossing books and papers about, breaking furniture and objets d'art in the heat of a hurried search.

"It is I who must apologize, Highness, for having called at an inconvenient time, and unannounced."

"To what do I owe the pleasure of your visit?" Marc asked, probing gently.

"I am a cousin of the late Princess Andronikov," he replied awkwardly, still uncertain of what to say.

"I see." Marc gestured to the chairs by the fireplace. "Please, have a seat baron. Can I offer you something to drink?"

"A cognac, perhaps?" he replied, with a charming smile.

"Luc, will you get a cognac for Baron Arakcheev, please."

"For yourself, your Highness?"

"Yes, actually…a Grand Marnier for me…thank you Luc."

"Highness." Luc bowed slightly in Marc's direction. He walked out of the drawing room, leaving the door open.

"As I was saying, Prince," Arakcheev continued. "I am a cousin of the late Princess Aleksandra Andronikov. I am here at the request of my grandmother." he paused. "This is most awkward for me, prince…were it not for my grandmother's request, I should not have come."

Marc looked at the handsome face, trying to read the genuineness of his words.

"You see, although my cousin was quite generous in her bequest to my family, at least in terms of money…neither my cousin, the Countess Apraskin, nor my grandmother and I, were allowed to remove any of the family mementos. According to Princess Aleksandra's will the estate was to be sold in toto, aside from those bequests specifically mentioned."

"I see."

Luc returned, carrying a large tray with two decanters and two glasses. He placed them on a console and poured the drinks, placing the filled glasses on a silver salver.

"In short, your Highness, my grandmother has asked me to offer to purchase certain of the family mementos."

"Well, Baron Arakcheev, I do not see why there should be a problem, at least not for my part." Marc paused, while Luc served the drinks.

"Luc, will you please ask Monsieur Renaud to join us?"

"Your Highness." Luc bowed slightly. Returning the silver salver to the console he went to fetch Paul.

"You see we had a break-in the evening after my arrival. The staff was off for the evening, and I had gone into St. Tropez to have dinner with friends. There were several things taken, a number of pieces of porcelain and crystal were also smashed or broken," Marc paused, trying to determine if this news had any effect on the baron. It did not, which to his way of thinking was not a good sign.

"So," he continued, in the same casual manner. "Perhaps it is best that you should deal with my secretary, Paul Renaud. Indeed, at the moment, Paul is more familiar with the property than I."

"You see." He took a sip of his Grand Marnier. "I only arrived on Sunday, with my dear friend Stephen Hampstead, who came down with me from Paris. Since then, others have joined us. Laurent Teyssier, an architect friend of mine from Paris, and his stepfather. Perhaps you've heard of him, Sergei Reisky, he is an artist of some note."

"I'm sorry to say I'm not familiar with his work, Prince," he paused, selecting his words with great care. "Your Highness is thinking of making changes to the chateau?"

Marc had struck a nerve, he could tell. At least Reisky's name was familiar to him. He decided to play out the game. "Not to house…" Marc pulled his cigarettes and lighter out of his trouser pocket. He offered a cigarette to the baron.

"No thank you, Prince."

Marc casually lit a cigarette. "However, the pavilion…well the gallery is so dark. I've asked Laurent to give me some ideas, some skylights or a few windows perhaps." The baron was hard to read. Well-trained, Marc thought, he is definitely hiding something, but what

Marc could not determine.

"As I was saying," Marc continued, in the same casual vein. "My sister and her family arrived this morning, and there are more guests arriving later today. Perhaps you know them, Prince Michael Romanovsky, Count Dimitri Karpov and his daughter Countess Irina. I believe they were acquaintances of your cousin, Princess Andronikov."

The baron took a sip of his cognac, avoiding Marc's gaze. "Yes, I believe we met at a ball my cousin gave shortly before she died; a brief meeting, to be sure. You know there are a great many noble families that left Russia after the events of 1917."

"Yes, of course." Marc had struck another nerve. "In any case, as you can well imagine, between my guests and the unfortunate incident of the break in, I have had little time to familiarize myself with either the house or its contents."

There was a knock at the open door.

"Ah Paul come in, come in...Baron Stephane Arakcheev, my secretary, Paul Renaud. Sit down Paul." He waited for Paul to take a seat. "The baron is a cousin of the late Princess Aleksandra Andronikov. He has come to pay us a visit, as his grandmother would like to obtain certain family mementos that were included in the sale. I have told him that you would perhaps be the best person with whom to speak. If you could assist him, I would be most grateful."

He turned to Arakcheev, "Are you staying in the neighbourhood?"

"I've only just arrived, and I came straight here. I haven't yet made any arrangements."

"I see," Marc replied. "Well, if you will give your list to Paul, you can return tomorrow afternoon, if that is convenient for you, and we can sort out any details then."

"Tomorrow afternoon would be perfect, Highness."

"Good, then it's settled." Marc stood up, Paul instinctively stood in concert with Marc's action. "Now if you would be so kind as to excuse me, my other guests are waiting."

"Of course, Highness." Arakcheev stood up.

"Baron," Marc added, as if an afterthought. "Perhaps you would care to join us for dinner this evening. Although the house is full, I'm certain there is room for one more at the table."

"I would be honoured, Prince."

"Good...dinner is at eight, cocktails will begin around seven...black tie of course."

"Of course."

"Good...well, it's been a pleasure to meet you baron...see you this evening."

"Paul," Marc continued, addressing Renaud. "Please do what you can to assist Baron Arakcheev...and if you would be so kind as to tell Brigitte that we will have another guest for dinner when you've finished here."

"Monsieur le Prince." Paul bowed slightly as Marc left the room.

"Inspector Leclerc," Marc spoke into the library telephone. He had waited until Arakcheev was definitely gone before making the call. "Marc Balanger here."

"Yes, Monsieur Balanger."

"I've just had a visitor, this afternoon, one in whom you have expressed an interest."

"Monsieur?"

Chapter Eleven – Settling Accounts

The dining room was exquisitely arranged. The plates were vermeil as was the cutlery. The table was set with the finest china and crystal, carefully placed on a cloth of fine white linen edged with lace; the service was elaborate in keeping with the menu. There was to be a soup to start, Soupe de pomme de terre glacée aux truffes. Following the chilled entree there was to be a warm entrée, Foie gras de canard poêlé & artichauts Poivrade. A fish course would come next, Daurade sauce cèpes, pommes grenailles truffées.

After the fish, Brigitte had prepared a meat course, Côte de veau du Limousin, served with a gâteau de pomme de terre and Légumes grillés couleurs sud for vegetables. To complete the meal she had prepared a triple dessert, Tarte à la crème de marron, a Gendarme de Saint Tropez au chocolat, and a Moelleux chocolat passion.

The wine list was equally imposing; a L'Estello rosé, Rosé Cuvée Sextant d'Or 2002 with the soup, with the duck and artichokes Luc had selected a Cuvée Château Roubine, Rouge millésime 1999, another L'Estello, Blanc Cuvée Sextant d'Or 2002 had been chosen for the fish, and a Cuvée de Bargemon, Rouge millésime 1998 had been selected to accompany the veal. The desserts would be washed down with champagne; Moët et Chandon, 1952.

There were only ten places; Paul had elected to have dinner with Brigitte in the kitchen, in order to better prepare for the evening's main event.

The table decorations were carefully selected to send a subtle message to certain of the guests. Marc instructed Brigitte to use one pair of the "Egyptian" candelabrum and the rock crystal urn, brought from the pavilion, as the centrepiece for the dinning table. The matching pair of candelabrum, taken from the hidden alcove, was to be used on the sideboard. Marc wanted to see just how much Arakcheev really knew, or had guessed, during his time in the house. Message or not, the "pavilion pieces" looked spectacular in their new setting.

To simplify the seating arrangements, Paul prepared place cards, which rested on miniature vermeil easels, a housewarming gift Chantal brought with her from Paris. Marc asked his sister to act as the hostess. They fiddled with the traditional custom of formal dining, seating by rank, so that Irina Karpov could sit next to her fiancé.

In the end, Chantal was to have Prince Romanovsky on her right and her husband, Edward on her left. Next to Edward would be Stephen, then the Baron Arakcheev. Irina Karpov would sit next to Romanovsky, and her uncle, Sergei, next to her. At the opposite end of the table, Marc would have Laurent on his left, and Karpov on his right.

Karpov and his party did not arrive until five; there was no time to introduce them to his other guests, as they needed time to settle in and change for dinner. Sergei was coming down the stairs as Marc greeted the arriving party. Irina ran forward to greet him warmly. Marc was glad to see the open affection the young woman held for her uncle. It further exonerated her from the questionable activities of her father.

The stage was set, as Stephen would say, and the players were gathering in the Green Drawing Room. The men, most of whom had already come downstairs, were wearing the traditional evening dress of the past hundred odd years; black tie, dinner jackets, white shirts and dark striped trousers.

Some, like Marc and Laurent, wore double-breasted jackets eliminating the need for a waistcoat. Others, like Stephen and Edward, wore single-breasted jackets. The single-breasted jacket required a waistcoat. Stephen and Edward were of the school that allowed the wearer to express his personality by the choice of fabric.

Stephen, who was known for his unusual and always elegant selections, was wearing a waistcoat of red velvet, embroidered with a baroque pattern in gold thread. Edward, on the other hand had selected a waistcoat that complimented his wife's dress, a deep emerald silk embroidered with a trellis pattern of fine gold thread.

Prince Romanovsky wore a double-breasted jacket. Hanging beneath his tie, suspended from a silk ribbon was a diamond-encrusted badge of the order of St Andrew.

The ladies had a much greater freedom of expression when it came to their dress. Chantal had selected an empire style evening dress of deep emerald green silk which fell from the high waist to a slight train at the back. The short sleeves were embroidered in a trellis pattern with gold beads, trimmed at the bottom with a narrow band of scalloped gold lace.

Chantal wore her grandmother's pearl choker that completely enveloped her long slender neck. Her earrings were graceful pendants; pear-shaped emeralds, bordered by small brilliant-cut diamonds, suspended on delicate diamond chains from square-cut, diamond-rimmed emeralds. On each wrist she wore one of her grandmothers bracelets, a matching pair; quadruple strands of pearls with emerald clasps.

At Marc's instance she wore the locket that Prince Felix had given to his wife on their wedding day. The diamond chain hung long, falling to the top of the high waist of her gown. The emerald silk of her dress served to highlight the diamond initialled gold of the locket.

Chantal's long blond hair was swept up into an Empire inspired coiffure. Here and there, sprinkled among the delicate curls and tendrils were placed little diamond rosettes, another Balanger family heirloom. She resembled a painting of a Napoleonic court beauty; a look she knew complimented her Anglo-French heritage.

Irina Karpov was a different kind of beauty. Her pale skin was set off by a mane of wavy jet hair, which she wore pulled back from her face, held in place by diamond studded bar clips. Her dress of white silk-satin was sleeveless; the bodice was fitted to the waist. The bias cut of its skirt moved gracefully as she walked, swirling delicately whenever she turned.

The base of her neck was circled by a band of platinum; channel set with large matched square cut diamonds. She wore pear shaped diamond studs in her ears, and multiple Art Deco diamond bracelets on each wrist. She was a vision in white and ice.

The baron arrived precisely at seven. Luc greeted him and showed him into the Green Drawing Room. "Baron Stephane Arakcheev," he announced the baron in a voice, loud enough to be heard over the cocktail chatter, but not so loud as to be offensive.

"Follow me S," Marc tugged at the sleeve of Stephen's jacket. "Baron, so good to see you again." This afternoon, he had been rather stiff, formal; now it was time to change tactics, keep the baron off guard. Now it was time for charm. "I should like to present my dearest friend in the world, Stephen Hampstead."

"Monsieur Hampstead." Arakcheev's full sensuous lips parted, becoming a broad smile. "I have seen you often on television. It is a pleasure to meet you in person."

"Stephen, please. Unlike most of the people in the room, I'm just a plain North Country boy, north England that is...no need to stand on formality."

"In that case, you must call me Stephane," Arakcheev replied, still smiling.

"Stephen," Marc cut in. "Perhaps you would take Stephane to the bar and fix him a drink, then introduce him round, that is if you don't mind."

"Pleasure," Stephen responded, with a grin.

"I'll drink to that," Arakcheev said suggestively, raising a perfectly arched eyebrow.

"Well then," Marc replied, taken a bit off guard. "I'll leave you in Stephen's capable hands."

"I'm certain they are." Arakcheev had the last word, and it was delivered with an unquestionable double entendre.

Marc joined the little group standing beside the backgammon table. Laurent was deep in conversation with Prince Michael and Irina Karpov.

"I am so happy to finally meet you Laurent." Irina's smile was charming, radiant almost. "As the only child of an only child...well, I have very few relations, none close to my age....I realize that you are uncle Sergei's son by marriage, but…I would like it very much, if…"

"I am an only child too…" Laurent interrupted graciously. "Irina, I would be honoured to be your cousin." Laurent felt strangely attracted to this young woman whose innocence genuinely surprised him.

Marc watched as Stephen introduced the baron to the group sitting by the fireplace; Chantal, Edward and Sergei. Arakcheev definitely knew how to work a room. He seemed to be charming everyone he met.

"We plan to be married in June, in St Petersburg."

Prince Michael's comment brought Marc's attention back to the conversation in his own group.

"I hope that you will both join us for the wedding," Prince Michael continued.

"I cannot speak for the Prince, of course." Laurent gave Marc's ribs an imperceptible nudge with his elbow. "But I am certain that Sergei and I will be there."

"Please forgive me, Prince," Marc said apologetically. "You know this is my first little party at Maure, I must plead guilty to the distracted concern of a host."

Marc was saved from further explanation by the arrival of Stephen and Arakcheev. "Prince Michael, Countess Irina, may I present Baron Stephane Arakcheev?"

"Your Serene Highness, Countess Irina." Arakcheev bowed slightly.

"Laurent Teyssier…Baron Stephan Arakcheev."

"A pleasure, Monsieur Teyssier, I've just met your charming stepfather Monsieur Reisky."

"Prince Michael and the Countess are engaged." Marc continued, "We were just discussing the wedding plans."

"Forgive me, Prince," Prince Michael interrupted. "I pride myself on never forgetting a face. We've met before have we not Baron?"

"Yes, Your Highness, I was presented by the Princess Andronikov, my cousin."

"I remember, it was a ball for the Assembly of Russian Nobility honouring the Grand Duchess."

"Quite correct, Highness. The ball was held in the Gothik pavilion on the grounds of this very chateau."

"That's one of the reasons I was so glad you included us in your invitation prince." Irina smiled appreciatively. "You see, that ball is where Michael and I first met. It was in your Gothik pavilion that I met my own prince charming and fell in love."

"We danced together all night." Prince Michael took his fiancée's hand in his, squeezing it gently. "For me she was the only person in the room."

"I would so appreciate it if we could visit the pavilion." Irina flushed slightly at the compliment.

"We shall go tomorrow," Marc replied. "Actually, did you not say, Prince Michael, that you have friends who live nearby?"

"Yes, I have cousins that live near Draguignan, and several friends near Fréjus and Toulon."

"Then we must have a party," Marc said enthusiastically. "Tomorrow you must telephone your friends and see if they can come to a party tomorrow evening. I will have my secretary arrange everything...Paul has been with me for years, I have no doubt he will be able to organize something to your liking. Perhaps we will not be able to live up to the Princess Andronikov's elegant ball, but certainly we can celebrate the results."

"Your Highness is too generous," Prince Michael bowed, acknowledging his host's liberal hospitality.

"Yes, indeed." Arakcheev looked Marc in the eye. "The Prince de Jonville is most generous. I was quite intrigued by the locket your sister is wearing. She told me it was a gift from Your Highness."

"It was just a little something I found recently," Marc replied.

"It reminds me of a locket that Prince Felix Andronikov gave to his wife on their wedding day."

"Indeed." Marc smiled pleasantly. "What a coincidence...my sister designs jewellery...when I find little things that might inspire her work, I cannot resist picking them up for her."

"Quite," Arakcheev replied, returning the smile.
"Count Dimitri Karpov," Luc announced Karpov, as he walked into the drawing room.

Karpov walked directly over to the group surrounding his daughter and her fiancé. The agitation in his approach was only just below the surface. "Arakcheev, what are you doing here?"

"Count Dimitri," Arakcheev stepped to one side, making a place for him in the group. "Like yourself, I am a guest of the Prince de Jonville."

"Father," Irina admonished softly, somewhat embarrassed by her father's abrupt manner.

"Forgive me, my dear, Your Highnesses, gentlemen." He was forcing himself to calm down. "I've just gotten off the phone with our attorneys in New York. It seems there are some problems with the negotiations of an exploration contract we're working on with an American firm. I may have to go to New York tomorrow."

"Oh, father," Irina expressed her disappointment. "The Prince de Jonville is arranging a party for Michael and me tomorrow night, in the pavilion where we first met."

"You need not worry, dearest," he said, reaching out and taking her hand. "Even if I have to go, you and Michael should remain."

Luc reappeared at the door and caught Marc's eye. "I see that dinner is ready," Marc announced. "shall we go in?"

The dinner was a great success. Each course was greeted with quiet enthusiasm. The conversation was as varied as the menu, flowing seamlessly from painting to theatre to collections. Marc offered options for the weekend, trips to the surrounding villages like Le Thoronet and Villecroze with their medieval fortifications and Romanesque abbeys, a drive down to Fréjus with its Roman ruins, visits to the neighbouring vineyards, and of course the party in the Gothik Pavilion to commemorate the meeting of Irina and Prince Michael.

By dinner's end, Marc's guests seemed relaxed and prepared to enjoy what promised to be a truly pleasant weekend in the country. As the last bit of the third dessert was eaten and the last glass of champagne had been drunk, Chantal suggested that everyone retire to the Green Drawing Room for coffee and liqueurs.

As the company began to move out of the dining room, Marc stopped Karpov. "Perhaps you would care to join Sergei and me in the library. I have something, which I think is of interest to you."

The real reason for his being here had finally surfaced. Karpov was not surprised that his host was in possession of the codebook, nor did the "show" which his host had organized fall on deaf ears. It was very like one he would have organized himself.

Karpov had read between the lines of Sergei's message. At least, with the Prince de Jonville's assistance, finding the documents would not be difficult. He assumed that the excursions planned for Saturday would provide them with the time to find the cursed things.

The library was prepared; the jewelled coffer placed prominently on the desk, a cozy fire in the fireplace, liqueurs and crystal snifters on a silver tray on the console. Marc entered the room first, going straight to the desk. "Please," he motioned to a chair before the fireplace, indicating that Karpov should take a seat. Sergei, who followed behind them, closed the door as he entered the room.

"Sergei." Marc took the key to the casket out of his pocket. "Would you pour us a cognac?"

"Certainly." Sergei performed his assigned task wordlessly.

"Would you care for a cigar, Prince?" Karpov reached into his jacket pocket for his cigar case. He knew he was no longer in control of the situation; Balanger's entry into the game had changed all that. He was resolved to play out the scenario that had been written for him. He had carefully observed his host throughout the evening; he had achieved his position by being able to judge the character of those around him. Perhaps it was folly on his part, but he trusted that this secret would remain secret.

"No, thank you…I'll have a cigarette instead." Marc paused long enough to take a cigarette from the urn on the desk and light it, while Sergei served the drinks and took his seat opposite Karpov.

"I told you I had something that would interest you." Marc

unlocked the jewelled coffer. "But before we conclude our business, I should like to be certain that once you have that for which you are looking...there will be an end to this affair. As we are all gentlemen here," he continued. "I want your word that once this business is concluded, that *will* be an end to it."

"You have my word prince," Karpov replied simply. "I assure your highness that no one wants an end to this unpleasant affair more than I."

"You have brought the diary?" Sergei asked.

"Yes." Karpov pulled it out of a pocket in his jacket. "I assumed that we would have need of it."

Marc lifted the Alastani diamond out of the casket. Karpov masked his surprise. Marc then pulled the codebook out of the coffer. "This is Prince Felix's codebook," Marc said.

Laying it on the desk, next to the diamond, Marc turned the key once more and removed the false bottom. He removed the documents, and walked over to Karpov.

"These are the documents that you have been searching for," he said, handing them to Karpov. "I assure you that these are all the documents, and that there have been no copies made. Monsieur Reisky can serve as my witness that this is the truth."

Karpov untied the ribbon that held them together; quickly he examined the pictures and the two documents that had been bundled with them. A look of relief came over him. "How did you find them without the diary?"

"The Prince is rather well-known for his mystery novels," Sergei replied, leaving the details unspoken.

"If I were you," Marc said, placing the false bottom back in the box, and locking it in place. "I would take advantage of the fire to put an end to this little saga between yourself and the Andronikov. Enough people have died for the sake of this secret."

"Exactly what do you mean by that?" Karpov said, quickly tearing the photographs and the two documents into small pieces and tossing them into the fire. He watched as they turned to carbon ash in the flames. Uriatkin's death could not be connected to either him or to the blackmail. His "accident" had been clearly and officially labelled an incident of inter-gang rivalry.

Marc placed the Alastani diamond in his trouser pocket; closing the lid, he locked the jewelled casket. "The first was Prince Felix himself." Marc walked over and sat on the sofa facing the fireplace. "I believe he was murdered by the Bolsheviks to keep the death of the Imperial family secret. Although the announcement of the Tsar's death was published in the local newspapers shortly after the fact, the family's deaths did not become public knowledge until the late twenties."

Marc took a sip of his cognac before continuing. "Then of course there was Pavel Uriatkin, although that could not be proved in a court of law…and lastly, there was Malinkov, who was perhaps too overzealous in the discharge of his duties."

"Malinkov is dead?" Karpov's face went white; he was visibly shaken. "What do you mean Malinkov is dead?"

"Yesterday," Sergei said, amazed at Karpov's reaction. "There was a murder in the village. I was asked to look at the corpse…Inspector Leclerc thought it might be the intruder we saw at the pavilion. It was the intruder…it was Malinkov."

"I had nothing to do with it," Karpov denied vehemently. "I had nothing to do with his being here, and nothing to do with his death." He downed the cognac in his glass and held it out towards Sergei. "Please, I need another cognac."

"Do you honestly think I would expose Irina to the scandal of a murder of one of my own employees on French soil? A man overboard on the Mediterranean is a much easier end to arrange, if, indeed, I had wanted to get rid of him."

"You're saying that you had nothing to do with his being here?"

"I said that to Sergei when he told me he'd seen Malinkov on the grounds. Malinkov asked for leave to return to St Petersburg on a family matter."

Sergei returned with the refilled glass, which Karpov took. He drank deeply.

"That would mean that Malinkov was acting on his own," Marc

said. He lit another cigarette. "Perhaps he wanted to obtain the documents himself, to take up where Princess Aleksandra left off."

"No, no, if he wanted to blackmail me he could have done it without the Andronikov documents," Karpov shook his head in disbelief.

"Is it conceivable that he was looking for the diamond?" Sergei asked, returning to his seat. "It's worth millions, he could have been a very rich man were he to have gained possession of the stone."

"It's possible," Karpov replied. "All I know is that yesterday morning he came to me and said that he had a call from St Petersburg, a family matter. He asked for a few days leave…I gave it to him."

"If he was after the diamond, he was not alone," Karpov continued. "You have the stone and Malinkov is dead, murdered you said." Karpov took another healthy swallow of his cognac. "His partner must have killed him…but why?"

"When you saw Arakcheev, this evening, you asked him what he was doing here. Why?" Marc asked pointedly. "How well do you know him?"

"Not well," Karpov replied. "Like Michael and Irina, I met him at the ball for the Grand Duchess. We met again after the death of the princess; I contacted him, as one of the heirs. He and his grandmother were living here at the time. I offered to buy the chateau but he explained the conditions of the will. He said it was being contested, and if things were decided to the satisfaction of the heirs…"

"Which of course they were not," Marc interjected.

"He said that he would consider an offer. I never heard from him again." Karpov pulled another cigar from his case. "I was just surprised to see him here…he was so determined in his fight to break the will. It seemed strange to me he would accept the hospitality of the person who was now in possession of something he considered to be rightfully his."

He lit his cigar. "Surely you don't think that Malinkov and Arakcheev…"

"Why not?" Sergei asked.

"Arakcheev is a…" Karpov hesitated.

"A what?" Sergei asked the question. "A homosexual?"

"Yes, a homosexual," Karpov said with difficulty. "And Malinkov was definitely homophobic. He sent his own brother to the work camps in Siberia for that very reason. I am certain there is no connection."

"Well, the prospect of wealth can make strange bedfellows," Marc said, extinguishing his cigarette.

"Not in this case," Karpov said, with absolute certainty.

"I've arranged for my bank in Monte Carlo to send an armoured car to collect the Alastani diamond and some other jewels, which were found with the coffer containing the documents and the codebook. They are coming on Monday morning."

"From there," Marc continued. "They will be sent to the Louvre. I am putting all the jewels on permanent loan to the object d'art collection. A museum is far better equipped to see to their security than am I."

"What about Malinkov's partner," Karpov asked. "How do you intend to avoid any further difficulties in that regard?"

"I've prepared a story for both Nice Matin and Varmatin, which will tell of the find and its destination. They are photographing the jewels at the bank on Monday afternoon. That should take care of the partner."

"What will you do with the diary?" Sergei asked.

"Destroy it," Karpov replied. "The diary and the codebook."

"I have another suggestion," Marc leaned forward. "Allow me to decode the diary."

"What?"

"Allow me to decode the diary."

"There could be references..."

"References to what, Dimitri?" Sergei said coolly. "To documents that no longer exist."

"Look," Marc said. "Prince Felix was close to the Imperial family. For all we know, there are other secrets with which he was entrusted, things that, if uncovered, could enhance your standing among the Assembly. Things we will never know if the diary is destroyed."

"If there are any unfavourable references to the Karpov's, which

I doubt," Marc continued. "I will destroy them myself."

"I will assist him," Sergei said. "You cannot possibly think that I would allow anyone to mar the happiness of my sister's only child."

A knock at the door to the library interrupted their conversation; Chantal came into the room. "Forgive me gentlemen, but the Baron is leaving, I came to fetch my brother to say his goodbyes."

"Of course, Chantal." Marc stood up. "We have perhaps been too long with our books and cigars." Marc took a book that had been sitting on the table in front of him, part of the carefully staged scene prepared earlier by Renaud. "In any case, Count Dimitri, I insist you accept this little gift as a token of my friendship, from one collector to another."

"Thank you Prince," Karpov said, taking the book. He opened the fine tooled-leather binding to the title page as his host followed his sister out of the library. It was a first edition of Tolstoy's "War and Peace," inscribed by the author to his dear friend Prince Andrei Andronikov; a princely gift indeed.

The guests were scattered in groups around the sitting room. Stephen and Edward were playing a game of backgammon. Laurent was talking with Arakcheev near the doors to the terrace, and Irina and Prince Michael were enjoying a quiet moment in front of the fire.

"You must forgive me for pulling you away from your guests, Prince...for the second time today." Arakcheev flashed a charming, apologetic smile.

"On the contrary, this time it is you who must forgive me, dear Baron, for you are one of my guests as well...and a shamefully neglected one at that," Marc replied, with an equally charming smile. "You see I know so little about Russian literature, and with such experts as Sergei and Count Karpov, I was carried away by the discovery of what is in my own library."

"Understandable, of course, your highness." The reference to "'my library'" struck a nerve, and Arakcheev had a hard time masking it. The house and everything in it should have been his, and the loss was very fresh in his mind."

"You are too gracious, Baron."

"I was thinking that perhaps with all your guests, and the proposed party tomorrow evening, we should postpone our appointment until Monday... if that is acceptable to Your Highness."

"Baron, you are as understanding as you are gracious," Marc replied. "Perhaps you would join me for lunch on Monday. We could sort out the details of your grandmother's request then."

"Thank you, Your Highness, lunch on Monday would be perfect."

"And you must return tomorrow evening for the party, Baron. It seems only fitting. Since you were present at the event at which our two lovebirds were first introduced, you should also be present at the party commemorating the event."

"Your Highness is too kind."

"I believe we will start the festivities around eight?"

"Till tomorrow at eight, Highness," Arakcheev replied with a slight bow. "Again, thank you for a most interesting evening."

"The pleasure was mine, I assure you," Marc said with a brief nod. "Laurent, would you be so kind as to escort the Baron Arakcheev to his car."

"Of course." Laurent replied.

Just as Laurent was escorting Arakcheev to his car, Chantal came up to her brother. "I think I'll go and check on Marc-Édouard. I'll be down in a minute."

"I'll go up with you," Marc said. "I have a little something I need to put away for the night." He patted his trouser pocket.

By the time he returned to the Green Drawing Room, Sergei and Karpov had rejoined the other guests. They were sitting with Prince Michael and Irina. The young woman seemed close to tears.

"Please Papa," she entreated. "Can't you wait until Sunday night?"

"Irina," Prince Michael said, taking her hand. "Certainly you understand that if your father says it is important, then he must go."

"Go?" Marc said, walking over to them. "Forgive me I could not help overhearing."

"Yes," Karpov responded. "I have just received another call on my cell...from my company's attorneys in New York. I must return to the Rosenkranz this evening and pack. There is a direct flight from Nice to New York, tomorrow at 10:30, I must be on it."

"But Papa," Irina implored. "The Prince de Jonville is planning this lovely party for us tomorrow..."

"And you and Michael will be here for it. You have your uncle Sergei, and your cousin Laurent," Karpov said, trying to soften the blow. "Please Irina, try to understand. This is a very important contract. The attorneys feel that if I am there in person we will get what we want."

"But Papa, you have no one to drive you. Michael drove us here today because Malinkov is away."

"If you must go, Count Dimitri, I will see if Luc can drive you."

"No, Your Highness," Karpov replied quickly. "It is not necessary. Irina, as you will remember I have not always had a driver, I drove myself in Moscow, and it was not so long ago that I have forgotten how to operate a car. If the prince would be so kind as to drive you back to St Tropez on Sunday..."

"Of course, Count Dimitri, I will drive them down myself. Laurent has to be back in St Tropez on Sunday evening, in any case," Marc replied.

"Then it is settled," Karpov said with finality. "You and Michael will enjoy the rest of the weekend, you'll have your party, your uncle Sergei will stand in for me, and I will see you when I return from New York on Thursday."

"Yes, Papa," Irina knew when her father took that tone of voice there was no changing his mind. She acquiesced with a meek smile.

"Thank you for your kindness, Highness," Karpov said. "And thank you for your hospitality. By the way, I have decided that you were right about the little matter we were discussing. That little collection is perhaps too precious to be exposed to salt water. I would appreciate it if I could leave it in your care. Sergei has it."

"I assure you count, I shall handle it with the utmost care."

Karpov headed south from Carcès on D13, looking for the turnoff to Le Thoronet. Just as he was beginning to think he'd missed it, he saw the sign in the headlamps of his Bentley. He turned east on the road heading for the village. The drive was not a long one. He followed the signs to the abbey and parked the car in the visitor's lot.

Quickly he walked down the path, which ran beside the chapel, crossing behind it to the ruins. The moon was full, casting an eerie light on the white stone of the crumbling walls that surrounded the pit. A tall shadowy figure in a black trench-coat stepped out of the shadow of the trees.

"Did you bring the notebook?" Karpov tried to get a better look at the face, hidden beneath the wide brimmed hat of the black-coated stranger.

"Did you bring the money?"

"I know about Malinkov."

"Did you bring the money?" The shadowed man's tone was brusque, abrupt.

"Yes, and the securities, Karpov replied. Carefully he felt for the small revolver in his pocket.

"Let's see it."

"Let's see the notebook." Karpov slipped his finger around the trigger.

"Here is the notebook." The stranger held out a black-gloved hand. Malinkov's notebook was in it. "Where's the money?"

"Do you think I would be stupid enough to bring it down here." Karpov kept his finger on the trigger. "We go back to the car so I have some light. I verify the notebook, then you get your payoff."

The stranger reached into the pocket of his trench coat. Slowly he extracted a revolver with a silencer screwed into the barrel. His gloved finger was on the trigger. He put the notebook back in his pocket. "You lead the way."

They walked back up the path to the car. Karpov opened the door. "Let me see the notebook."

The black-gloved stranger hung back out of the light. He stretched out a hand with the notebook. Karpov quickly flipped through it. It was Malinkov's notebook, a compendium of skeletons; names, dates, places and events.

"The money," he growled, shoving the gun into the light with a threatening gesture.

"It's in a briefcase in the trunk," Karpov said. "Let me press the trunk release." Karpov leaned forward; slipping his hand in his pocket, he exchanged the notebook for the gun. He pressed the trunk release. He felt the stinging of the first bullet as it entered his arm. He turned, his gun in his hand.

A second bullet struck Karpov in the chest, but as he fell backwards, he heard the sound of his own gun discharge. As he fell, he felt the car slowly start to move forward. The front of the Bentley bumped one of the concrete pylons that separated the parking area from the walkway in front of the abbey chapel, setting off the car alarm.

The black-clad man ran quickly to the trunk of the car. He spotted the briefcase in the flashing trunk light. A light came on in the caretakers lodge. He grabbed the briefcase and ran back towards the ruin behind the abbey. Karpov's bullet had found its mark, his assailant clutched at his side as he ran to the black sedan parked in the shadows.

Chapter Twelve –
A Father's Tale

It was a beautiful sunny spring morning; the azure sky was dotted here and there with soft bits of white cloud. The gentlest of morning breezes caught the scent of the flowers in the garden, transporting it up to the terrace where tables had been set up for breakfast. The buffet table was covered with Provencal fabric, blue stylized flowers on a sunny yellow background. It was laden with the bounty of Var arranged on locally produced earthenware; fruits, melons, and berries, cheeses and sliced meats shared space with baskets full of fresh baked croissants and sliced baguette. Butter, homemade jams, fruit preserves, and cubed raw sugar filled bowls of locally produced glass. From elegant earthenware tureens, the aroma of scrambled egg and hot sausages escaped into the morning air.

Glass pitchers of freshly squeezed orange juice, milk, and heavy cream mingled with silver pots of steaming coffee, Russian tea, milk, and hot chocolate. They were conveniently placed on the eating table, within easy reach of the breakfasting guests.

Marc-Édouard and his parents, having breakfasted early, had gone to the pool for the promised swim. Sergei had also breakfasted earlier and escaped to the library to begin deciphering Prince Felix's diary.

Marc, Laurent, and Stephen were well into their breakfast before Irina and Prince Michael came onto the terrace, accompanied by Renaud. The mood was light, and the events of the day; a trip to the Roman fortifications of Taradeau and to the medieval abbey of Le Thoronet, and the upcoming party in the Gothik pavilion that evening, dominated the conversation.

"How are the plans coming for the party?" Marc asked, as Paul took a seat at the table.

"Done and done," Paul said, preparing a large café au lait. "Caterer arranged, sound system and DJ organized, guests confirmed."

"How many guests?" Marc poured himself another juice.

"Around a hundred, including your house guests."

"So, who's going to be riding with whom?" Stephen finished off his coffee.

"Pardon?" Irina sat down to the table with her breakfast.

"To visit the abbey, Stephen replied.

"I'll take you, Irina and Michael with me in the Jaguar," Laurent began. "Chantal, Edward and M.E. will take their car...Chantal's suggestion."

"What about you, Prince?" Irina poured herself a cup of the strong fragrant Russian tea.

"Marc, please, Irina. We are all family here, or near enough to it." He smiled.

"Besides, Stephen chuckled. "Every time I hear someone call Marc prince, I feel like they should be adding a whistle." He added a quick little whistle by way of illustration. "And a here boy."

Stephen had a golden retriever named Prince as a child, and the two images, Marc and the dog always became entwined when formality came into play. "Although Marc may sometimes be a bitch, as we all know, he is neither a dog nor a boy."

"Thank you S, for that enlightening set of imagery," Marc said, slightly annoyed.

"As you say," Laurent gently brushed a stray hair from Marc's forehead. "We are all family here, or near enough."

"Well I for one," Prince Michael added. "Am quite glad to forgo the formality...Stephen does have a valid point. I must confess that I often feel collared and on a lead when people address me as prince."

Irina raised her glass of juice, first to Marc, her host, then to Michael, her fiancé. "Gentlemen, I toast to your freedom from the kennels." She smiled charmingly. "But to return to my original question. With whom will you be riding...Marc?"

"Actually, I won't be going. I've got a *little family gathering this evening*, and as capable as my staff may be, I want to oversee some of the final details myself."

"Sounds like we have a surprise in the offing." Stephen grinned. Marc was planning to present the couple with a truly impressive wedding gift. It was difficult not to let the cat out of the bag.

"It won't be a surprise for long, if you drop any more hints." Marc looked at his friend with a raised eyebrow. "If you'll excuse me, I have some phone calls to make, and a surprise to organize." He flashed a broad grin, stood up and unceremoniously left his guests on the terrace to finish their breakfast.

"Le Thoronet was built over a thirty year period, between 1160 and 1190. It has been called one of the three jewels in the crown of the Cistercian order." Laurent the architect had been called on to serve as the guide, and he was quite pleased to do so. "Regarded by architects as the finest example of Roman Architecture in Provence, the acoustics of the chapel are renowned. It is the setting for a series of international concerts of medieval music."

As Laurent indicated the pointed arches in the nave, the trapezoidal form of the cloister and the perfectly cut stones, fitted without mortar, Edward was doing what he loved best, at work or at play, snapping photographs of the company as they admired the simple elegance of the Cistercian monks homage to God.

Irina was as impressed by her cousin's knowledge of his field, as she was with the simple and enthusiastic way he shared it. The circumstances of her life had made her feel rather solitary and alone. She was genuinely happy to have found a new family, her mother's brother, so kind and caring, and this marvellous stepson of his, handsome, charming, and honest about himself and his feelings. Between this and her beloved Michael, she felt the loneliness of her childhood, the pain of not being accepted, slowly melting away.

"I believe you are right." Sergei looked up from the diary as Marc entered the library from the terrace. "Andronikov was a shrewd young man. If this diary is correct, the 'memorial jewels' were only, as the expression goes, 'the tip of the iceberg.'"

Sergei had spent most of the morning decoding the diary. He started with an entry marked February 24, 1917 and decoded through to May 3, 1917.

"This entry is dated February 24, 1917. Andronikov was using the old Julian calendar, a habit he changed two days later, when he switches to the Gregorian date," he read the entry to Marc, who made himself comfortable in the empty wing chairs opposite Sergei.

"The workers now own the streets of St Petersburg. The Cossacks called out to assist the police, have shown no enthusiasm for their task, the police stations have been raided for their arms and have been put to the torch by the crowds. The tsar will call out the army, but I have little hope. Nicholas will not survive this storm. Thank God I had the foresight - thanks to Felix Y - to be prepared for the worst.

"The entry for the 25th reads; 'Only one cart made it to the wharf, to be safely loaded on the ship which waits to take us away from this madness, the others were taken by roving gangs of workers before they could arrive at their destination. Our cases and trunks have been emptied of our clothing and filled with our most precious portable things. Even Elena's corset and the hems of her dress are filled with jewels we have taken from their settings. I allowed only two changes of clothes for each of us, but I have promised Dearest that she may buy whatever she needs when we arrive in Paris.'

"The entry for February 26th," Sergei continued. "I received the word from cousin that the troupes had taken certain areas back from the workers, thank God we were ready. I followed cousin's route, and we were able to make it to the ship in safety. What a sorry band we were, Dearest and I, Fedor Mikhailovich, our old steward from Alastani, Marie Junot, Dearest's maid, and Agafia Olekhnovna, Aleksandra's nurse. Dearest held our little Aleksandra wrapped in her sable lap robe to keep her warm. Tears flowed from all of us as we stood on the deck and said good-bye to our beloved homeland, knowing we would never return.

"Our journey will be a long one, St. Petersburg to Gothenburg by sea, again by sea from Gothenburg to Newcastle. Then by train we will go to London and to Dover. From Dover to Calais we will again travel by sea, then from Calais to Paris by train. The plan is to proceed without stopping until we arrived in Paris."

Marc extinguished his cigarette, the story of their exodus was poignant; he was beginning to feel an immense respect for the young man, who struggled so valiantly to take his little family away from certain disaster, whose cautious planning to provide a new future, in the face of certain ruin, placed him well above his peers.

Sergei skipped over the next few entries to Prince Felix's arrival in Paris. "March 16th, 1917," he read. "We arrived in Paris two days ago. Dearest was very tired and slept for almost a day. Maitre Noyer, my agent in France, met us at the Gare du Nord and took us to our rooms at the Ritz. Happily the letter of credit from our bank in Zurich had preceded us by two days. Thanks to Papa's careful attention to his investments abroad, and to the good training he had given me, we will not have to part with any of the jewels nor the few things we were able to salvage from the palace in St Petersburg. Little Aleksandra will not be poor, nor will any of her children. We will leave for Lorgues tomorrow to start our new life in the little chateau that Maitre Noyer has bought for us. The warmth of the south will bring Dearest back to life, and keep the roses in little Aleksandra's cheeks."

"I am beginning to quite like this Prince Felix," Marc said thoughtfully, pulling out another cigarette. "He is not as I imagined him."

"The most interesting part is still to come," Sergei said, taking an offered cigarette from Marc's pack.

"Would you care for something to drink." Marc leaned forward to the coffee service on the small butler's table between their chairs.

"Yes, a coffee would be nice about now."

"Two sugars and white?"

Sergei nodded, continuing, "The next entry of importance to our search is dated October 17, 1918." He read, "The work of modernization is almost finished. The electrification has been completed, as well as the plumbing. The additions to the Gothik pavilion with the secret alcove are done. Only the hidden room remains to be completed, our Treasure Chamber, as Dearest calls it. Then I will bring the jewels and precious trinkets from St. Petersburg, now safely locked in a Paris bank vault, here, to the chateau. Dearest is thriving in her new home, far from the civil war that is now raging in our beloved homeland.

I receive frequent letters from cousin, who entreats me to return and fight for the 'Whites'. But I cannot leave my Dearest nor our little Aleksandra, who is blossoming daily like the flowers in our beautiful garden."

"So the Chateau de Maure held two secrets built by the Prince Andronikov." Marc reached for the unlit cigarette that he had laid on the table some time before. "What else does he say?" Marc asked, lighting the cigarette.

"October 30, 1917," Sergei read. "The architect has completed his work on the secret room. The entrance is ingeniously concealed in the small passage that leads from our bedroom to the sitting room, where my Dearest takes her morning tea. The panel concealing the steel door is so cleverly done that not even I, who know the location of the lock, can easily find it. Once the latch cover is slid open, the silver key turns the lock effortlessly, and the door opens to reveal a steep stairway that leads up to the treasure room.

The architect is so clever; above the sitting room he has added a little room, facing the garden. Though it has no windows, which allows it to escape notice, he has put skylights to provide us with illumination, and a little spiral staircase so that I can go onto the roof and keep the glass cleaned. He has also contrived an electric light to come on when the door is opened, thereby lighting our way safely to the top of the stairs."

"November 15th, 1917," Sergei continued. "It has taken two days, but the task is done. Labourers un-crated the furniture and moved the things to go into the pavilion gallery into place. They brought the rest of the furniture and objets d'art up to Dearest's sitting room. The messengers from the bank brought all our cases in which our precious things had been stored since we left St Petersburg. I had them taken up to Dearest's sitting room as well.

With Fedor's help, I set up Papa's memorial in the secret alcove in the pavilion gallery. There beneath his portrait, I placed the crown that great-grandfather had made for the coronation of Nicholas I, which each of us have worn at the coronations since that time. Beneath the crown, I placed the order of St Andrew, and the jewelled coffer that once contained the Alastani Diamond, symbol of our suzerainty over Alastani from the time of the Byzantine emperors.

The diamond was stolen the day before our flight, doubtless by one of the servants with Bolshevik sympathies. The gold samovar and tea service was placed in the pavilion, so that we can have tea on Saturdays and remember Papa and the sovereign position that was once our family's heritage.

With great difficulty - as the furniture, though not yet assembled, was quite heavy - Fedor and I moved the pieces to go into the treasure chamber. Poor Fedor, he is getting quite old, and I was loath to ask for his help; but he is the only one I can trust with the secret of our Treasure Chamber.

We positioned the furniture as Dearest wished it, and then assembled each piece. Then we brought up the cases and placed the jewels in the great Empire jewel cabinet, which was given to my great-great-grandfather by Alexander I, in appreciation for his services during the war against Napoleon. It was said to have been made for the Empress Josephine. Dearest came up and placed the jewelled bibelots and objets d'art where she wished them to be; and our little Treasure Chamber was finished."

"There are no further references to the Treasure Chamber" Sergei said, putting the cigarette out in the ashtray. "Shall I read the entries regarding the documents?"

"In for a penny in for a pound."

"Pardon?" Sergei looked puzzled.

"Just an old English expression." Marc chuckled. "Please go on Sergei."

"I think you are going to find this extremely interesting," Sergei began. "September 21st, 1918, the son of mama's sister, Alexandr Andreivich Arakcheev arrived today with his Hungarian wife, Baroness Léna Horváth, and their little Andrei. He has come to ask for help in settling his family in Budapest, as the Horváth family is numerous, and they are not able to help, being somewhat in a strained position themselves.

Alexandr also brings news of the civil war, and has hopes that now that Russia has made peace with Germany, perhaps the Whites may yet bring down the Bolsheviks and restore the monarchy. I do not share his optimism, for the Tsar is dead, as is the Grand Duke Mikhail Alexsandrovich, and Prince Y writes from his confinement near Sevastopol, that the 'Whites' are disorganized and scattered, and that if it were not for the Germans and the Treaty of Brest Litovsk, they might now all be dead. He said in his letter, that he prays daily that they might be rescued, for the British are not far away."

"September 22, 1917," Sergei continued. "The day was beautiful, Dearest is quite happy to have the company of Léna and the little family. It reminds her so much of the times we used to spend together in our place in the country near Alastani, before the tragedy…always a house full of family and friends. The children, now that they are safe, are a constant joy to their mothers. Agafia Olekhnovna kindly looks after little Andrei as well as our dear Aleksandra.

I have tried to persuade Alexandr Andreivich to settle here in France and to do as Dearest and I have done, to try to build a new life for the sake of our children. But he resists all my efforts, saying that it is better for Léna to be near her own family, as he plans to return to fight with the Whites, as soon as he has settled them.

I have decided to offer my help to establish his little family in Budapest. I requested a letter of credit for 150,000 pounds to be issued to him by my bank in Zurich. They are most grateful and will leave as soon as the letter arrives. We will be sorry to see them go. Dearest so enjoys the company of dear Léna, and the children are a constant source of pleasure.

Alexandr Andreivich says that he has documents that will raise the indignation of the entire world against the Bolsheviks. He is adamant that once this Great War is over, these documents will raise such a cry of outrage, that it will bring the armies of Europe to the aid of the White's cause; but he will not show them to me. He insists that they must remain secret, even from me, until the time is right.

"October 1, 1917...Alexandr Andreivich is leaving tomorrow for Budapest with his family. He asked me to hold the documents in safe keeping for him. I will put them in the Alastani coffer in the secret compartment. They will be safe there till he returns for them."

"The documents are not mentioned again until 1920," Sergei continued. "And the entry concerning them is also the last entry in the diary. 'November 30, 1920. Alexandr Andreivich has finally contacted me about the documents, which I have kept for him for so long. He has asked me to meet him, but says that I am not to bring the documents, as he fears that agents of the Bolshevik government have followed him on his return from the Crimea. He said that he would make plans for obtaining them when we meet. I will leave for Nice tomorrow morning. I have kept my promise to Alexandr Andreivich and not broken the seal on the envelope. But I cannot help but wonder, what it is that could force the world to leave it's euphoria of peace for a cause that is now all but defeated.'"

"Dimitri's secret is safe."

"Yes," Sergei confirmed.

Their walk through the past was interrupted by a knock at the door. "Monsieur." It was Paul. "Inspector Leclerc is here. He'd like to have a word with you."

"Show him in, Paul, please."

Marc stood up as the inspector entered the library. "Inspector, please," he indicated a seat on the sofa beside them. "You know Sergei Reisky, of course. May I offer you something to drink?"

"Yes, I am rather thirsty." He settled himself on the sofa. "Some juice if you have it."

"Paul, do you mind?"

"Of course not, Monsieur," Paul replied graciously. "Apple, Orange, Cassis?" he asked the inspector.

"Cassis would be nice, thank you Monsieur Renaud."

"To what do we owe the pleasure, Inspector?"

"I am afraid the reason for my visit is not a pleasant one," Leclerc began. "Do you mind if I smoke?" he asked, taking a pack of cigarettes from his jacket pocket.

"Not at all, in fact I think I'll join you. Sergei?" Marc offered Sergei a cigarette.

"I understand that Count Dimitri Karpov was one of your guests for the weekend."

"That is correct, Inspector." Marc lit the inspector's cigarette then his own. "He received several phone calls after his arrival yesterday. Business calls from New York I believe."

"I see." Leclerc nodded his thanks as Paul returned with a small silver tray, holding a small crystal pitcher of juice and a glass, and placed them on the table in front of the sofa. "So Count Karpov did not stay?"

"No, actually the second call came about 11:00. He said that it was necessary for him to go to New York, something about an oil deal on which he was working with a US firm."

"Do you know at what time he left?"

"I didn't notice the exact time, did you Sergei."

"No, not the exact time, but it must have been around a half an hour after the second call."

"He left alone?"

"Yes," Marc replied. "His daughter and her fiancé are still here…we are having a party for them this evening. It seems they first met here, at the chateau, at a party given by the Princess Andronikov…The party this evening is a sort of commemoration of their meeting."

"And Arakcheev, he was one of your guests for dinner last evening?" Leclerc poured himself a glass of juice.

"Yes he was." Marc wondered at the question, as he had phoned Leclerc yesterday purposefully to tell him that Arakcheev had arrived on the scene; to let the inspector know that one of the people he wanted to question about the break-in was to be a guest. "Why do you ask?"

"Do you remember what time the Baron left?"

"A good half hour, forty-five minutes before Karpov." Marc was burning with curiosity.

"Do you know how I can contact Baron Arakcheev?"

"Actually, no, I don't," Marc replied. "He did not tell me at which hotel he was staying."

"You mean you think he is still in the region?"

"Well, I think so," Marc said. "He is invited to the party this evening…and he is coming to lunch on Monday to discuss the business of his grandmother's request…"

"Monsieur Balanger, the Baron Arakcheev's grandmother died three weeks ago, shortly after they returned to Budapest." He paused, taking a deep drink of his juice. "Do you recognize this book?" He pulled a little black book from his pocket and handed it to Marc.

"No, inspector." Marc returned the book to Leclerc. "I've never seen it before."

"Monsieur Reisky?"

"No inspector," Sergei replied.

"The handwriting is little better than a scrawl, and it is, I believe, written in Russian."

"May I see the book inspector? Perhaps I can decipher some of it for you."

"I was hoping that you would ask, Monsieur Reisky." Leclerc handed the book to Sergei.

Sergei flipped through several pages. It was a catalogue as it were. Names, dates, special tasks Dimitri had Malinkov arrange for him. Uriatkin's accident, the break-in, both were there and much more besides. "Inspector, this little notebook contains information that could prove very damaging to my brother-in-law, and disastrous to the future of my niece."

"Count Karpov was your brother-in-law?"

"Yes, Inspector," Sergei replied, his sense of foreboding growing with every passing second. "Dimitri was married to my late sister, Irina is their daughter and my niece. It has been many years since my brother-in-law and I have spent any time together…you see I fled Russia many years ago…before Irina was born."

"Yet you arrived in St Tropez on board the Count's yacht only a few days ago," Leclerc interrupted. "There are now two men dead in my district, in less than forty-eight hours, both foreigners, both Russian."

The colour drained from Sergei's face. "Dimitri is dead?"

Marc sat motionless, stunned.

"Yes, that is correct. Count Dimitri Karpov was found dead in the front seat of his Bentley at around one o'clock in the morning. He was discovered by the caretaker of the Abbey of Le Thoronet, who was roused by the sound of a loud car alarm. Count Karpov was killed by the same gun as the man who was murdered in Lorgues."

Leclerc put out his cigarette, and refilled his glass. "There are some things that you are not telling me Messieurs, things which I need to know. I think it is time you let me in on your little secrets."

Chapter Thirteen – The Best Laid Plans

The chateau was filled with light. Torches burned in the entrance court, illuminating the path of the guests from their cars to the steps, leading to the broad terrace that stretched across the front of the chateau. A string quartet played baroque chamber music on one corner of the terrace. Intimate groupings of tables and chairs had been scattered around the terrace for the comfort of the recent arrivals.

Suzanne and Marie served champagne, vodka, and caviar to the guests while they waited for the hired carriages to make their continuous circuit between chateau and Gothik pavilion. Marc, Sergei and Laurent stood at the top of the stairs to the courtyard; host, uncle and cousin of the feted couple, welcoming the people as they arrived.

The carriages were one of the surprises that Marc had arranged; hired from neighbouring villages. Though the walk from the chateau to the pavilion was not far, everyone was in evening dress. The carriages, with their candle-lit lanterns, gave an air of romance and elegance to the festivities, and ensured that no heels were broken in transit. Irina and Michael waited on the terrace of the Gothik Pavilion, outside the ballroom, welcoming their friends and relations as the carriages arrived from the chateau.

The attire was festive, though formal; Irina had asked Renaud if he would organize a celebration rather than a ceremony. Nevertheless, the women wore flowing evening dresses, some short, some long. All were bejewelled, and the jewels, though impressive, were worn in innovative ways. It was a glittering evening.

Prince Felix's Treasure Chamber was no longer hidden. The prince's diary was quite specific as to its location. Though it took some doing to find the concealed lock, the key was easy. It was on the ribbon that held the keys to the Gothik pavilion.

The sheer volume of jewels and precious objects was astonishing. It would take weeks to catalogue the contents of the room. The discovery of the real Andronikov treasure had given them the idea. Marc had phoned the inspector. The plan was risky, but the inspector agreed. The jewels would serve to bait the trap. Marc, with Chantal's help, selected jewels for everyone, putting the first steps of the plan into action.

Marc stood on the terrace at the top of the stairs, the first in the receiving line. He wore a black raw silk double-breasted suit with a simple knit t-shirt of black silk. Around his neck, he wore a large square cut diamond ringed with small, square cut sapphires. The pendant was suspended on a diamond chain. On the lapel of his jacket he wore a brooch; an immense cabochon sapphire surrounded by small brilliant cut diamonds. A fifteen-carat diamond shot its fire from the little finger on his left hand, and a large cabochon sapphire ringed with round diamonds decorated the ring finger of his right hand.

His hair was pulled back on the sides, fastened into a ponytail that hung down over the loose hair in back. The ponytail was secured with a square cut sapphire mounted in a frame of brilliant cut diamonds.

Laurent stood next to him. He looked dashing in a double-breasted, silk twill evening suit. Under the jacket he wore a black silk-knit turtleneck. On Laurent's lapel was pinned the twin of the sapphire brooch that Marc wore in his lapel.

Sergei wore an exquisite rose bud pin in the lapel of his white double-breasted dinner jacket. The stem and the leaves were green gold; the petals of the rosebud were made of pale pink sapphires.

Marc was secretly amused at the reactions of some of the guests as he welcomed them. He knew that by Monday evening, the department of Var would be abuzz with stories. He would become a cross between the Count of Monte Cristo and Karl Lagerfeld. He found the prospect of such a comparison pleasing.

The diversity of Michael's circle of friends was a bit of a surprise. When Marc had suggested the party, he had expected a smaller version of the Princess Andronikov's ball. He had been quite wrong. There were Russian aristocrats, to be sure, but they were not the largest contingent. Mixed among with them were members of the French aristocracy, actors, painters, owners of local nightclubs and vineyards. Much to his surprise, some of their guests were people that Marc had met during his own forays to the south, in the years before he'd moved to Canada.

As the carriages with the guests arrived at the Gothik pavilion, they came to a stop at the ballroom end of the terrace, where Prince Michael and Irina stood waiting to welcome them. Torches had been stuck into the ground bordering the terrace to provide illumination.

Small round tables, intimately arranged, were covered with white linen cloth, falling in luxurious folds onto the terrace's flagstone surface. The tables had lit pillar candles, in large hurricane glass cylinders, ringed with fresh cut flowers. Light from the large crystal chandeliers in the ballroom filtered through the open gothik arched French doors.

Prince Michael wore a white double-breasted dinner jacket with a crew neck navy t-shirt in knitted silk. Resting on his shoulders was Prince Felix's diamond chain and badge of the Order of St Andrew, an order of which Michael was also a member.

Irina was a vision of raven-haired beauty. Her dress was long; white Fuji silk with a deep décolleté and thin little straps. She wore a diamond choker. Its lace-like design wrapped her neck, starting just below her delicate jaw and falling to her collarbone. Beneath that, resting on her shoulders, she wore a diamond necklace from which hung pendant-set, carved cabochon rubies, ringed by smaller round brilliants.

She wore earrings, bracelets, one on each wrist, and a ring. They were part of a matching suite made for the ruby and diamond necklace. Irina's raven tresses were pulled back and up, tendrils falling loosely here and there, through a necklace of large alternating square cut rubies and diamonds, which she wore as a tiara.

Arakcheev was the last to arrive. As he stepped out of the open Victoria carriage onto the terrace, he could feel his blood coming to a boil. Andronikov jewels were everywhere in evidence on the houseguests of the Prince de Jonville; jewels that should have come to him, hidden jewels he had been unable to find after two years of searching. He forced himself to conceal his feelings, smiling a charming smile, complimenting his host and hostess on the splendour of the evening.

Inside, a disc jockey was playing a mix from the Caves du Roy; the floor of the ballroom was filled with dancers. Champagne flowed, and little groups of people conversed, keeping time with the music.

He met Stephen just inside the door to the ballroom, noting the pavé diamond, open petal rose in his lapel. Another Andronikov jewel, like the square cut yellow diamond Stephen wore on the little finger of his left hand.

"Spectacular," Arakcheev said, taking a champagne filled crystal flute from the proffered silver tray of a uniformed caterer's waiter. "The Prince de Jonville has outdone himself."

"A man has to do what a man has to do." Stephen chuckled. "Can't let the new relations think he's a country cousin from the frozen wilds of the North."

"New relations?" Arakcheev asked, with a charming smile.

"Perhaps I'm jumping the gun just a bit; but yes, Laurent is Sergei's stepson, as you know, and Sergei is Irina's uncle."

"Ah!" he smiled knowingly. "And Laurent is…"

"Yes." Stephen grinned. "My money's on a fall wedding. But enough about him, I'm more interested in you." He slipped his arm through Stephane's. "Something to eat?"

"Sounds great," Arakcheev replied, allowing himself to be manoeuvred towards the gallery and the tower room. "I haven't eaten since this morning."

"So that's how you keep your boyish figure." Stephen reached over and poked Arakcheev in the ribs.

Arakcheev barely suppressed the look of agony as a pain shot up his right side. He forced a smile of appreciation at the compliment.

The gallery was filled with a soft luminescence from the candles. The console had been moved from the secret alcove into the room. It resembled a Russian palace, the soft light reflecting off the highly polished surfaces of the lapis lazuli, mahogany, and gold.

As they walked into the tower room, set up for the supper, Andronikov stopped short. The tables were laden with a bounty of Provencal cuisine, elegantly presented in Andronikov silver and silver gilt. But that was not what stopped him in his tracks. It was Chantal. If Irina was the image of a Russian princess, Chantal was a Russian Empress. Her dress was the same kind of Fuji silk, cream coloured, long and flowing. Her jewels were of such exceptional magnificence that he noticed nothing else but the brilliance of the candlelight, playing in the reflective depths of the large stones.

Diamond necklaces were layered from the deep décolleté of her dress to the top of her long elegant throat. Large pear-shaped diamonds hung from diamond bows in her ears. Pairs of bracelets covered her bare forearms. And in her hair, coiffed in the style of an Empire beauty, was a diadem that married the purest canary and white diamonds in the form of entwined wheat sheaves.

Andronikov recognized the tiara and the jewels, which the Princess Andronikov had worn at the ball given for the Grand Duchess. Without question Marc had found the Treasure Chamber that had eluded him.

A plan quickly formed in his mind. According to family history these jewels were nothing compared to the loose stones plucked from their mountings, which Prince Felix had shoved into the cases they had brought with them from St Petersburg. He would have a part of this bounty before the night was over.

The music from the ballroom stopped; the pre-arranged signal for the waiters to gather everyone to the ballroom.

"Curtain in five minutes." Stephen grinned. Stephen, now on Stephane's right side, slipped his arm through Arakcheev's. This time Arakcheev could not conceal his discomfort. He winced visibly at the sharp twinge of pain.

"Something wrong?" Stephen asked, releasing Arakcheev.

"Nothing." He summoned a smile. "Really, I slipped getting out of the shower this evening. It's probably just a bruised rib." This flirtation was useful, Stephane thought, it would keep him in the intimate circle. "The left side is fine." He winked and this time it was he who slipped his good arm through Stephen's. "Shall we go in? We wouldn't want to be late for the show."

The five of them stood in front of the musician's gallery; Irina in the centre, Michael and Sergei on her left, Marc and Laurent on her right.

"I promise this won't take long," Marc began. "And for those of you that know me…I promise this won't take long." Marc waited for the laughter to subside. "When I discovered that Countess Irina Karpov and her fiancé, Prince Michael Romanovsky met for the first time at a party in this room, I was determined that they should celebrate that meeting with a little party, which is why you were all asked here this evening."

He paused a moment and waited for Luc and Paul to appear at the door of the gallery. "I recently acquired a Russian collection, which contained some rather splendid items of religious significance…to be honest, I was uncertain as to what use I would make of them."

As he spoke, Luc and Paul walked across the ballroom, coming to a stop next to the little group in front of the balcony. "However, the arrival of my guests gave me the perfect solution to my little problem. Irina, Michael, I hope that you will accept these tokens of my affection and of my hope that you will have a long and happy life together."

Luc and Paul removed the scarves that covered the Andronikov wedding crowns. Irina had tears in her eyes; even Michael was moved. There were little gasps, and a round of generous applause, after which Marc spoke again.

"So much for my little surprise." Marc felt Laurent's arm encircle his waist. "If I may paraphrase a line from Genesis…the book, not the musical group…let there be music."

The music began again. As the guests came forward to congratulate the couple and admire the wedding crowns, Marc and Laurent melted into the crowd making their way over to Stephen and Arakcheev.

"Baron, what a pleasure to see you." Marc smiled warmly.

"The pleasure is mine, I assure you, Prince." Arakcheev concealed his mounting anger. "Unfortunately I cannot stay for long."

"Oh?" Marc said, with an air of disappointment.

"I was just telling Stephen that I had a little fall getting out of the shower this evening."

"I'm so sorry, you are all right I trust," Laurent expressed his concern.

"Actually, I think I may have bruised some ribs."

"Perhaps we should find some comfortable chairs and sit," Marc said.

"Thank you, but it's probably best if I return to my hotel."

"I need to go back to the house for a few minutes," Marc said, thinking on his feet. "We can share the carriage."

"We'll go with you," Laurent jumped in.

"Don't be silly," Marc replied. "I'll just accompany the baron to his car, make my phone call, then I'll be back. I won't be long."

Chapter Fourteen – Final Accounting

Marc was in the library. He'd said good-bye to Arakcheev on the terrace, and then come into the library to wait. Marc filled up his cigarette case, taking his time. He returned his case to his jacket pocket. He heard the sound of footsteps coming up the stairs of the garden terrace. Lighting a cigarette from the pack, he picked up the phone, as if preparing to make the call.

"You're being very generous with my inheritance."

"I was wondering how long it would take you to circle back."

"Put the phone down and turn around...slowly."

Marc did as he was asked. Stephane Arakcheev was standing close; the gun trained on him was equipped with a silencer. "Is that the gun you used to kill Malinkov...and Karpov?"

"You have been busy haven't you, Monsieur mystery writer."

"Not nearly as busy as you," Marc replied coldly, exhaling a long stream of smoke.

"How long have you known?"

"If you mean that you had a part in the break-in, Leclerc suspected it. I became suspicious when you paid your first visit." Marc took another long drag on his cigarette.

"That's why your sister was wearing Prince Felix's locket."

"Yes. I knew you would recognize the initials, even if you'd never seen the locket itself."

"I see." Stephane backed up slowly, putting his back to the wall, keeping the gun trained on his host.

"Even though I wasn't sure...I always like to give a person the benefit of the doubt...I knew that the locket would draw you out, if indeed you had played a part in it."

"Tell me something," Marc said, putting out his cigarette. "How did you hook up with Malinkov? Dimitri Karpov said he was a homophobe."

"It wouldn't be the first time a repressed homosexual tried to cover up his own orientation by disparaging the very thing he is himself." He paused, glancing furtively at the French doors leading to the garden terrace, looking for any movement outside.

"You're right there," Marc said, with a degree of sadness. "Do you mind if I have another cigarette."

"Take one from the pack," he said, as Marc reached for his pocket.

"My lighter is in my pocket."

"Use the matches," Stephane said, menacingly. "Actually it was easy. He was with Karpov when Karpov came to make his offer to buy the chateau." He smiled malevolently at the memory. "The first time he saw me, I could see it in his eyes…the hunger for what he had always wanted but never dared have. You know he informed on his own brother. The poor bastard was sent to a re-education camp in Siberia."

"You know about that?" Marc lit his cigarette with the matches on the desk.

"He told me about it while I was seducing him for the first time."

"And he told you about the Princess Andronikov's blackmail…"

"And his little black notebook."

"So the two of you decided to get the diamond."

"And the diary and codebook. But then you came along and bought the house before we could find it."

"So you changed your plans."

"Not really changed, rather, I modified them to account for the change of circumstances," Stephane paused, listening carefully; he thought he heard the sound of someone on the terrace.

"You see I knew what Malinkov knew." Stephane continued, "Sergei was dispatched to find the codebook. I knew about Laurent being Sergei's son, and about Laurent and you. It was not a far stretch to assume that Sergei, trying to protect his stepson, would confide in you…and I knew you would find the codebook, and the Treasure Chamber."

"What if I hadn't?"

"A risk, to be sure, but a calculated one. You see I've read your mysteries…" His breathing was shallow, normal breathing was becoming more difficult.

"Thank you…I think."

"Why did you kill Malinkov?"

"Quite simply, he was a liability. Anyway he was lousy in bed…and…I've never been one to share."

"And Karpov?"

"Malinkov's notebook was handy; even with the Alastani diamond, I was going to need some ready cash," Stephan paused, looking towards the open French doors to the terrace. "You can come out now, Laurent…that is unless you want your lover to join Malinkov and Karpov."

Laurent walked slowly into the room.

"Why don't you join Marc over there by the desk." Arakcheev motioned with the gun. "Karpov, well…he was a boorish ex-Bolshevik…he got what he deserved."

"What now?" Laurent took Marc's hand and gave it a reassuring squeeze.

"We're going to the Treasure Chamber, before, as they say in American westerns, the cavalry arrives. And I'm going to collect the part of my inheritance you haven't been displaying all evening…for my benefit. Then with the two of you as guarantees for my safe passage out of this rather precarious position, we will drive to the Toulon-Hyères airport, where a chartered plane awaits to take us to a more hospitable destination."

"And then?" Marc asked, still holding Laurent's hand.

"If you are both good little boys, and if the police who I am certain are on their way, if not already here, keep their distance…I will board a plane to my final destination and you will be free to resume your lives."

Marc noticed a look of discomfort on Arakcheev's face. His jacket was open; Marc could see a moist red spot on Stephane's shirt. Leclerc had said that Karpov fired a single shot from his gun. It must have found its mark. He could tell from the gentle squeeze of Laurent's hand that he had seen it too. They had an advantage, now they had to figure out how to use it.

"Shall we proceed to the Treasure Chamber?" Stephane smiled menacingly. "It's rather sweet, the way the two of you are holding hands, but I think that it would be better if only one of you leads the way…Laurent that will be you. Marc, I trust you will forgive my informality Prince…you will walk with me."

"To ensure your cooperation, my old friend here," he made a little motion with his gun. "Will be trained on the leader…I am sure you will both remember, I do not hesitate to use it."

Prince Felix "little Treasure Chamber" was large, rectangular, roughly the same size as the sitting room beneath it. Due to the quick attention provided by Luc and Paul that afternoon, the furniture and exposed objets d'art were free of dust and the glass of the twin display cabinets was clean.

The furniture was the finest example of Russian cabinetry of the Empire style. It's inspiration clearly taken from the Empress' jewel cabinet. The polished wood and ormolu mounts gleamed softly in the light of the large electrified crystal chandelier, an antique French Empire piece.

The shelves of the display cases were laden with fine examples of the goldsmith's art of many centuries and many countries. A pair of cups made entirely of rubies set in gold frames, was placed next to a collection of gold and jewelled snuffboxes. One shelf was filled with Fabergé eggs that rivalled those of the Imperial collection, another contained a collection of Fabergé figures of Russian inspiration made of gold, precious and semi-precious stones; jade, amethyst, rubies, emeralds, diamonds and lapis lazuli, yet another displayed a collection of Fabergé animals in the same materials.

One console table contained a lady's gold toiletry set inlaid with diamonds and rubies. It was complete with all it jars and bottles, brushes and combs, its ewer, basin and mirror. The centre table held an 18th century French-made gold centrepiece of frolicking cherubs, and a pair of matching candelabrum.

The floors were covered with rare Persian carpets of pure silk. It was the cave of Ali Baba filled with treasures the Andronikov had collected over centuries.

Marc had not fully appreciated the wealth and power that were the birthright of the Andronikov princes until he was in this room, a room that contained only a fraction of what they had once owned; trinkets hurriedly assembled and tossed into suitcases. He wondered what had been in the carts that had not made it to the ship.

From the bedroom below, they had brought up two large, soft-sided, LV totes. Marc held one, Laurent the other.

"Put the totes in the chairs," Arakcheev barked, indicating the chairs placed around the centre table. "Start with the jewel cabinet. Open the drawers." He was beginning to exhibit signs of the pain from his wound. "Open the drawers," he repeated forcefully, waiving the gun.

Marc and Laurent did as they were instructed, offering no resistance. To say they were anxious, would be an understatement. Yet sang-froid was the order of the moment, and they were doing their best to maintain it. One by one they pulled out leather cases and velvet drawstring bags, carrying them to the table.

"This is taking too much time," Arakcheev muttered, barely audibly. "You, Laurent, you bring the cases from the jewel chest, you Prince, open them and fill up the traveling cases."

They had been in the room earlier, Marc, Laurent and Chantal, selecting the jewels to be worn that evening. They did not have any time to begin to inventory its contents, nor had they taken the time to open all of the drawers and doors of the great jewel cabinet. Marc was amazed at what he saw as he opened the containers and placed their contents into the large, LV tote.

The sheer quantity of loose precious stones was astounding. One jewel case contained twelve loose diamonds, none of which was less than forty carats each. There was one mogul cut stone, that he could swear was at least a hundred. Velvet drawstring sacks contained loose pearls. Each one was filled to the brim, each one a different colour; black, grey, pink, cream and purest white. There were leather cases filled with loose emeralds, rubies, and diamonds, some faceted, some carved.

Then there were the fitted cases of mounted jewels; necklaces, rings, brooches, bracelets, and tiaras. One tiara was fitted in such a way that its large, white, teardrop pearls could be changed for black ones; the black pearls were carefully placed in a little velvet sack beside the tiara, in its box. Another tiara, similarly fitted, had diamonds that could be changed for rubies or emeralds, which rested in their own leather cases inside the tiara's large leather box.

"Look," Marc said, feeling the weight of the traveling case. "If we keep this up we won't be able to carry them. This one must weigh at least 50 pounds and it's only half full."

The look of discomfort on Arakcheev's face was now clearly visible, he reached inside his jacket and placed his hand over the wound in his side. This time when he drew his hand out from under his jacket, there was blood on it. The wound from Karpov's bullet had opened again. "All right, that's enough, let's get out of here. You, Laurent, you go first...carry the bag. Prince you walk with me."

The entrance hall was filled with armed police, their weapons drawn. Arakcheev and his hostages stood at the top of the stairs; Laurent with the bag of treasure, Marc next to Arakcheev, the gun in his side. Leclerc and Stephen were at the door leading to the front courtyard. Marc could see that Luc and Paul were standing behind them.

"Put down your gun, and surrender, Baron." Leclerc said in a clear voice. "Even if you should get past us, you will be picked up at the Toulon-Hyères airport. Mr. Hampstead was listening outside the doors to the library, we know about your escape plan. The plane is no longer waiting for you."

Arakcheev knew there was no escape. He also knew that he was loosing blood fast, the bullet from Karpov's gun was still in him;

he had not dared risk a visit to a hospital. His options flashed rapidly before his eyes. Even if he killed one of his hostages, he would not get out of the chateau alive.

Slowly he lowered his gun. "Ils n'ont rien oublié, ni rien appris," he murmured softly. "Napoleon was right you know." He looked at Marc with one last charming smile. "I should have quit while I was ahead."

He let the gun fall from his hand and shifted his weight to the staircase railing. The steps were marble, the angle relatively steep. Life in prison was not an option. If he fell properly he could end this. Leaning forward, he fell rolling down the stairs. He landed on his back at the foot of the staircase.

One of the officers ran over to Arakcheev. He bent down, feeling for a pulse at his neck. "He is still alive."

"Quickly," Leclerc called out. "Get him to the hospital in Draguignan."

Several officers ran forward, carefully they picked Arakcheev up from where he lay bleeding on the floor and carried him out to a waiting police van.

Marc and Laurent came slowly down the stairs. The three musketeers, as he had come to call them, waited at the bottom step with Leclerc. Marc was rather shaken, but he had Laurent's arm to steady him.

With a trembling hand he reached inside his jacket pocket for his cigarette case. "It's not every day I have a gun poking in my side," he said, trying to muster a smile. "I'm afraid it has left me a bit unnerved."

Laurent took the case out of Marc's hands and pulled out two. He lit one for each of them.

"Paul," Laurent handed him the bag. "Would you please return this to the Treasure Chamber and lock it up. We can deal with the mess tomorrow."

"Of course, Monsieur," Paul said, taking the bag. He waited for Laurent and Marc to move from the staircase before ascending the steps to the second floor.

"I think I need a drink before we rejoin our guests." Marc was still a bit shaky. It was the first time he'd ever had to face the threat of real physical violence; he hoped it was the last.

"Grand Marnier?" Stephen asked.

"Doubles," Laurent replied. "On the garden terrace?"

Marc nodded his agreement. He stopped; he noticed some blood on the floor at the bottom of the stairs. "Luc," he said. "Could you find something to clean this up? It wouldn't do to have one of the guests see it."

"Right away, Monsieur," he answered, going towards the kitchen.

"Inspector, will you join us in a drink?" Laurent asked courteously.

"No, Messieurs. I thank you, but I think I should go to the hospital and follow the progress of my prisoner."

"As you wish, Inspector."

"I will return tomorrow to inform the Countess of her father's death."

Marc was beginning to regain control of himself. The trembling had stopped; relief was taking the place of anxiety. "I'm glad the plan worked, inspector," he said with conviction.

"It could not have done without your courage Messieurs," Leclerc replied. "I regret that I had to place your lives in danger."

"All in a day's work, eh Inspector!" Marc smiled.

"Yes, Monsieur, all in a day's work."

It was a beautiful sunny day on the southern coast of France. The sky was a clear azure blue, dotted with little white clouds. It was picture perfect. St Tropez was alive with the activity of a holiday resort at the beginning of the season. Marc and Stephen sat on the terrace of L'Escale, sipping their Pastis, waiting for Laurent to return from the meeting with his client and join them for lunch.

Irina had left from Nice this morning with the body of her father. He was to be buried in St Petersburg. Sergei and Prince Michael accompanied her on the sad journey. At least something good had come out of poor Irina's tragedy. She had come to lean heavily on Sergei after the news of her father's death. Sergei was clearly up to the challenge, protective of his beloved sister's only child.

Chantal and her family had returned to Paris Sunday evening, none the worse for wear. They would be coming back next weekend; Chantal and Marc-Édouard would stay for a couple of weeks. Chantal was, after all, a gemologist. There was an inventory to take, and a valuation to be made. Governments and insurance agents alike wanted to know the value of Granny's Chips, as Stephen had come to call the collection of loose gems from the Andronikov hoard.

The Alastani Diamond, and the other objects from the secret alcove had been transferred to the bank this morning, as planned, and the story of the find and the loan to the Louvre of the articles, was in the Nice Matin that lay on their table. There was no mention, however of the incident at the Chateau de Maure on the night of the party.

A small article at the bottom of page one, told the inhabitants of the Var that the murderer of two tourists had been apprehended. It went on to say that the murderer had died in the hospital at Draguignan, of gun shot wounds inflicted by one of the tourists, shortly after being taken into custody.

The pages of Malinkov's little black notebook met the same fate as the Andronikov documents; cinders in the library fireplace. There would be nothing to mar Irina's future happiness. Marc was glad that Inspector Leclerc had been so cooperative in the matter. After all, Irina was an innocent in all this.

Laurent walked onto the terrace, all smiles. "She loved the plans, so we are to go ahead with the work. I meet with the contractors tomorrow." He leaned down and kissed Marc lightly on the lips. He couldn't help but notice the trace of melancholy on Marc's face. "Still thinking about Arakcheev?" he asked, sitting down.

"Can't help it...it's tragic really."

"Bonjour Messieurs." It was the waiter from last week. "So good to see you again. Will you be having lunch?"

"Yes, please," Laurent replied.

"Messieurs, you seem so serious today," the waiter said, distributing the menus. "It is too beautiful a day for such gloomy faces."

"You're absolutely right," Stephen said, sitting up. "Tell me something, my good man," he began, imitating the voice and mannerism of Mae West to perfection. Looking the waiter up and down, he let his eyes come to rest at crotch level. Looking back at the waiter's handsome face, he grinned. "Is that a gun in your pocket or are you just glad to see me?"

The waiter grinned broadly. "I assure you, Monsieur, it is definitely not a gun."

Marc laughed in spite of himself. They all laughed. It was a beautiful day.

Printed in the United States
1549400001B/122